Satin Falls

Part One: The Submission Virus

&

Part Two: Feminized And Humiliated

Combined!

by Ann Michelle

Please visit my website:

www.annemichellesworld.blogspot.com

TABLE OF CONTENTS

"Introduction by Ann"

—o—

Dear Readers,

Satin Falls is a story I've been working on for a very long time. This story is about a small mountain town where the males slowly lose their ability to resist any command given by the females after an unknown virus infects the water supply. Naturally, the women take advantage of this.

But there's more.

Guiding the women in this is a psychiatrist with a grudge against the masculine half of the human race. She decides that the best revenge against *male*kind would be to encourage the women of Satin Falls to feminize and humiliate their helpless males. Will she succeed? Well, you'll have to read the story to find out. I will tell you this, however, that the one person who might be able to stop her is her former female lover who is now set to marry a man who would rather be the one wearing the dress at their wedding. Unfortunately, she may not want to save the men.

My goal in writing this story is not only to

provide you with an erotic tale that hopefully will thrill each of you throughout the story, but also to provide you with an entertaining bit of genuine fiction as well... a true feminization novel. To that end, this story follows several couples as their lives change in this brave new world of silk and high heels and female domination as the men slowly sink into feminization and their chances of being rescued hang by the well-manicured fingertips of one young woman.

What's more, I've combined both parts now in one book! I hope you enjoy reading this as much as I did writing it.

With love,
Ann :)

P.S. Thanks for signing up for my monthly newsletter. If you haven't signed up, you can do so here: https://annmichellebooks.wixsite.com/website. All you need is an email address. You won't regret it.

Part One:
The Submission Virus

"Prologue"

—o—

Nestled in the mountains away from the big city and the overpopulated ski resorts, Satin Falls is the kind of place they make movies about. From its small shops populating its picturesque downtown to the gorgeous scenery to its friendly people, Satin Falls is about as perfect as a town can get. It's the kind of place where everyone knows everyone else and they all consider each other friends. It's the ideal place to raise children, to retire, or just to live.

But something has gone wrong in Satin Falls, something strange.

Fortunately, the community has Dr. Melanie Morgan to lead them through this crisis. She was the first to identify the problem and she's been a steady voice in letting the others know exactly how they need to handle this situation. Today, she will report on her most recent research and she will provide further guidance on how the community should proceed.

The crowd gathered in the town hall waits anxiously. There is an unease in the air. All of the prominent women of Satin Falls are here. A few even brought their husbands, who sit sheepishly at their wives' sides in overly feminine dresses and high-heeled shoes. These men are obviously embarrassed to be here and to be dressed the way they are, but they had no say in whether or not they would come... nor in how they would dress. Those decisions belong to their wives now.

The wives, by the way, mostly wore pants to the meeting, and many of them seem more than a little happy to be in charge. This virus has been good for quite a few of them.

Melanie Morgan stepped up to the podium. She was so close to achieving her goal now, and still no one suspected a thing. She looked out over the assembly. A feeling of euphoria swept over Melanie as she saw the humiliated males and she giggled; she immediately cleared her throat to hide her giggle.

She smiled.

"Good evening, Ladies. Let's talk about what happens next."

Chapter 1: "It Begins"

—o—

Six months earlier...

Life was not treating Melanie Morgan particularly well. She'd moved to Satin Falls to get away from a failed marriage to a man who soured her on men only to find herself on the verge of losing a female lover she thought was "the one" to yet another man. This was eating her up on the inside. Fortunately for her, events were about to offer her a chance for a little payback.

—o—

Melanie kissed her lover Sidney Drake on the neck and gently cupped her firm breast. Sidney, however, did not reciprocate. Melanie cringed on the inside. She could feel Sidney's reluctance to embrace her and it tore her up. Melanie tried kissing Sidney again, but again Sidney remained still.

"You really mean it, don't you?" asked Melanie. A tear appeared in her eye.

"I'm sorry," said beautiful Sidney. A tear appeared in her eye as well. "I just can't do it anymore, not with the wedding coming up. It wouldn't be right to Eric. I can't do that to him."

"But, it... it wasn't a problem... not before," said Melanie, choking on the words.

"I'm sorry," repeated Sidney.

Sidney spun on her four-inch heels and started toward the door. Melanie grabbed her lover's hand and stopped her.

"Sidney! Please, don't go," pleaded Melanie.

Sidney wiped away a tear with her free hand. "I'm sorry... I can't," she said sadly without turning around. Then she yanked her hand free from Melanie's grip and she kept walking. Melanie followed her. She kept up easily with Sidney despite being a good deal shorter because she wore sneakers and yoga pants, whereas Sidney wore four-inch heels and a pencil skirt.

"Please don't go," Melanie practically begged. She thought about placing her hand on Sidney's shoulder to stop her again, but she didn't want to do anything that might agitate Sidney.

"I can't," said Sidney still without turning around. Tears were streaming down her face as she made her way to the door of Melanie's house.

"Don't do this," said Melanie before quietly adding, "not over a man."

"I'm sorry," repeated Sidney one last time, and she walked out the door.

Melanie watched her leave.

The image of Sidney walking away burned

in Melanie's mind as she drove herself to her office half an hour later. Sidney had been the perfect lover for Melanie after the ugliness with her ex-husband. Melanie truly believed she had found happiness with Sidney and she wanted to spend the rest of her life with that gorgeous woman. But now Sidney was leaving her *for a man*, and that ate her up. She was so upset she almost decided to stay home today, but she knew how rare clients were in Satin Falls and one wanted to see her.

"Need to make the rent," she said to motivate herself to leave for work. She repeated this several times in the car too to keep herself from turning around or bursting into tears.

Melanie parked outside her office. She got out of the car, a small pink sports car, and she started up the concrete steps to her building. Her heels clicked off the concrete as she went. When she reached the office, she unlocked the door, passed through the reception area to her inner office, and then crashed down on her leather couch to cry. She only had a few moments before she heard the door opening to the reception room.

Her tears would need to wait

Melanie wiped her eyes, straightened her psychiatric certificate where it hung on the wall, and went to greet her client. Her client was Jason Cole, the son of Greg Cole, who lived with his new wife Brenda and her daughter Cindy. They were concerned with some of Jason's recent behavior. Melanie invited them all to her office and bade them to sit down. Cindy waited in the lobby.

"Please, have a seat," said Melanie and she sat down in a dark leather chair. She leaned back and casually crossed her legs, allowing her tan open-toed pump to dangle from the ends of her toes.

Greg, Brenda and Jason sat down on Melanie's couch.

"So tell me what I can do for you," said Melanie.

"Well, this is a little odd," said Greg Cole and he hesitated to continue.

"I'm used to odd," said Melanie reassuringly. "Please continue."

Greg ran his tongue over his teeth. "Well... until about a week ago, Jason was perfectly normal. Then we started noticing little things... strange things. And then yesterday... well, yesterday was just too much. That's when we called you."

"What types of 'little things' did you notice?" asked Melanie.

"Well—" started Brenda before Greg cut her off.

"Just lots of little things. I'm not saying Jason's not a nice kid, because he is. He's always been courteous and he's never really been a rule breaker or anything like that. But he's suddenly got *really* helpful." Greg furrowed his brow and stared at Melanie's knees as he spoke.

"Helpful is good," said Melanie.

"Not like this."

"Oh?"

"Yeah. Look, I don't know how to put it, except he's become a big pussy," blurted out Greg.

Jason blushed and Brenda rolled her eyes. Melanie bit her tongue and her nostrils flared. There were many ways to say what Greg meant and most of them did not require insulting women in the process, yet Greg, like so many of the other men Melanie encountered, could only reach for the one way to say it. It bothered Melanie that so many men seemed to see women as something beneath them, an inferior state of being, but she also knew that was unlikely ever to change. Still, she didn't have to like it.

"Mr. Cole, that description doesn't really help," said Melanie coldly.

Greg shrugged his shoulders. "How else am I supposed to say it?"

Melanie tapped her pencil against her notepad angrily. Meanwhile, Brenda scowled at her newly-wed husband, who remained unrepentant even though everyone else in the room clearly was showing their disapproval.

"Dr. Morgan," said Brenda, "about two weeks ago, Jason started becoming more helpful around the house. It wasn't all that strange, because he's done that before. But it started getting strange after a couple days. Whatever chores I asked him to do, he did, without fighting me in any way – no resistance at all. Then, about a week ago, he seemed to become even more helpful to the point of becoming... well, *submissive*, if that's the right word?"

Greg shrugged his shoulders again. "Like I said: *a pussy.*"

Melanie squeezed her pencil and gritted her teeth. Greg reminded her more and more of her ex-husband by the minute, and that was not a good thing. She physically turned toward Brenda at this point to send a subtle signal of disapproval to Greg, though she doubted he was observant enough and self-aware enough to understand.

Brenda continued: "*Submissive.* I think that's the right word," she said softly. "He became almost servile. It seemed that anything I asked him to do, he did without question."

"That's not unusual for teens and pre-teens. It is a little less common in young adults like Jason, but it's not entirely unheard of. Perhaps he's trying to earn a favor," speculated Melanie.

Jason shook his head. So did Brenda.

"No, it wasn't like that," said Brenda. "I can

tell when he wants something. This was more... it's hard to explain. It's like he was brainwashed. It was like he just automatically did anything I suggested, whether I meant for him to do it or not and whether he should have done it or not."

"Can you give me an example?"

"No, unfortunately I can't. All I can say is that I know the difference between him doing the things I tell him because he wants something and this. It was almost like he had no will of his own—"

"Then there's the incident from yesterday with his stepsister, the one we told you about," said Greg, interrupting his wife, and he rolled his eyes. "She's out in the lobby right now if you want to talk to her."

Melanie glared at Greg. She really didn't like him and she decided to be rid of him now. "Perhaps it would be best if I met alone with Jason at this point," said Melanie. She looked Jason Cole up and down. He seemed like a normal young man. She could still see a hint of mascara just above his right eyelash, however.

Greg and Brenda both nodded their heads. Melanie showed them out and then closed the door. She returned to her seat and crossed her legs. Once again, she let her open-toed tan pump sway gently from the ends of her toes.

"Jason, you claim you acted involuntarily

with your stepsister," she said.

"Yeah," said Jason. His eyes couldn't meet Melanie's.

"Can you explain that?" asked Melanie.

"What do you mean?"

"I mean, if you didn't want to do it, then why did you do it?"

Jason furrowed his brow and shrugged his shoulders. "I don't know," he said. "She just told me to do it and I did it."

"So you followed her order?"

"Yeah, I guess."

"Why did you follow her order if you didn't want to?"

Jason shook his head. He kept looking at the floor. "I don't know... I didn't think about it," he said hesitantly.

"You recognize that each of us has choices in all our actions, correct?"

Jason shrugged his shoulders.

"Are you saying you had no choice?"

Jason shrugged his shoulders again. "I just didn't think about it," he said defensively.

"You mean you didn't think about the consequences or you didn't think about whether you should—"

"I mean, I just didn't think about it. She said do it, and I did it. I never stopped to even think about if I should do it or not. It just happened," he said, interrupting her. He was clearly highly embarrassed to be discussing this.

Melanie raised an eyebrow. Normally, this type of explanation indicated either that the subject was lying or that he was showing signs of a disassociation condition. But two days prior, Melanie sat in this same chair as a slightly younger version of Jason gave identical answers. That young man too found it impossible not to obey any order given by his sisters, his mother, or his sister's friends. Yet, like Jason, he didn't seem to understand he was following orders either. Instead, he claimed he just acted without giving it any thought. Afterwards, he was able to feel shame about how he had acted, but at the time it simply never occurred to him that he had a choice. It was *highly* unusual to run into two such cases at the same time.

Melanie flexed her toes, which caused her pump to swing back and forth. "Tell me Jason, how long have you felt compelled to obey your stepsister's commands?"

Jason cringed. He clearly didn't like the inference that he was obeying his stepsister. "I'm not compelled," he said, though his tone was unsure. He ran his fingers through his hair nervously; Melanie could still see traces of the nail polish on his cuticles. "Like, I don't have to do anything anybody tells me," he said, contradicting his earlier claims. He looked up. "I mean, I don't need to *obey* anybody."

Melanie considered this for a moment. Jason seemed normal. He looked healthy. He sounded reasonable. There were no obvious problems with him and no apparent breaks from reality, yet something was clearly wrong, just as it had been with the other male she saw two days prior.

"I'm going to run a test," she said.

"A test?"

"Yes. It's a very simple test. All I need you to do is resist my command. Do you understand?" asked Melanie.

"Yeah."

"Can you do that? Can you resist my command?"

Jason shrugged his shoulders. "Sure."

Melanie wiggled her toes, causing her high-heeled shoe to fall to the floor. "Pick up my shoe," she commanded.

Without a moment's hesitation, Jason did exactly as instructed. He slid off the couch to one knee and grabbed the shoe. He picked it up off the floor. He now held it in his hand.

"I asked you to resist my command," said Melanie.

"Oh sorry," he said.

"You do realize that you just obeyed my

order, right?"

Jason furrowed his brow. "I... well... look, I just picked it up. I'm sorry, I didn't know I wasn't supposed to," he said and he blushed.

"Are you saying you did this voluntarily?"

"Yeah, I guess. You asked me too."

Melanie raised an eyebrow. "All right, if you think you did this voluntarily, then let's make the test harder, shall we? Get on your knees, return the shoe to my foot and lick my toes through the shoe." If Jason had any power to resist, Melanie was sure this would be the moment he did.

He didn't.

Just as before, Jason slid off the couch to his knees before Melanie. He took her nylon-covered foot in his hand and slid the high-heeled shoe onto it. Then he leaned over, stuck out his tongue, and lapped up her toes like they were water. Melanie felt a tingle race through her pussy seeing this young man do something so humiliating on command. She briefly saw an image in her head of her ex-husband on his knees doing this in public and that filled her with exhilaration. She knew right then and there that she needed to figure what this was and how it had happened... and how to recreate it.

"Ok, you may return to your seat," said Melanie a few licks later.

Jason did.

"You're blushing," said Melanie.

He remained silent.

"Did it humiliate you to kiss my shoe?"

Jason bit his tongue and nodded. "Yeah."

"Then why did you do it?" asked Melanie.

"You asked me to."

"I asked you to resist my commands as well, why didn't you resist?"

Jason scratched his head and looked at the floor. "I don't know. I didn't think about it."

Melanie smiled. His responses continued to amaze her. "Jason, I want you to walk me through your thought process. What were you thinking when I asked you to resist my orders?"

"That I shouldn't do whatever you said."

"Then what happened."

"You dropped your shoe and asked me to put it back on your foot and lick it," said Jason.

"And you put it back on my foot and then you licked my toes."

"Yes."

"What were you thinking when you licked my toes?"

"That you wanted me to do that."

"And that it was humiliating?" asked Melanie.

Jason nodded his head.

Melanie took a deep breath. She tossed her

shoe back on the floor. His eyes didn't follow her shoe, they stayed on her eyes. "Do you like women's shoes, Jason?" she asked.

"No... gross!"

"Feet?"

"No."

"Did you want to touch my feet?"

Jason looked disgusted. "No."

"In hindsight, does it bother you that you picked up my shoe and kissed it?"

Jason blushed. The answer was obvious.

"You *may* pick up my shoe and hold it *if you want to*," she said.

Nothing happened.

"Interesting," said Melanie and she wrote a note. When she finished, she casually said, "Jason, I'd like you to hold my shoe."

Jason leaned over, pick up her shoe and clutched it in his hands.

"Fascinating," she said to herself and she wrote another note. "He could resist when my desire was presented as an option, but not when I implied a specific desire that he act." She turned to Jason and spoke: "It would make me happy too if you got on your knees, kissed my toes again and then returned the shoe to my foot."

Once again, Jason slid out of his chair onto his knees. He bent over and kissed her foot. Then he slid the shoe onto her foot and returned to his chair. He blushed again. "Can we please stop doing that?" he asked.

"Doing what?"

"Picking up your shoe and kissing your foot. It's gross!"

"You can stop any time, Jason. All you have to do is resist my command." She tossed her shoe to the ground again. "Pick it up and kiss it. This time, sniff it deeply and rub it against your face."

As before, Jason retrieved the shoe. He placed it to his nose and took a deep whiff with his nose. It smelled of sweat and leather. Then he rubbed the shoe all over his face.

"Please stop," he said.

Melanie ignored him. "Now beg me to let you put it back on my foot."

Jason instantly dropped to his knees before her. "Please let me put your shoe back on your foot! Please?!"

"Interesting," thought Melanie. "So I can make him do more than physical acts too. I can make him verbalize things I want him to say. Query: can I make him believe something is true? Can I implant a thought?" Melanie took a deep breath. "All right, put it back on my foot," she told him.

He did and he returned to his seat.

Melanie now placed both feet together and leaned forward on her knees. "Jason, did it humiliate you to pick up my shoe? Answer me truthfully."

"Yeah, a lot," he said.

"No, it didn't, Jason. You enjoyed it," said Melanie.

Jason's face went blank for a moment.

"Tell me again, Jason, did it humiliate you to lick my shoe?" asked Melanie.

"No. I liked it." As Jason said this, he blushed and Melanie saw him become erect.

"Why are you erect, Jason? Answer me truthfully."

Jason blushed even deeper. "Because it turned me on." This was something even Jason didn't know until he had said it.

Melanie raised her eyebrow again. "Amazing!" she thought. "I was able to implant an idea and uncover a deeply humiliating turn on." She scribbled another note. She then returned her attention to the embarrassed young man. "Tell me again why you licked my foot even after I told you to resist my commands."

"You told me to."

"Are you telling me you had no choice?"

"Choice about what?" he asked.

Melanie leaned back and bit the end of her pencil. Jason was clearly obeying her orders, but seemed unaware of this. Instead, he seemed to see her orders as something other than orders, something he simply did without question without ever realizing that he was obeying a command. What's more, there seemed to be few limits on her power to issue orders. This was fascinating and definitely required further study. In the meantime, however, she needed to place him in competent hands for his own protection... and she knew exactly whose hands those were. In fact, she found the idea rather "appropriate," given her recent humiliations at the hands of various males.

"Tell me why it bothers you to obey your stepsister," said Melanie.

"It's humiliating. She's a brat," replied Jason honestly. "Besides, she's a girl."

"There's nothing wrong with obeying women, Jason, even your stepsister. Let's talk about that Jason."

For the next twenty minutes, Melanie explained to Jason why he should accept his stepsister's authority willingly, not that he had the power to resist her in any event. When she finished, she instructed him that everything said in their sessions was confidential and she told him that if he was asked what they had discussed, he was to state that they discussed personal responsibility and only personal responsibility. She gave him examples to repeat. She then dismissed him and she spoke with Cindy for several minutes.

Jason's life was about to change.

Chapter 2: "The Problem Grows"

—o—

Although Melanie was the first person to recognize the wider issue affecting Satin Falls, she wasn't the first person to notice that something was going on. Two weeks before she met Jason Cole, several of the girls of Satin Falls first noticed that their bratty brothers weren't quite as bratty anymore. A few days later, teenage girls began to notice that their boyfriends were becoming more courteous and eager to please. A few mothers also noticed that their sons were suddenly becoming almost helpful. No one questioned any of this. To the contrary, the women of Satin Falls counted themselves lucky and happily accepted the changes.

For the next week, things ran smoothly.

With each passing day, however, it became more and more clear that something was going on. Indeed, right around the time Melanie met with Jason, it was becoming clear to many of the women of Satin Falls that the boys weren't just being helpful or courteous, they were becoming downright obedient.

Within a few days after that, it was obvious that some sort of line had been crossed. Girls everywhere were noticing that their boyfriends and their brothers could no longer resist even the slightest demand. The boys claimed nothing had changed and they said they felt no differently, and among their friends they acted just as they always had, but add a girl to the mix and suddenly the boys found themselves hopping to perform every command she gave. A few days after that, it wasn't just commands anymore, even hints had become enough to make the boys jump. Within a week, mere expressions of speech had become enough.

Suddenly, things were changing all over the city. The balance of power had shifted and the girls realized they were now in full control.

At first, only a few girls took advantage of this amazing change, but as more did, it became acceptable among the rest to join in. Soon, the boys were handing over the remote controls for the televisions. Others found themselves doing their sisters' chores. An unlucky few found themselves waiting on their sisters and their girlfriends hand and foot. A few even learned just how tyrannical and vindictive girls can be when they receive unlimited power.

That's why David Carlson appeared at school at the local junior college, Satin Falls Academy, on a Monday morning wearing his ex-girlfriend's best Sunday dress and her highest heels. His face was made up, his nails were painted, and his longish blonde hair was done in a permanent wave of curls.

"What are you wearing, David?!" demanded college Dean Max Dwyer.

David blushed. He was surrounded by students, all of them gawking at the frilly pink dress and the silver high-heeled sandals he wore. He looked like he wanted to disappear into a hole and never come back. He couldn't bring himself to reply.

"Why are you wearing a dress and heels? What's going on?" asked Dwyer. "Answer me, David!"

David swallowed hard. "My, uh, ex-girlfriend made me wear it."

"She 'made' you wear it?" asked Dwyer incredulously.

David nodded his head.

"Did she threaten you?"

David shook his head.

"Did she force you physically?"

Once again David shook his head. He shifted from foot to foot as the high heels were difficult to stand in.

"Did she blackmail you?"

Again, David shook his head.

Dwyer looked perplexed. "I'm confused, David. If she didn't force you and she didn't threaten you and she didn't blackmail you, then how did she 'make' you wear the dress?"

David ran his tongue over his teeth nervously. "She told me to wear it."

"She 'told you'?"

"Yes, sir."

Dwyer glared at the young man in the dress. "This sounds like some sort of joke, young man. But the joke's on you. You probably want me to send you home, but I'm not going to. I'm going to let you attend class all day long dressed just the way you are. Maybe next time, you'll think twice."

With that, Dwyer walked off, leaving the humiliated young man to endure his day in the dress and heels. Unfortunately, this proved to be a rather large mistake on Dwyer's part, for almost every girl in the school saw how David had been dressed that day, and it gave them ideas. Consequently, the next day, two more male students showed up wearing dresses and heels. Three more did so the day after that. More followed them. And each time, they claimed only that their girlfriends or sisters "told them" to dress that way.

At first, Dwyer saw this as some sort of joke, and he tried to punish the boys to stop them from further disrupting the school. But he soon realized that something strange was going on. He had a problem, and it was unlike anything else the school had ever faced before. He needed help. So he decided to call for help... he called the town psychiatrist, Dr. Melanie Morgan.

—o—

As things slowly began to spin out of control at Satin Falls Academy, life continued normally everywhere else in Satin Falls. Sidney Drake and her fiancé Eric Miller, for example, went to Eric's parents' home for dinner, as they did every other Friday night.

Sidney hugged her fiancé tightly. They were in the living room at Eric's parents' house. Eric's mother Violet was working in the kitchen putting the finishing touches on the meal. Eric's younger sister Kayleigh helped his mother in the kitchen. Eric's father Henry was off in his study waiting for dinner to be served; he never came to the table until the others were seated. Eric's father Henry just happened to be Sidney's boss at the law firm where she worked: Hunter Miller. Henry and Sidney did not see eye to eye... not about anything.

"Everyone's busy. That means we're alone," said Sidney and she smiled.

"They should be busy until they finish the roast," said Eric.

Sidney looked over her shoulder one more time to make sure they were alone. Then she kissed her fiancé on the lips while simultaneously placing her right hand on his rear. She felt for his pantylines.

"Hmm, a thong. What color?" asked Sidney.

"Pink, Miss. I know you like me to wear pink when we come here," said Eric.

"I do indeed," she replied and she kissed him again.

Eric smiled. By all appearances, Eric was a strong and masculine young man in his late 20's. He stood erect with a proud bearing. He spoke with a strong, authoritative voice. He had excelled at school, and he played sports in high school and in college. No one doubted his masculinity. But Eric had a secret he kept hidden from everyone, everyone except Sidney that is. Sidney knew his secret and actively encouraged it because it turned her on just as much as him.

"Your toenails?" asked Sidney.

"Red, Miss."

"Which red?"

"Rose, Miss."

Sidney ran her hands up his back and felt for his bra through his heavy black sweater. She smiled when her fingers found it. "Good girl," she said with a laugh. "What would Henry say if he knew?"

"My father would be very upset at what I'm

wearing, Miss."

"Oh, he'd be more than just upset," said Sidney with a chuckle. "He'd be furious, the old bastard. I'll bet he'd flip his lid." She wrapped her arms around Eric and pulled him close. "Of course, he'd probably blame me. 'What have you done to my son, you feminist bitch?!' Oh, how it would kill him to know about you. Heck, just the fact you follow my orders would kill him even without all the rest. He can't stand the idea of women being in charge."

Eric said nothing. His father was a difficult person and he'd never been able to tell him the truth, but he did love him so he tried not to take sides between his father and Sidney. They clearly did not like each other one bit, and both could get carried away in their dislike of the other, as Sidney was doing now.

Sidney got a distant look in her eyes and a vicious smile crossed her lips.

"I should make you stand up in the middle of dinner and show him your panties," growled Sidney. "That would serve him right to know you're a sissy and there's nothing he can do about it."

"Please don't do that, Miss," said Eric pensively.

This snapped Sidney back to reality and she realized what she'd said. She blushed. "I'm sorry, dear. I was just upset at how things are going at work. Your father tried to make me look like a fool again and it frustrates me, but that's no excuse for taking it out on you." She kissed him on the lips. "Forgive me?"

Eric smiled and nodded. "What did he do this time?"

"He's back to whining about my clothes: I 'don't dress conservatively enough' to be a 'real lawyer.' My skirts are too low and my heels are way, way too high according to Henry."

Eric looked down at the platform sandals Sidney wore. They were black with lots of straps and had a five-inch heel. She wore black stockings, but her perfect toes with their red-painted nails, the same color as Eric's toenails, still could be seen clearly through the stockings. These were beautiful shoes, but hardly something lawyers would wear around the office.

Sidney saw her fiancé looking down at her shoes doubtfully. She shook her head and she chuckled. "No, honey, I wasn't wearing these. I was wearing basic black pumps with wide three-inch heels. They're very professional. Female lawyers wear shoes like those all the time. But he started whining that they were too high."

"Dad can be very conservative when it comes to these things, Miss."

Sidney rolled her eyes. "Hardly. He's fine

with the secretaries wearing four and even five-inch heels and short skirts. Heck, they could probably wear lingerie if they wanted. He just doesn't like a woman being an attorney, that's all it is, and he's trying to humiliate me to keep me in my place. So he attacks me in public every time my skirt is shorter than twenty inches or my heels are higher than two and a half inches as if I'm some sort of slut."

"You make it sound like he follows you around with a ruler, Miss."

Sidney smirked cynically. "It feels that way sometimes. I swear that man spends his day staring at my shoes. He must want to wear them or something."

This made Eric blush at the idea of his father wearing women's shoes.

"Do you know what would be hilarious?" asked Sidney.

"What, Miss?"

"If old Henry had to wear high heels. We should make all the wedding guests come dressed as women."

A look of horror passed over Eric's face. Sidney saw this and she laughed.

"Relax, baby, I'm kidding. There's only room for one sissy in my life and that's you!" She kissed her fiancé again. "Could you imagine it though?"

"I think it would kill him," said Eric.

"That it would!"

Then Eric said, "I'm sorry my father's so hard on you, Miss. I wish I could help."

Sidney smiled and shrugged her shoulders. "That's sweet, dear, but there's nothing you can do. It's just the way your father is and I'll have to deal with it. But he better hope he never ends up working for me, that's for sure! I swear I'm going to be merciless!"

—o—

Over the next two weeks, Melanie did intensive study. Dean Dwyer and the college's Board had called her in and asked her to investigate. So she had. She researched everything she could find on the topics of mind control, loss of will, hypnosis and conduct disassociation. She even looked briefly into female domination as a fetish in the event the males had just been turned on by something and were now playing some sort of sexual game. Nothing anywhere ever acted like this.

She decided she needed to broaden her researcher, so she called in two friends: a chemist and a geneticist. With their help, Melanie managed to find the cause, but she had no clue as to a possible cure. Of course, she wasn't looking for one either. Indeed, finding a cure wasn't exactly her goal at all. If anything, she wanted to find a way to spread and expand the effect. But she had to keep that secret, as it would not be well-received by anyone in the town. In the meantime, she needed to stop the town elders from seeking help from the outside world, because that help might expose her plans and might find the cure she never wanted found. If she could do that, then she would remain in charge of this situation and she could do as she wanted. That was her main goal when she met with the college Board that Monday morning.

It was Monday.

Melanie sat in a large, ornate conference room where the university Board normally met. She wore a beige pantsuit with nude pumps. Her shoulder-length brown hair was tied in a bun on the back of her head. Two scientific reports sat on the table before her. She was still alone. She looked at her watch.

"Running late as always, Dwyer," thought Melanie.

She tapped her fingernails nervously on the desk and she looked at her phone. Sidney had ignored her messages. She knew she would, but she sent them nevertheless in a moment of weakness. That Sidney ignored them made her sad. It also made her angry.

"I can't believe she left me for *him!*" growled Sidney.

A moment later, in walked Dean Dwyer, an affable man in his early fifties. He sat down across from Melanie at the center of the table. With the Dean came a much younger woman, Assistant Dean Sondra Stern. She wore a fitted black dress and black stilettos. Melanie thought she was pretty, but she came across as a little harsh or cold. She sat to the Dean's right. Behind the Dean and Stern came the three member Board: two middle-aged women and an older man. They sat to the Dean's left.

Dwyer picked up his gavel and he struck the table.

CRACK! CRACK!

"Let me call this meeting to order. I've asked Dr. Morgan to come brief us tonight on her findings to date, with the understanding that her efforts are only preliminary at this point." He set down the gavel. "Thank you for coming."

"Thank you for having me, Dean," said Melanie.

"I think it's safe to say that there's no doubt something is going on, and it seems to be getting worse," said Dwyer.

"What do you mean 'worse'?" asked one of the Board members.

Dwyer looked at the woman. "It seems the

boys are losing the ability to resist commands from women: any command... from any woman. At first, this was only clear and direct commands. But now it's gotten to the point where even suggestions or hints of commands are being acted upon," said Dwyer.

"What do you mean 'suggestions or hints'?" asked the male Board member.

Dwyer leaned back and folded his arms. He wore a brown sweater, brown slacks and loafers. "To give you an example. When this started, a woman would need to say, 'Rick, fetch me that book.' The boy would then do it. Now we've reached a point, where a woman could simply say into a crowd of boys, 'I wish I had that book,' and every single boy in the crowd would automatically go get the book for her."

The Board members looked at each other uneasily.

"Is there a danger?" asked one of the women.

"Yes and no," Dwyer said cautiously. "So long as everyone acts reasonably and carefully there's no danger. But not everyone has acted reasonably and carefully. We are talking about young people after all."

"And you think we need to say something?" asked the woman.

Dwyer started to nod his head, but he was

cut off.

"What?! Wait a minute!" protested the male Board member. "That will only make things worse by letting the genie out of the bottle!"

"The genie is out of the bottle. The girls know something is wrong and more of them are discovering their newfound power every day. We can't hide this and hope it goes away. We need to address it," said the other woman.

The man shook his head. "We can't do that. If we announce what's happening, it will be open season on the boys. They'll be completely at the girls' mercy."

"They already are."

Dwyer raised his hand to stop the argument. "We don't we hear from Dr. Morgan. I've asked her to come brief us. Maybe she can help us. That is why we called her after all."

Sensing she had two allies in the room in the women, Melanie dove right in. "To cut to the chase, you ladies are correct. The genie *is* out of the bottle. The girls know something is wrong and are flexing their newfound powers already. It would be irresponsible to ignore this and hope it goes away. We need to address it. And that means we need to tell everyone what is happening and put in place a program to smooth the transition."

"The 'transition' to what?" asked the man

cautiously.

Melanie laughed to herself. *"To a world run by women, you stupid man,"* she thought, but she actually said: "Transition to the new reality we need to establish. We need to teach the girls how to use this power wisely so they don't injure the boys by accident or intent, and we need to help the boys accept their new status."

"Can't we cure the boys instead?" asked Dwyer.

Melanie tossed the two reports onto the table. "We don't know how yet. I have here two reports, one from a chemist and one from a geneticist. Our problem comes from a retrovirus, which was created when two chemicals combined in the water supply and then mutated a virus. That virus attacks the Y chromosome, which is why the boys have been affected, but not the girl. When it attacks the chromosome, it makes the changes we are seeing. So we know what is causing all of this, but right now, we have no way to stop the virus or to reverse what it has done." She paused. "Unless and until we can solve that riddle, this is the new reality."

The room went silent, except for the sound of Sondra Stern tapping the sole of her high-heeled shoe against the tile floor.

"How much worse could this get for the boys?" asked one of the women.

Melanie shrugged her shoulders. "We're not sure yet. Since it tinkers directly with the Y chromosome, it could do almost anything. It's theoretically possible they could undergo a great many changes still, including new behaviors or new mental or physical traits. There's just no way to tell what could happen, or when it might happen. It could even reverse itself, though that's unlikely. The geneticist I've consulted actually believes this is how human evolution happens."

"So there are no limits? Is that what you're saying? They could grow wings or turn green?" asked the older woman.

Melanie shook her head. "No. While that's *possible*, something that radical is highly, highly unlikely. The geneticist thinks it's more likely that if other changes occur that the boys will simply become more feminine as the X chromosome compensates for the damage to the Y."

The room went silent again.

"What do you mean more feminine?" asked the man nervously.

"More feminine means exactly what it sounds like: more like women," said Melanie. "That means potentially loss of strength and muscle mass, loss of size, shrunken penises, breast growth... those are all possible. In effect, they could take on the characteristics of their mothers, who gave them the X chromosome. But, of course, it's much more likely nothing will happen."

The Board members looked at each other nervously.

"And you say this was in the water?"

"Yes, we found it in the water. The chemist is still finishing his report, but it appears to have been a combination of a natural organism coming into contact with two separate but reactive chemicals that wouldn't normally be found together, but came into contact when one was dumped accidentally and the other was used to try to kill an algae growth."

"And this is permanent or not?"

"We don't know."

"This is a catastrophe," said the younger woman.

Melanie nodded her heard. "Yes, but we're just speculating about the future now. Right now we need to deal with the issue at hand. These girls have power over these young men and unless you want to keep them separate 24/7, then we need to do something. What I'm proposing will help them cope."

"What are you proposing?" asked the male board member. He seemed shaken by the presentation.

Melanie smiled to herself. This was what

she had been waiting for. Here was her chance to take control over this issue and to use it to get the revenge she felt she deserved against the males of this world... the males who humiliated her in her divorce and now took away her lover Sidney. And best of all, no one, not Dwyer, not the Board, had the slightest idea what she was really up to.

"First," said Melanie, "we need to recognize that this power the girls have now is real. That means we need to teach them to use it wisely. Secondly, since the boys can't resist, we need to make it easier for them to accept that they are powerless."

"I mean, what are you proposing specifically?" asked the man.

Melanie ran her tongue over her teeth. She felt nervous. If they were going to reject her plan, this was when they would do it. She saw all their anxious faces staring at her. She held her breath and continued.

"I'm proposing that we explain this power to the girls so they understand what is happening. Then we assign each boy a female guardian. Their job will be to watch the boy while he's in public and act as a protector. And we need to teach the boys to accept the authority of the girls. We need to ease their sense of shame and soften the blow to their masculine egos to make this easier for them to accept."

"Can't we teach the boys to resist these commands?" asked the male.

Melanie shook her head. "It doesn't appear possible. This is a genetic change which is stronger than mere will power. These boys are literally programmed to follow the girls' commands now." Plus, thought Melanie, "*That would ruin my plans.*"

"Then it's foolish to tell the girls how much power they have!" said the man. "That would only encourage them to take advantage of this situation!"

Sondra suddenly scowled at the man. "It's foolish to ignore this and hope nothing horrible happens. The girls will discover this. Many of them have discovered it already. Putting your head into the sand will leave both the girls and boys unprepared for how to handle this. That's foolish."

The room burst into claxon of voices. For over an hour, they argued. When they finished, the Board voted. Melanie would be given the responsibility for training the boys, the girls, and the parents. What's more, as Melanie suggested, they would do their best to keep this secret from the world outside Satin Falls, except for the scientists Melanie decided to hire to help work on a cure. Melanie had gotten everything she wanted and more. She was firmly in charge of this issue now.

Chapter 3: "Amber and Jason"

—o—

It was Saturday, and Amber Drake, Sidney's younger sister, went to see her boyfriend Jason Cole. Amber had been home sick for the past few days with a cold and she hadn't heard much about what was going on with the boys. All she'd heard at this point was that some of the boys were acting "weird."

"But when don't they?" she thought. She was in for a surprise.

Amber knocked on Jason's door. Jason's parents were out of town shopping for the day, and Jason was home with his stepsister Cindy. Amber thought they could do their homework together and then spend some time sitting by his pool. Jason, however, seemed hesitant to be with her starting the moment he opened the door.

"Amber, hi," said Jason with a hint of trepidation.

Amber wrapped her arms around him and hugged him tightly. "I missed you," she said and she kissed him.

Jason smiled politely, but didn't return her affections. This was unusual. Amber was a beautiful girl, with wavy brown hair to the middle of her back, almond-shaped eyes, hints of dimples in her cheeks, curvy yet athletic legs, and a robust figure. She also excelled at accentuating her features with the right clothing and makeup. Today, for example, she wore a pleated white mini-skirt, a tight pink v-neck sweater and pink slides with a two-inch heel. Just seeing her always brought a smile to Jason's face, and that was before he even thought about how much he loved being with her. Seeing her had not made him smile today, however.

Amber raised an eyebrow. "What's wrong?" she asked.

"Nothing. Everything's fine," he said cautiously.

"Are you sure?"

Just then Jason's stepsister Cindy came around the corner, wearing denim shorts and wooden clogs. They had only just become stepbrother and stepsister as their parents only married a few weeks prior. Unfortunately, they didn't get along. Jason blamed this on Cindy; she was only a year younger than Jason, but she seemed even younger do to her bratty attitude, and she especially seemed to like doing things that annoyed Jason. She and Amber were cordial, though they certainly weren't friends.

"Hey Amber, how are things?" asked Cindy.

"Fine, how are you?" replied Amber and she stepped inside the home.

"Cool, everything's cool. Right, Jason?"

Jason bit his lip. "Yeah, everything's fine."

Amber furrowed her brow. Something seemed wrong, but clearly she wasn't going to get any answer from either of them. She decided to press ahead. "I brought my homework with me. I figure we could do that together," she said to Jason as she patted the bag she carried.

"Sure," said Jason and he shot a glance at Cindy, who nodded her head. Amber missed this.

"Well, lead on," said Amber.

Jason led Amber to the living room. Amber, who walked behind him, admired his tight rear as they went. She liked his butt a lot. As they turned into the living room, however, for the briefest of moments, Amber thought she saw the outline of a pair of panties beneath Jason's tan walking shorts. This startled her. But before she could look again, what she saw vanished as he sat down.

"That's impossible," she thought, and she dismissed this as her imagination.

For the next hour, Amber and Jason slogged their way through various math and science questions while Cindy watched television from a nearby recliner. By the time they finished, both felt mentally exhausted.

"Do you know what we should do now?" asked Amber.

"What?" asked Jason.

"I'd love to sit by your pool!"

Cindy sat up at this. A huge smile appeared on her lips. Amber thought this was strange. Even more strange, Jason seemed hesitant. Jason had never refused to sit by the pool before, so what made him so nervous now, she wondered.

Jason bit his lip. "Uh, I'd rather not go outside."

"Why not?"

"Yeah Jason," asked Cindy in a mocking tone, "why not?" A wicked smile crossed her lips. She looked directly at him; he seemed nervous. Then she said, "Jason, go change and then go sit outside by the pool with Amber."

Jason started to rise. Amber saw this and cocked her head to one side. How had Cindy, of all people, gotten him to agree when he seemed so opposed? And why did he agree without even a hint of resistance? This was all very strange.

Cindy turned to Amber. "You can borrow my mom's swimsuit if you want."

"Thanks."

—o—

Five minutes later, Amber walked out back to the small pool in Jason's backyard. She wore a canary yellow two piece bikini and her pink slides. She's found some suntan lotion in the bathroom and was busy applying it to her chest and arms when Cindy appeared. Cindy wore a blue and white-checkered bikini. On her feet were blue flip-flops. Her long black hair was tied back in a ponytail.

"Jason will be out in a minute," said Cindy. She seemed to stifle a giggle.

Amber thought this was suspicious and she almost went inside to check on Jason to make sure nothing had happened to him, but then Jason appeared and Amber's jaw dropped.

"Oh my God!" gasped Amber.

Cindy laughed.

"I'm sorry," Jason said. "It wasn't my idea." Jason wore a red bikini with a flower pattern. On his feet were tan wedge-heeled sandals with a three-inch wedge heel; he walked in them like a pro, as if he had been wearing them for some time. What's more, as he neared, his erection was obvious as was the fact he already had tan lines which matched the bikini! Clearly, he had been sunning himself in this very bikini before.

Amber rose and inspected her boyfriend. The bikini left nothing to the imagination, including his erection.

"Why are you wearing that?" she asked as she tugged at the bikini.

"It wasn't my idea," he repeated. His face was so red it almost looked like a crayon.

Amber pulled the bikini away from his chest so she could see his tan line. "You wore this to get a tan?" she asked, sounding confused. "I don't understand. What's going on, Jason?"

Jason looked at her and he cringed. Suddenly, he sang: "I love wearing sissy clothes! I'm a little sissy. I'm Sissy Jason!" Then he turned on his heels and he skipped inside.

Amber stood there stunned. Behind her, Cindy was doubled over laughing. Amber shook her head at Cindy's nasty display and she followed Jason into the house. He had locked himself in his bedroom and would not come out.

"Jason, what's going on?!" demanded Amber.

"I'm sorry. Please leave," he said.

"Can we talk?"

"Please leave me alone."

Amber took a deep breath. She thought about trying to force him to talk about this now, but changed her mind. She would let him calm down and then she would speak to him later.

"I'll call you later," she said.

With that, she left. As she did, the image of her boyfriend in the bikini and the heels filled her mind. She had no idea what this meant and she was still in shock. Interestingly, she also felt a very strange feeling deep within her. It was almost a tingle deep inside her crotch. She didn't know what this meant and she wasn't sure she wanted to find out.

—o—

Amber returned home to wait for her sister Sidney. She was deeply confused and she needed advice, and Sidney was the best person to give it to her. Sidney was a few years older than Amber and had been appointed her guardian when their parents died. They now lived together in an apartment Sidney rented as Amber finished school and Sidney got her start in the law. With Amber being legally old enough now, and Sidney planning to marry Eric, Amber and Sidney agreed that Amber would get the apartment to herself once Sidney moved in with Eric after the wedding. Amber had no idea that Eric was a cross-dresser or that Sidney dominated him. She didn't know that Sidney had been Dr. Morgan's lesbian lover either.

"It was really weird," said Amber. They were in the kitchen. Sidney still wore her skirt suit and heels from work. She leaned against the kitchen counter eating an apple. Amber wore shorts and sandals. She still looked stunned from her experience with her boyfriend a few hours prior. What stunned her most, perhaps, was that she felt a very strong desire to masturbate. She tried to put that out of her mind.

"Weird in what way?" asked Sidney. She stepped out of her four-inch heels, heels which had once again drawn the ire of Henry Miller. This time, she came within an ounce of self-control of asking him if he had "a thing" for her shoes. The only thing stopping her was that she was pretty sure he would fire her, even if she was to be married to his son.

"You won't laugh?" asked Amber.

"I won't laugh. We're sisters. You can tell me anything. What happened?" asked Sidney.

"From the moment I got there, he seemed nervous," said Amber. "I'm not sure why, but he was. Then we did our homework. When we finished, I asked him if we could sit by the pool. He said he didn't want to. That was strange."

Sidney shrugged her shoulders. "Maybe he just didn't want to sit by the pool."

"He always does, that's why it seemed strange. But that wasn't the only thing. Right after he told me he didn't want to, Cindy told him to do it and he instantly agreed. He just got right up and went to change. It was weird. At first, he seemed really opposed and then he just did it when she told him to."

Sidney shrugged her shoulders again and she fished a drink out of the refrigerator. "So he changed his mind?"

"Just wait, it gets worse," said Amber. As she prepared to discuss the next part, she felt her pussy becoming wet. This troubled her as she had no idea why any of this should excite her. She had felt the same way on the walk home: excited and horny, but also ashamed and confused. She tried to focus on her concerns about Jason. "After he agreed, I changed into a swimming suit and I went outside to wait by the pool. A few minutes later, he comes waltzing outside... and... well, get this... he's wearing a bikini and high heels!"

Sidney almost spit out her drink. "He what?!" she blurted out. Her thoughts instantly turned to what her fiancé was likely wearing at this very moment at his apartment. No doubt, that too involved high heels... and a feather duster. Her face turned bright red.

"Don't laugh!"

"I'm not laughing. Trust me," said Sidney. She bit her lip and blushed. *What are the odds that Amber found a cross-dresser?* wondered Sidney.

"Why would a boy do that?" asked Amber.

It wasn't clear if this question was rhetorical or not, but Sidney assumed Amber would want an answer. Unfortunately, she wasn't sure how to address this, not without running the risk of exposing Eric. She took a deep breath. She ran her tongue over her teeth. She thought about dodging the question, but Amber needed guidance. Finally, she spoke.

"Some guys just like to wear women's clothes," said Sidney as calmly and as reassuringly as she could.

Amber seemed surprised. "Really?! Why?"

"I'm, uh, not sure. I just know they do."

"How do you know? Do you know any?"

Sidney blushed. "Well, I mean, it's not an uncommon thing," she said, evading the question. "I've read about it at times. It's called a 'fetish' and some guys just have it. It's like women who want to be submissive or guys who get off on women's shoes," she said.

Amber furrowed her brow. "Guys get off on women's shoes?" she asked doubtfully.

Sidney realized that this conversation was not headed in the right direction. It was one thing to talk about the birds and the bees with her little sister; it was another to become Amber's Encyclopedia of Fetishes. She decided to try to force the conversation back on topic.

"Look, Amber, there are guys who get off on wearing women's clothes. There's nothing wrong with it."

Amber raised an eyebrow. "There's nothing wrong with it?"

"No. They're just clothes."

"Then why don't they do it openly?"

Sidney bit her lip. She really wished Eric was handling this conversation. "Well, sometimes they can't because some people don't react well. So it's safer to just keep that quiet. But it doesn't make it wrong or anything."

There was a pause.

"What about women?" asked Amber cautiously.

Sidney nodded her head. "Yes, some women wear men's clothes."

Amber blushed. "No, I mean, are there women who get excited by men wearing women's clothes?" asked Amber carefully. She felt that tingle again.

Sidney simultaneously felt terror at this question and a strange thrill. "*Yes,*" she wanted to scream, "*I love seeing Eric in women's clothes!*" but she knew that was the last thing she could say. She decided to shift the conversation away again. "Yeah," she said, "I guess so. But the issue is Jason, right?"

"Right. And you think this is something that turns Jason on?"

Sidney nodded her head. "Yes, I do. And you can either accept that as part of who he is, or you can leave him and find another man. But if you really do love him, then honestly, this shouldn't bother you."

Amber scratched her chin. "I'm not so

sure."

Sidney furrowed her brow. She was surprised Amber wasn't more accepting of this. "Look, I know it's a difficult decision, but keep in mind that he's the same Jason you fell in love with even if he is prancing around the house in heels and a dress," said Sidney and she instantly regretted using the word "prancing." She had gotten into the habit of teasing Eric about his feminization, because he liked it, and that meant she often found herself describing male feminization in quasi-insulting ways or in ways that implied weakness or that suggested it was weird. This was a hard habit to break, and she did not want to send this signal to Amber. Amber, however, had something else on her mind and had been misinterpreted by Sidney.

"What? Oh, that's not what I mean," said Amber before Sidney could correct the "prancing" comment.

"What do you mean?" asked Sidney cautiously.

"I don't think he likes wearing women's clothes. I think he's being forced."

Sidney bit her lip and placed her hand on her sister's shoulder. "Listen little sister, the world is full of people with issues. Trust me on this, I'm a lawyer, I've seen it all. There's no reason to get upset about this just yet. What you're experiencing is called denial—"

"No, I get that, but that's not what I'm talking about. When I asked him why he was wearing those things, he said he was a sissy," said Amber. "Actually, he sang that he was a sissy."

"See."

"*But* he seemed angry about it and he clearly didn't want to say it or let me see him in those clothes. So why would he say those things and dress like that if he didn't want to? I really got the feeling it was like he was being blackmailed into putting on this show for me and it wouldn't surprise me if Cindy was behind this!"

Sidney took a deep breath. "People act strangely at times like that." Amber started to speak, but Sidney cut her off. "All I'm trying to say is that until you know exactly what's going on, there's no reason to judge anything. It could have been a prank gone wrong. Or maybe he's just one of those guys who likes your closet as much as he likes you. For now, if you love him, just keep an open mind and wait for it all to shake out."

Amber nodded her head. "I will," she said, but she clearly wasn't satisfied. Everything about the incident struck her as strange or wrong. Jason was acting against his will, of that she was sure. Amber vowed to get to the bottom of this.

—o—

A day or so later, Sidney sat down on Eric's couch and kicked off her heels. She leaned back and rubbed her eyes. Eric brought her a cup of hot tea, as he often did when she came home tired and frustrated. He wore a black satin maid's uniform with a low cut square top, a white pinafore apron, and open-toed black slingbacks with a four-inch heel. This was Sidney's favorite uniform of his.

"Thank you, dear," said Sidney, and she took the tea.

"Hard day, Miss?" asked Eric and he wiped his hands on his apron.

"You don't know the half of it," she said.

Sidney patted the seat next to her and Eric sat down, smoothing his skirt before he did and then pulling his feet close together and resting his hands on his knees. He was the perfect picture of femininity in his motions. Indeed, when he first told Sidney about his cross-dressing and she insisted that he show her, she was floored at how feminine he was in his appearance and how he carried himself when he was dressed. That came from all the practicing he had done once he moved out of his parents' house and into this apartment, and it turned her on something fierce to think that this was a man. Of course, it turned her on even more to realize that he had chosen to share this dangerous secret with her. Not only did the sense of power she felt from knowing this about him make her happy, as did the sense that he had delivered himself into her power, but the amazing feeling of trust it gave her made her feel warm and loved. She had never felt so close to another person.

Right now though, she felt annoyed.

"So what happened?" asked Eric.

"In a word: Tim Johnson. He's the biggest pain in my rear. Add in your father and together they make everything so amazingly difficult. Let me tell you, your father really does not like women working as lawyers."

"Dad's like that, Miss."

Sidney rolled her eyes. "Don't I know it? Do you know he actually asked me today if I would have time to work full-time even with my wedding coming up? Can you believe the nerve?"

Eric smiled. "Well, weddings are a big deal and he probably figured you wanted to take some time to work out all the details, Miss."

Sidney laughed. "That's exactly what Henry was thinking all right." A sly smile crossed her lips and she leaned over and wrapped her arms around Eric. "But that's what I have you for, my little house hubby. You can do all that girly stuff for me."

Eric felt his penis become erect and he

blushed. "Yes, Miss."

Sidney saw him blush and she smiled. "Oh oh, is someone hard?" she asked.

Eric smiled but didn't answer.

"Bad girl," said Sidney with mock chastisement. "You know you're not supposed to get hard without permission."

"I'm sorry, Miss," said Eric and he giggled.

"We'll see about that."

Sidney slid her fingers beneath his skirt and dexterously pulled his erection from his panties. It now stood straight up in his lap. She looked down and smiled. "You have such a pretty penis," she said and she rubbed its tip with her finger. Then she ran her nails over its head, which caused Eric to shudder. Finally, she took the shaft between her fingers and she started stroking.

Eric seemed to melt.

"Do you like that, sissy?" asked Sidney.

"Oh yes, Miss, I do," purred Eric.

Sidney stroked a little harder and a little faster. She could see the pleasure in the far away look in her fiancé's eyes and she felt it in the throbbing in his penis. He was enjoying this a lot.

"Could you imagine what Henry would say if he saw this, sissy? Heck, imagine what he would say if he knew you were planning the wedding for me and that you were going to be my househusband?"

"He would be upset, Miss," said Eric between breaths.

"That is the understatement of the year," said Sidney. She stroked her fiancé even faster and she now twisted her foot around, flexing and unflexing her toes. "That man simply cannot accept that the world isn't like caveman times anymore. There *are* women professionals now."

"Yes, Miss," said Eric. He was breathing hard now.

"There are women bosses too," she said. Then she smirked. "Some women even run the lives of their little sissy husbands, don't they?" She kissed her fiancé on the cheek.

"Oh yes, Miss," moaned Eric. He felt his balls jiggling and his penis throbbing. He was so very close to cumming.

"You like hearing me talk like that, don't you?" asked Sidney, though this was more of a statement to herself than a question to Eric; she knew that Eric liked gentle humiliating reminders of his forfeit masculinity.

"Oh yes, Miss," exclaimed Eric. "It makes me very happy when you say those things."

"Does it excite you?"

"Yes, Miss!" His breathing was labored and he was starting to tremble.

"I'm sure it does. You like having me in charge, don't you?"

"Yes, Miss!" His chest heaved and his balls bounced. His penis throbbed.

"You like that I want to make all the decisions for you, don't you?"

"Yes, Miss, it excites me. It makes me feel like your property when you make decisions for me, and that turns me on." Eric's erection not only throbbed, it positively lurched in his fiancée's hand.

"Tell me you like being my little sissy girl."

"I like being your sissy girl, Miss. I want to please you."

"Tell me what you want, dear."

"I want to be yours, Miss. I want to be helpless without you. I want you to control everything about me!" His penis jumped and he stopped breathing.

Sidney leaned in close and whispered in his ear: "Tell me you're mine."

"I—" he gasped as his erection made one giant throb. "I—" he tried again and again his erection jumped. He knew what this meant. They both did. "I'm yours!" he exclaimed as his penis exploded. C um shot straight up into the air, almost as high as his chin. Then it came crashing down right on his skirt and his stockings.

Sidney smiled. "Did you like that?"

"Yes... Miss," said Eric between breaths.

Sidney then wrapped her arms around him

and held him tightly as he slowly caught his breath. Eric felt a warm glow pass over him as she did. He felt intensely happy and calm. Finally, she let go.

"Now go put on that cute little red dress with the black stilettos. I like seeing you in that," said Sidney.

"Yes, Miss," said Eric and he stood up to go change. As he did, Sidney slapped his rear with her open palm.

SLAP!

He giggled in response and he raced off on his heels. Sidney watched him wiggle his way to the bedroom.

"You really are the perfect man," she thought to herself.

—o—

Eric returned a few minutes later in a red dress which always reminded Sidney of a Spanish dancer. It was gorgeous and it turned her on that her fiancé would wear it for her. Tonight, he'd paired it with some beautiful black high-heeled stilettos with very high heels and red soles. They had roses over the toes. All told, he looked incredibly sexy and Sidney could not wait to release the tension she felt by having him lick her to orgasm.

"Very sexy, baby," said Sidney. She drank her fiancé in with her eyes.

"Thank you, Miss," said Eric and he grabbed the skirt of his dress and shook it. He spun around to let Sidney see the dress from all sides. His toes looked so delicate sticking out the front of the shoes.

"Beautiful. Now come here, girlfriend."

"Yes, Miss," said Eric.

He knew what she wanted, so he sauntered over to his fiancée as she sat on the couch. He swung his hips widely and did his best to seduce her with his eyes. Then he carefully kneeled down on the floor before her. As he did, she uncrossed her legs and spread them as wide as she could in the pencil skirt she wore.

"I definitely need this," said Sidney.

Eric placed his hands, with their dark red nails, on her calves and slowly worked them up her legs and beneath her skirt. As they ran up her legs, they pulled back her skirt, allowing her legs to spread wider. Finally, her legs were spread wide enough that he could reach her pussy with his face. He leaned over and kissed her pussy through her panties. Then she raised her rear off the couch and he pulled her panties down her legs and then off her legs, one leg at a time. That left only her stockings and her garterbelt. He then rubbed her thighs and slowly moved his lips between her legs.

As Eric's lips worked their magic, Sidney felt a sense of exhilaration run over her. She leaned back and took a deep breath.

"You are an amazing lover, girly," said Sidney.

Eric kept licking.

"Oh, by the way, I meant to tell you that I know another cross-dresser in town," said Sidney.

"Really?" asked Eric.

"Yep. It's my little sister's boyfriend!"

Eric stuck his head up from between Sidney's thighs. "Really?!"

"Yeah. He came out to Amber a couple days ago. I guess he told her he would meet her at the pool and then he showed up wearing a bikini and high heels with a huge hard-on beneath the bikini."

"How did Amber take it?"

"She freaked out. She didn't know how to respond."

"That's too bad."

"Isn't it though?" asked Sidney. "I tried telling her about all the benefits of having your own sissy, like having total freedom and having a huge wardrobe full of gorgeous clothes you can share, but she's in denial." Sidney pointed at her crotch again. "Hey, no one told you that you can stop, Mister!"

Eric smiled. "Sorry, Miss," he said.

He got back to work.

"She might still come around," said Sidney. She then focused on what she was feeling from Eric's tongue. Sidney came a few minutes later... and it was good.

Chapter 4: "Melanie Strikes"
—o—

Melanie's mid-heeled black pumps made a loud cracking sound with each heel strike as she walked across the wooden stage to the podium. She'd intentionally dressed conservatively and professionally today, in a mid-calf skirt suit, a loose white blouse with a high collar, and a tailored black-checkered jacket because she needed the audience to see her at her most "clinical." After all, she was about to provide some shocking news and some very strange advice, and she needed to come off as trustworthy as possible when she delivered it.

When Melanie reached the podium, she set down her notes and her phone. She checked one last time for any reply to her messages to Sidney. There were none; Sidney had ignored her. She had been desperate to see Sidney again and she finally gave in to her need and sent Sidney a text... several actually. Apparently, Sidney did not feel the same. Melanie felt a twisted feeling in her stomach as she looked at her phone. Still, she knew she couldn't focus on that right now. Right now, she needed to put her plan into motion. Here was her chance. She was going to show the men of Satin Falls what it felt like to feel powerless and at someone else's mercy, and she was going to do it by striking at the very thing men treasure above all else: their manhoods.

Melanie took a deep breath and she looked out over the assembled men and women. They looked pensive. She had already seen some of them in her practice; she recognized the Cole's, for example, and she snickered to herself at how "macho asshole" Greg Cole would react to what she was about to say.

"You want to see a 'pussy,' do you?" she thought angrily. "Well, get ready for this."

Melanie smiled reassuringly and began...

"Good evening. Thank you for coming. We've asked you all to come tonight because our town faces a crisis..."

Melanie's speech lasted only a few minutes. The question and answer session that followed lasted almost three hours. By the time it was over, everyone in the room knew exactly what was going on and what the plan was for tackling this problem. That didn't mean, however, that everyone approved... especially the fathers.

Greg Cole sat on the edge of his bed and kicked off his loafers. He and his wife Brenda had just come from the meeting with Melanie. It had been a lot to take it and even more to accept.

Greg in particular had asked several pointed questions during the meeting and he still wasn't satisfied.

"I don't even know what to say," growled Greg to his wife.

Brenda stood before her mirror and removed her jewelry. She didn't respond. She wasn't happy the way Greg had acted during the meeting.

"Does any of this make sense to you?" asked Greg. "DNA damage?"

"It would explain what's been wrong with Jason."

Greg unbuttoned his shirt. "It just seems so far-fetched. Seriously, a new microbe in the water which makes boys do whatever girls tell them? That's science fiction garbage. That's not real."

"Is it really so hard to believe, Greg?" asked Brenda with a hint of frustration in her voice. "They have pills now which can alter moods or memories or break down your will to resist. Why can't nature do the same thing? And it's not like women's DNA hasn't made them prone to be submissive in the past. Maybe it's just the boys' turn now?"

Greg shuddered at the thought of his boy being submissive to a girl. Brenda, on the other hand, actually felt a tiny thrill at what she'd just said. The idea of nature turning the tables and making males submissive held a certain appeal to her. It was only too bad, she thought, that it hadn't happened to her husband instead.

"Why just the boys? Why weren't the girls affected?!"

"You heard Dr. Morgan. It has something to do with the Y chromosome," replied Brenda calmly.

"Well, if it's something about the Y chromosome, then why have just the boys been affected but none of the men? I have a Y chromosome. Nothing's happened to me or any of the other men I know."

Brenda felt that tingle again, only this time it was a little stronger. She imagined her husband waiting on her hand and foot, doing everything she told him. He needed to be put in his place and the idea of having absolute power over him really did excite her. In fact, she realized that she was becoming wet. If only, she thought, this had been more than a fantasy.

"Dr. Morgan said they think the boys were just more susceptible because their bodies are still growing," said Brenda.

Morgan didn't mention that her geneticist friend said that adult males might still be affected over time, nor did she mention the possibility of other changes. She told the Board she didn't want to cause a panic, but the truth was that she didn't want to say anything that might spur greater action on the part of the town's males. The last thing she needed was them demanding to see outside doctors, who might then find a cure and ruin her plan.

"Yeah, I guess," said Greg doubtfully. He pulled off his pants. Then he clenched his fists. "This just— this isn't right. It should be girls who have to do what boys want, not the other way around. That's how it's always been. That's the natural order of things."

Brenda rolled her eyes. "Like I said, women's DNA made them prone to be submissive in the past. Maybe it's just the boys' turn now?"

"My son should be giving orders, not taking them. Especially from girls!"

Brenda rolled her eyes again. She didn't respond this time.

Greg pulled off his shirt and his underwear. He was naked now. Brenda, meanwhile, had slipped into a nightie and she sat down at her vanity to remove her makeup.

"I'll tell you another thing," said Greg angrily. His face was bright red as if he were embarrassed. "I don't like the idea at all that girls are going to be appointed as 'guardians' of the boys. That sounds like some feminist jerk-off fantasy to me! That woman just wants to emasculate the boys!"

"It has to be this way," said Brenda coldly. She'd had just about enough of her husband and his insecurities. He couldn't stomach the idea that a woman might be in charge because it made him feel inadequate as a man, and that was why he was lashing out now. Brenda, who generally just turned the other cheek whenever Greg acted this way, was reaching her limit.

"No, it doesn't. It doesn't have to be this way," growled Greg.

Brenda spun around to face her husband. She had had enough. "Yes, it does, Greg! It needs to be this way. Right now the boys are extremely vulnerable. Any order from any girl, even an accidental order, will make that boys do whatever the girl said. That means that even simple expressions of speech like 'go play in traffic' can be dangerous. Without a girl protecting each boy, bad things could happen. You heard Dr. Morgan. She made it clear why they need to do this."

Greg was taken aback by his wife's tone. She rarely blew up at him as she just had. Still, that wasn't going to stop him from speaking his mind. "Well tell me this, why can't they just separate the boys?"

"How?" demanded his wife.

"Like separate classes."

"Dr. Morgan covered that, *if you had listened*. They could put the boys in separate classes, but how do you stop the boys from running into girls between classes or on their way home? Besides, you heard her idea about the nurture reflex. Dr. Morgan thinks that giving the girls an official role in protecting the boys will trigger their natural nurturing instinct and will keep them from trying to take advantage of the situation."

Greg folded his arm. "Maybe we should leave town?"

Brenda put her hands on her hips and glared at her husband. "Greg, can you imagine what would happen to Jason in another town where he was the only boy who felt completely compelled to do anything any girl even suggested?"

Greg grumbled something to himself. "This is a nightmare."

Brenda stepped into her wedge-heeled slippers. She looked at her husband. "Frankly, this sounds like it could be a good thing. The girls get a little self-esteem and the boys learn a bit about humility. What's so bad about that?"

"What's so bad?! It's just not right. A boy like Jason needs to learn to be his own man, not take orders from some girl."

"Well, dear, you better get used to it, because unless something changes, Jason will always find himself under the control of women from now on."

"We need to find another doctor, a real doctor," growled Greg.

"You know what, Greg? Just stop talking. I don't want to hear it," said Brenda.

And he did.

Neither seemed to notice that he had just obeyed his wife.

—o—

Amber got to class early the next day. She was hoping to have more time to talk to Jason before class, but he was later than normal. As she sat waiting for him, she noticed that everything seemed a little strange to her. Granted, when one is gone from a place for a few days, it always feels a little different when you return, but this was something else. This was more than that. Indeed, as Amber looked around the hallways and then her class, she noticed that it was much more quiet than usual. The boys in particular seemed very quiet. They were almost sheepish. The girls all seemed happy, but their conversations were whispered conversations too. It was like the boys and girls had separated into two camps and the boys waited pensively for an assault from the girls. At least, that's how things felt to Amber.

"Hey Beth, what's going on?" asked Amber

to her friend who sat next to her.

"Haven't you heard?" replied Beth.

"Heard what?"

Beth blushed and shook her leg excitedly. "You mean you missed it all?"

"I've been out sick. You know that. So what's going on?"

Beth now flashed a sharp smile. She looked over her shoulder at several boys. They averted their eyes when she did. "Well—"

"Whoa, hold on. Jason's here!" said Amber and she got up to greet her boyfriend, who had just entered the room. As she approached, she looked him over. Apart from being uncomfortable meeting her eyes with his, he looked quite normal. She saw no traces of anything out of the ordinary. "Are you ok?"

Jason nodded his head.

"I'd like to talk to you," said Amber.

Just then, Professor Black walked into the room. He set down his bag and he brought the class to order. "Settle down, class. Everyone take your seats."

They did.

"There's going to be an unannounced assembly this morning," said the Professor. "What I need right now is for the girls to remain seated as the boys head straight for the auditorium."

With that, the boys were dismissed and they made their way to the auditorium. An hour later, the girls were called to the auditorium. The boys were nowhere to be seen. Amber walked into the auditorium with her friend Beth. They sat in the middle, toward the front.

"Any idea what this is about?" asked Beth.

"No idea."

"I didn't see any of the boys, so I didn't get a chance to ask them either. Did you?" asked Beth.

Amber shook her head. "No. I wanted to talk to Jason, but he never came back to class."

Suddenly, a loud tapping sound came from the stage. Dean Dwyer was tapping the microphone at the podium. "Ladies, settle down... settle down." Dwyer waited a few seconds for the room to grow quiet. "Before we begin, I want you all to know that I have the greatest faith in each of you that you can handle these events like adults."

This brought a murmur from the crowd.

Dwyer continued: "In a moment, I'll introduce Dr. Melanie Morgan. You need to pay careful attention to everything Dr. Morgan is about to tell you. This is extremely serious."

The room grew quiet and still.

When Dwyer stepped aside, Melanie Morgan took his place at the podium. She was dressed about the same as the prior night – a conservative navy-blue skirt suit with simple black pumps, though her heels were higher today. A small strand of pearls hung between the open collar of her royal-blue blouse. She looked out over the assembled young women.

"I wasn't quite sure how to start this speech," she began. "I thought about using a metaphor about a caterpillar emerging from a cocoon and finding its new life as a butterfly, but this really isn't the time for metaphors. So let me cut right to the chase and be blunt. Your world has changed and you will be asked to change with it."

Without a doubt, she had their attention now.

Melanie continued: "When you were born, there was a natural order to the world. Men and women were equal under the law, but nature made men more aggressive and controlling and it made women more passive and accommodating. This meant that men tended to be in charge." She paused. "For you, that's no longer true. Indeed, for you, the world is now very much reversed. Because of a virus introduced into the water in Satin Falls, the boys you go to school with... your boyfriends, your friends, your classmates, your brothers, have lost the ability to resist even the slightest suggestion made by any woman."

The room erupted in a combination of shocked voices and giggles. Some girls were shocked, but more already knew about this, as evidenced by the things they had made their brothers or their boyfriends do over the past few days.

Amber was shocked. She looked around with her jaw open until her eyes came to rest on Beth, who was grinning.

"That's what I was trying to tell you," said Beth.

The giggling began to grow throughout the hall.

"Ladies... settle down, settle down," said Dwyer as he stepped to the front of the stage. That seemed to help as the girls quieted down once more. He retreated to his chair and Melanie continued.

"Pay careful attention, ladies, because this is important. This change gives you great power, but it also gives you great responsibility. The boys literally cannot disobey you."

The hall burst into more giggles and murmuring. This made Melanie happy because the girls were responding the way she had hoped. Rather than being horrified by this change, they seemed to be relishing the idea; to them, this was exciting – a marked contrast from the boys who sat in stony silence as she told them how their world was about to change. This would make it easier for her to achieve her goal.

"Girls, calm down!" said Dwyer.

Melanie stepped over to him and placed her hand on his arm. "It's all right, Dean. This is a natural reaction."

Dwyer pursed his lips. "If you say so." Then he returned to his seat.

Finally, the giggling and murmuring slowed and the hall grew silent once more.

"What this means," said Melanie, "is that we need to work together to help the boys through this transition to their new submissive state." The word "submissive" sent a tingle through Melanie's pussy and it seemed to have a similar effect on a number of the young women. "You must learn to be very careful what you say to them. You must not say anything the boys will interpret as a command, unless you mean it as a command. To do that, you must learn to take command."

More murmuring.

"From now on, each of you will be assigned to a boy. Your job will be to watch out for the boy and to take care of him, *by taking control of him.* You must help him learn that following your orders is not a bad thing."

Dwyer perked up. He was not aware Melanie intended to suggest that the girls actively control the boys. He thought that she would only suggest that the girls act as a guardian for the boys. He suddenly felt nervous.

Melanie wasn't finished yet either. "*You must help them adjust to the new reality, where you are his superior and he must obey you. Think of this as a challenge. You must embrace your new status as the dominant superior person and you must help guide the boys as they learn to be submissive and inferior to you.*" The tingle in Melanie's panties grew with each sentence. It was so strong now that she almost felt compelled to touch herself. "Teach him that being submissive is not such a bad thing... it is his future, a future in which girls rule."

Dwyer looked like he wanted to jump out of his chair at this point, but Vice Dean Stern held his arm and whispered in his ear that the Board had placed their full trust in Morgan.

"But this is way beyond what she told the Board she would do," he whispered back.

"You need to trust her," said Stern.

As she said this, a strange look came over Dwyer's face and then he chuckled. He leaned back in his chair and said, "I trust her." Stern had no idea what had just happened. She put it off to Dwyer realizing that the Board had put this issue out of his hands. In any event, his objections seemed settled.

"Are there any questions?" asked Melanie.

A blonde girl in a yellow sundress and white sandals stood up. "How long will this last?"

"We don't know yet, but it looks like it could be permanent," said Melanie.

"Is this happening everywhere?" asked another girl.

"No, just here," said Melanie. *"So you must maintain this as a secret.* This is vital and you all need to cooperate with this. No one outside of Satin Falls can know about this. If you told this to anyone outside of Satin Falls, these boys would fall prey to any number of bad people and they could be seriously hurt or exploited."

A girl in a green blouse, white shorts and neutral open-toed high-heeled pumps stood up. "So, like, you want to assign a boy to each of us and they're like what? Like a slave or something?" she asked.

"EXACTLY!" thought Melanie. **"Now you get it!"**

Of course, she couldn't say that. So she tried to talk around it and agree with the sentiment without actually saying so. "Well," said Melanie, "I think that's a loaded word, so I wouldn't put it that way. But fundamentally, you are essentially correct about the nature of the relationship."

"So they are slaves?" asked the young woman.

A huge murmur arose.

Dwyer shot out of his chair and came to the microphone. "Now, girls, let's not think of it that way. These boys need your help. Think of yourselves as nurses, and they are the patients who need you to guide them."

"That's right," said Melanie as she took back the microphone. "Think of yourselves as the ones who need to guide these young men. They need to be taught to accept that their new place is to be submissive to you."

"But we still need to treat them with respect, compassion and equality, right?" asked Amber from the crowd.

Everything went silent.

Melanie glared at Amber. She ran her tongue over her teeth. "I'm sorry, what was your name?"

"Amber Drake."

This shook Melanie for a moment. She had never met Sidney's sister, but she recognized the name instantly. She also knew that Amber was a do-gooder and would not approve of her plan.

"Well, Ms. Drake," said Melanie. "Of course, those concepts are relative and they should only apply, which of course they do, to the extent they do not interfere with the lessons that need to be taught."

"So they do apply?" asked Amber.

Melanie looked at her watch. "Thank you for the question, but we are short of time and, at this point, I think it would be best if we moved to the next phase. In a moment, we will be calling each of you up to the front one by one, where Miss Stern will assign you to a boy and she and I will provide further instruction. Please remember that this is important and if you need assistance, my office is always open."

With that, she stepped back from the microphone.

Amber folded her arms. Something seemed wrong to her here.

Chapter 5: "The Humiliation Begins"
—o—

Sidney sat on the sofa reading the newspaper. She wore a black and white sheath dress. The black sandals she had worn with it sat on the floor before her and her legs were curled up beneath her. Eric scurried around preparing dinner in a purple nightie with matching high-heeled mules. This outfit had been an engagement present from Sidney. She enjoyed buying her fiancé women's clothes because she said it turned her on to think of him as her life-sized Barbie.

"Strange," said Sidney as she turned the page in her newspaper. "I would have thought there'd be something about the parents meeting at the school last night."

"What meeting, Miss?" asked Eric as he bent over to check the roast.

Sidney watched him bend and saw his panties appear beneath his nightie. She became instantly wet. "You look amazing, honey. Come here."

"But dinner's almost ready!" he protested.

"Come here," she repeated.

Eric walked over to his fiancée as commanded. His heels clicked off the hardwood floor and his feet slapped against the mules as he walk: ***CLICKSLAP!*** ***CLICKSLAP!*** ***CLICKSLAP!*** That sound made Sidney even wetter. It also made Eric harder... though he was always hard when dressed.

"You look so sexy," said Sidney.

"Thank you, Miss," purred Eric.

Sidney ran her hand up the back of his thigh up under his nightie. She slipped her fingers inside his panties and tickled his butt with her fingertips. She saw his erection throb and bounce beneath the nightie as she did this.

She giggled.

Soon, Eric began breathing hard and his penis looked increasingly tense. This made Sidney smile, but she wasn't going to let him cum yet. So after a minute or so, Sidney removed her hand and slapped his butt cheek: ***SLAP!*** This made his cheeks jiggle and it actually caused a jot of precum to burst out into his panties. A wet spot formed.

"Go finish dinner, sissy," she said.

"Yes, Miss," said Eric. He was still breathing hard. He felt very turned on at the moment, so it was with some reluctance that he returned to the kitchen.

"To answer your question, by the way, the meeting I was talking about happened at the school last night. They had a meeting and they wanted all the parents to attend. I couldn't make it because of work, but I figured they would cover it in the newspaper because they always have and because it sounded important, but they didn't. I guess I'll have to ask Amber if she knows what it was about."

Eric pulled the roast from the oven. "Dinner's almost ready, Miss, if you'd like to move to the table."

Sidney folded her newspaper and stood up. She straightened her dress, slid her pretty feet into her shoes, and walked over the table. She left her drink sitting next to the couch. Eric fetched it and brought it to her at the table. He held the glass out for her to take.

"Your drink, Miss."

"Thank you, dear. How are the wedding preparations going?" she asked.

"Fine, Miss."

"And when can I see my choices?"

"I'm still looking for one more option, but I can show you the rest at any time," he said. "Would you like to see them now?"

"Yes, I think I'd like to see them while we eat," she said and she sipped her drink.

"Yes, Miss."

Eric scurried off to the bedroom on his heels and grabbed a folder from his small computer desk. This was wedding material. He returned to the dining area with the folder and handed it to Sidney. Then he served the food. Meanwhile, Sidney opened the folder as they began eating. She saw a variety of wedding dresses, shoes and bridesmaid's dresses. There were also cakes and a number of dining accessories. Sidney had told him to find three alternatives for each item they needed to buy, then she would make the selection from those three alternatives. Sidney looked over each photo. They were all amazing.

"You're going to make this a hard choice, aren't you?" she asked with a laugh.

Eric blushed.

"You really have incredible taste," she said proudly.

"Thank you, Miss."

"Have you looked at any of these in person yet?"

Eric blushed again. "I think I would be too embarrassed to walk into a wedding shop and start looking at dresses, Miss."

Sidney smiled sweetly at her fiancé. "Would you do it for me, Eric?"

Eric felt suddenly helpless. He never could say no to her and she knew that, but would his resolution hold when it came time to visit the shop or would he chicken out? He wasn't sure.

"I'll try, Miss," he said cautiously.

Sidney smiled. "Good girl," she said and

she slid her foot out of her shoe and ran it up Eric's leg to his inner thigh. Her toes slipped beneath his panties and she grabbed his erection between them. Then she slowly moved her foot up and down his shaft, bending it at the ankle.

"Oh that feels so good," said Eric.

"I'll bet it does."

Sidney brought Eric right to the point that he would cum. In fact, she could feel his erection throbbing away. But she stopped before he came. Instantly, all those amazing feelings of anticipation came crashing to a halt. "Why don't you go tomorrow and call me from the shop," she said. "We can finish this after you get home." She then pulled her foot out of his panties and away from his shaft.

Eric sighed. "Yes, Miss."

—o—

"What happened at the meeting?" asked Sidney. Sidney was back at her own apartment the following day. She and Amber were making dinner and Sidney was quizzing her about school. Amber seemed distracted from her studies by whatever was going on at the school.

"They told us the boys are like brainwashed or something," said Amber. She sounded troubled by this.

Sidney raised an eyebrow. "'Brainwashed'?"

"Yeah. They have to obey us now," said Amber.

Sidney's jaw dropped. She couldn't believe her ears. She wondered if this was some sort of joke on Amber's part. "'Brainwashed'? 'They need to obey you'? Are you pulling my leg, Amber?"

Amber shook her head. "No."

"Seriously?"

"Seriously, I'm not kidding. They brought us all into the auditorium and then this woman told us all about it. She said something had happened in the water and now the boys needed to obey us. She's got a plan to handle it and everything, though I think her plan sounds kind of crazy."

"What was her name?" asked Sidney.

"Dr. something or other... Morgan, I think."

Sidney raised an eyebrow. "Melanie Morgan?" she asked cautiously.

Amber nodded her head. "Yeah, that's her. Do you know her?"

Sidney blushed. She absolutely knew Melanie Morgan. In fact, she had half a dozen messages from Melanie on her phone right now. And the mention of her set a spark to something inside Sidney which suddenly made her want to see Melanie again, though she knew that would be a horrible idea. She bit her lip.

"We were friends," said Sidney.

"Well, she's the one who told us about it and she's the one who came up with the plan."

"What plan?"

"The plan where the girls treat the boys like slaves!"

Sidney furrowed her brow. "I think you better tell me more about this plan."

—o—

The boys were given a couple days off from school to adjust to their new status. Eventually, they had to return, however. Things were pensive but calm the morning of their return. The boys seemed in shock more than anything and the girls seemed both anxious to exercise their newly given responsibilities and powers, but simultaneously afraid to be first and to step out of line. No one knew the boundaries yet... but they would learn fast.

Amber caught up with Jason in the hallway. His stepsister Cindy, *his new guardian*, was looking through her locker about ten feet away; he stood there waiting for her. Amber thought about throwing her arms around Jason and kissing him, but something stopped her. Things were just a little too weird at the moment.

"Hey," said Amber.

Jason bit his lip and looked down at the floor. "Hey, Amber."

"I've been looking for you," she said. She folded her arms tightly.

He nodded his head, but said nothing.

"Are you doing ok?" she asked.

"Yeah, I guess."

Amber bit her lip. The true answer seemed to be "no," but he clearly didn't want to tell her that. She kicked her heel against the floor nervously. "I can tell you're upset. What's bothering you?"

Jason shrugged his shoulders.

"Answer my questions, Jason," said Amber. She wasn't sure if this counted as using this new power they supposedly held or not, something she swore she wouldn't do, but she thought it was important to find out the truth. If Jason didn't want to date her anymore, then she needed to know. Otherwise, she wanted to help him.

Jason looked Amber straight in the eyes. "They made Cindy my guardian!" he exclaimed in an exasperated tone.

Cindy heard this and smirked. She was clearly enjoying her new position of authority.

"I know," said Amber and she hugged her boyfriend.

"Why can't you be my guardian?" he whined softly in her ear.

Amber twisted her lips and held him tighter. "You know they picked family first and unrelated girls were only chosen when there wasn't any family."

"But I don't want her, I want you!"

Amber smiled. "That's so sweet!" Then she frowned. "But there's nothing we can do."

Jason hung his head.

Amber saw how sad he looked. She sighed. Suddenly, she had an idea. If Sidney knew Dr. Morgan, then perhaps she could use that to get an exception to their rule on guardians from Dr. Morgan. She smiled.

"Let me see what I can do," said Amber.

"This is touching an all," said Cindy, "but little Jason needs to get to class. Come along, Jason."

Cindy started down the hallway. Jason immediately turned and walked after her. Amber watched them go. She felt angry at Cindy and bad for Jason. Delivering him into the hands of someone so immature, someone who disliked him so much just wasn't right. Amber needed to fix this.

—o—

A few minutes later, Amber made her way to the temporary office the school had given Melanie. She knocked on Melanie's door.

"Dr. Morgan? I have a question," said Amber.

Melanie looked up and saw the girl who had identified herself as "Amber Drake." She knew who Amber was. What she wanted to know now was why she was here. This promised to be interesting.

"Come in, Ms. Drake. What can I do for you?" asked Melanie.

"I don't know if you know this, but you and my sister were friends, apparently," said Amber.

Melanie cringed at the word "friends." It angered her that this was how Sidney was describing her now, especially with the verb "were" attached. Still, she maintained her calm. "Yes, I did know that. We were good friends in fact."

"Well, I'm wondering if I can ask you a favor," said Amber.

"What kind of favor?"

"My boyfriend was assigned his stepsister as his guardian. They really don't get along and she's been very cruel to him already. I was wondering if I could replace her as his guardian. I can promise you that I would take my responsibilities very seriously," said Amber and she nodded her head as if she were willing Melanie to agree.

Melanie leaned back in her chair and folded her hands before her in the air. Under normal conditions, there would be no way she would agree to this. Indeed, why in the world would she replace a cruel little stepsister with a loving girlfriend? That was exactly the opposite of what she wanted. She wanted all the girls to become cruel little stepsisters! Figuratively, of course.

But this wasn't a normal situation.

Amber's request presented Melanie with a special opportunity. *"If Sidney won't answer my messages, then maybe I can make her come back to me through this stupid young girl?"* thought Melanie. *"There's no way she could ignore me if I pull this Amber girl to me."*

She slowly nodded her head.

"And if she doesn't come to me voluntarily," added Melanie and she left the rest of the thought unspoken in her head, though she knew exactly what she was thinking. She was thinking that if Sidney did not come to her voluntarily, then she could use Amber to punish Sidney.

She smiled at Amber.

Amber smiled back. She had no idea what was going through Melanie's head at the moment.

"I wouldn't normally agree to this," said

Melanie, "but seeing as how Sidney and I are close friends, I think I will make a special exception in your case."

Amber smiled even more broadly. She started to thank Melanie, but Melanie stopped her by holding up her hand.

"That said, there are conditions. First, you can tell no one that I have agreed to this... other than, of course, Sidney and your boyfriend. Secondly, I will expect you to provide me with progress reports every few days. That means you and I will meet here, every few days so I can monitor the situation. After all, I need to be sure this young man gets all the treatment he needs." She paused. "You will also need to promise that you will execute any instructions I give you, even if they seem distasteful. If you don't, then our deal will end. Do you understand? Is it a deal?"

Amber felt uncertain about this, but she had no choice. "It's a deal," she said.

Melanie almost seemed to chuckle when Amber agreed.

Jason was relieved when he learned of this later that night. Sidney, however, didn't seem the least bit pleased, though she claimed she was, when Amber told her about the exception Dr. Morgan had made for her and Melanie's desire to meet regularly with Amber from now on.

—o—

On the surface, things seemed to go well the next few days. No one quite knew yet how to handle this new reality, so everyone was on their best behavior. But as the hours passed and it became more and more clear to the girls that the boys truly were helpless to resist them – that this was not some trick or game – the girls started becoming bolder.

The boys, on the other hand, were learning that resistance was futile. No matter how much they tried to resist, they lost. Every single time, they lost. Worse yet, it wasn't even a challenge for the girls to win. A few simple words was all it took and any boy would find himself a slobbering slave begging to be punished or doing humiliating things like kissing feet or sashaying through the hallway hand in hand with some other unlucky boy. They learned very quickly that they had no chance. All of this made the boys increasingly shy, because they realized that not getting noticed by the girls was the best way to avoid humiliation.

The girls, on the other hand, grew in confidence quickly. Actually, a better word might be "arrogance." With each passing day, the girls came to realize that they had become all-power and they seemed determined to set out to prove the old adage that power corrupts and absolute power corrupts absolutely. A good example of this was Cindy Cole, who was relishing the power she now had over Jason. Indeed, even though she had been removed as his guardian, she still had control over him when they were home alone.

Cindy lounged in the sofa chair. She was drinking an ice tea and watching a teen soap. She wore a white bikini with red polka dots and a pair of cheery-red mid-heeled slides. Her legs were crossed over the arm of the chair, with one foot resting on the edge of an end table and the other hanging in the air. Her slide dangled from her toes.

"Ah, life is good," said Cindy.

As Cindy sipped her ice tea, Jason scurried around the room sweeping. He wore a white tennis skirt, a pink bikini top and white high-heeled wedge sandals with a cork heel. Even more embarrassingly though, he had an obvious erection that stood up tall beneath his skirt.

"When you're done there, fold the laundry, boner boy," commanded Cindy.

"Leave me alone," said Jason as he kept sweeping.

"Why are you talking back to me, slave?"

"Don't call me that," he said.

"Why not? It's true, isn't it? Aren't you my slave now?" she laughed.

"No."

"Of course you are, because you need to do anything I tell you. That makes you a slave. It's simple."

"I do not," he said, despite the evidence to the contrary.

Like the other boys, his ego still made him resist even when the cause was hopeless and when he knew it would make the situation worse. It just felt better somehow to resist than it did to surrender.

"Don't make me prove it, slave boy," said Cindy with an evil. "Oh, and get me another drink. This one's getting warm."

Jason set the broom down and took the glass from her hand. He started toward the kitchen to make her another drink. "I'm not your slave," he repeated as he left the room. Cindy heard this.

"Ug!" grunted Cindy. "Get back here!"

Jason immediately reappeared at the door still holding the drink he was to replace.

"Get over here," ordered Cindy and she swung her legs to the floor. Her high-heeled slides landed on the hardwood floor with a loud *CRACK!* "I thought we settled this already!"

Jason swallowed hard and walked over to her. The idea of resisting never even entered his mind, though he definitely did not want to get anywhere near her at the moment. Cindy saw this and snickered at his helplessness against her commands. She then took the drink from his hand and set it down on the table next to the chair.

"Are you or are you not my slave?" she asked.

"Leave me alone, Cindy."

"That's not a 'yes,'" she said in a sing-song voice. "I think it's time we settled this once and for all... kiss my toes, slave." She pointed to the floor before her and she wiggled her toes inside her open-toed slides.

Jason bent over and kissed them. She had asked and he wanted to do as she said. A moment later, however, he realized that he really didn't want to do this, though he couldn't stop himself.

"Keep kissing, slave boy," said Cindy.

Cindy picked up the television remote and flipped around through the channels as Jason kissed her toes again and again. She let him go for several minutes just to make her point.

"All right, stop," said Cindy finally.

Jason's face was red with shame. He wiped his tongue on his shirt sleeve.

"Not a slave, huh? You should be glad I let you stop or you would have done that all day. Face it, slave boy, you need to do whatever I tell you and that makes you my slave."

"I'm not your slave," he said defiantly.

"Grrr! Yes, you are!" said Cindy with clear frustration.

"I'm not."

Cindy glared at Jason. "Stop trying to ruin this for me. Whether you accept the fact or not, I have absolute control over you, and I can make you agree with me. So tell me. I want to hear you say it. Say, 'Yes, Miss Cindy, I am your slave.'"

"Yes, Miss Cindy, I am your slave," he repeated.

She smiled. "Oh, I like that. Say it again."

"Yes, Miss Cindy, I am your slave."

"Now tell me you're insignificant and that you're lost without me to rule over you."

"I am insignificant, and I'm lost without you to rule over me."

"Still think your girlfriend is going to save you?" she asked with a laugh.

Jason blushed but remained silent.

"Answer me, slave boy. Do you still think she's going to save you?"

"Yes, she will."

"You better hope so, slave boy." Cindy picked up the drink again and she touched the hem of his tennis skirt. "I'm tired of this outfit. Go upstairs and take off all your clothes. Then go put on my mother's yellow sundress, the one with the white collar and the cute little daisy buttons down the front. Make sure you put on a pair of panties too... I'll let you pick the color."

Jason headed toward the stairs.

Cindy laughed behind him. "And don't forget to pick out some shoes before you come back down. Make 'em heels too. I like my slaves in heels. And they better be cute too or I'm going to punish you. Now run along little sissy, I expect you back in five minutes fully dressed."

Despite himself, Jason was determined to find a pair of cute heels to go with the yellow sundress he was going to put on. It never occurred to him that he didn't have to put those items on. Oh, he knew in the back of his mind that he didn't want to do this, but somehow that didn't seem to influence him. Interestingly, as he made his way up the stairs and he thought about what he was going to wear, he strangely found himself becoming erect. He wondered what that meant.

When Jason left, Cindy looked at her watch. Jason's father would be coming home from work soon and then her mother. She decided that it would be safer to make Jason change back into his boy clothes now. Thus, she rose from the chair and went upstairs. Jason was upstairs zipping up the yellow dress she had mentioned. On the floor were a pair of high-heeled black sandals with really tall heels. Cindy smiled at what he had picked.

"Sadly, we'll have to wait," she said. "Your father is coming home soon. Take off your fingernail polish, but leave the toenail polish. Then get dressed in your normal clothes. You know the rules... don't say a word about anything."

—o—

A couple weeks had passed since the guardian system was put into place and things seemed to be going well at school. Indeed, everyone seemed to be adjusting well. The number of known incidents had fallen to almost nothing, though there was still much the teachers didn't see.

The boys' lives were changing rapidly, however. For one thing, their parents no longer trusted them to leave the house alone. Nor were they trusted with money, for obvious reasons. They also weren't allowed to drive because that was considered too dangerous. All of this meant they needed to rely on their sisters and their mothers to take them where they needed to go, to buy them things they needed, and to generally give them permission to do whatever it was they needed to do. As a consequence, they now spent their time doing their homework, doing chores, and helping out around the house rather than playing games or wandering the streets. Interestingly, this made them better students, but they were losing their independence.

The girls' lives were changing rapidly as well. They found a new sense of freedom now that they no longer needed to compete with the aggressive boys. This caused many of them to come out of their shells and embrace life more fully. But it wasn't all positive changes. They were also learning to embrace their new power. Slowly but surely, they were coming to like having someone follow their commands. And they were beginning to take the things they wanted without restraint.

For example, many began dictating what they wanted their boyfriends to do on dates or they began changing the boys little by little to accommodate their image of how the boys should be, all without ever considering the boys' feelings or desires. The girls also learned very quickly that the boys could not keep secrets, so they took the opportunity to demand to know everything the boys had kept hidden... all their private thoughts. Of course, the girls did not reciprocate.

Some girls, simply enjoyed flexing their new muscles with malicious intent, girls like Gwen Wilson. Gwen Wilson hid behind the door as Coach Johnson passed out jerseys to the football team in the equipment room. They would wear these jerseys to the rally, which would begin in twenty minutes. Last year, the team finished 9-1 and came within a game of the conference championship. Hopes were high for this year as many of last year's stars had returned.

"All right, you guys know the drill. Stay here until you hear me announce tonight's game, then come running through the banner," said the Coach. "Let's see if we can't make everybody a little happier than they've been lately."

The players nodded their heads and the Coach left the equipment room. The moment he left, Gwen rushed over to her friends who waited hidden in the nearby girl's locker room. They had plans for the boys.

"He's gone," she whispered.

The three girls immediately emerged from the locker room. They were pushing a laundry cart normally used for jerseys and towels. They made their way to the equipment room, where the boys waited for the rally.

"Hey boys," said Gwen as she walked into the equipment room. Her two friends followed close behind. They had blushing grins on their faces.

The boys cringed. They knew what was coming and they were helpless to prevent it.

A few minutes later, the last of the students who would attend the rally piled into the bleachers. The gym was decorated in red and white streamers, and the cheerleaders and the pom-pom squad were gathered together in the center of the floor. The new football season kicked off this weekend with a game against arch-rival Lakewood and everyone was excited.

The lights dimmed.

A spotlight came on.

Dean Dwyer and Coach Johnson came out and took the microphone. They spoke about team pride and what the achievement of the school's students meant for the community. They talked about remembering days like this for the rest of everyone's lives.

"And on that note," screamed Coach Johnson in his gravelly voice, "let me introduce to you this year's *Satin Falls Tigers!*" He turned and pointed toward a large banner held by two cheerleaders at the edge of the darkness beyond the spotlight. Through it would run the players.

And they did.

The first was the team's star linebacker, Chet Redkin. Only, it wasn't the Chet Redkin everyone remembered. This Chet Redkin wore a garterbelt, high-heeled sandals, a bra, a long blonde wig, and nothing else. His erection bounced around as he ran; it was adorned with a pink ribbon. His face was bright red with shame as he blew kisses to the crowd.

Quarterback Danny Trejo followed. He wore crotchless panties, high-heeled mules, a tight sweater and a red wig. He also had a pink ribbon wrapped around the head of his erection. His face too was bright red.

More boys followed. Each boy wore high heels, lingerie, some other feminine item and a wig. Each also displayed their erections, each of which was wrapped in a ribbon. And each of them burned bright red with shame as they all ran to the middle of the gym and bounced around like cheerleaders. And when they were all out, they began hugging and kissing each other... as they had been told.

Most of the girls in the bleachers doubled over laughing. The boys in attendance didn't.

Dwyer would consider expelling Gwen Wilson and her friends for this, but Melanie would talk him out it, claiming it was merely an uncontrollable psychological reaction to a "nonconforming situation."

Chapter 6: "Henry Miller"

—o—

Henry Miller sat behind his large desk with a look of contempt in his eye. This was a look he saved for interns who had offended him and needed to be chastised before being summarily dismissed. Sidney sat across from him with a look of defiance in hers. She never let him intimidate her.

"I wanted to speak to you away from everyone," said Henry in his deep voice which had served him so well in court for so many years.

"About what?" asked Sidney.

"About my son Eric."

This was a surprise to Sidney. "What about Eric?" she asked cautiously.

"I'm happy Eric has decided to marry you," said Henry, though his tone suggested otherwise. Indeed, it was hardly a secret that he did not approve of his son marrying a woman who wanted to be an attorney, especially one who wanted to keep working after they were married.

"I'm gla—" started Sidney equally disingenuously, but Henry kept speaking over her.

"But I wanted to make it clear that there would be no special treatment around here," he said.

Sidney glared at him. Obviously, there would be no special treatment, she thought. She had never asked for any, nor would she accept any. She wanted to be judged on her own merits and to make her own name for herself. Henry made her so angry. He'd been rude to her since the day his partner Thomas Hunter hired her, and he'd only gotten more rude since the engagement had been announced. He spoke down to her, he often tried to humiliate her publicly, he kept her off of the good projects, and he seemed to require her to meet a level of performance he required of no one else in the office. All of this wore her down and upset her deeply, but she was never going to let him know that.

"I've never asked for special treatment," she said through gritted teeth.

"Well, don't expect any," he replied. He then picked up a file and started reading through it. This was how he dismissed people after chastising them and it angered Sidney further that he did this to her now.

"What a rude bastard," she thought. Still, she knew she could say nothing, so she rose to her feet and made her way to his door. When she reached the door, however, he took another shot at her.

"There is something else," he said.

Sidney turned and looked at him.

"Obviously, the firm would never fire anyone for this, as it would be illegal, but *off the record*, I wonder how you intend to satisfy your obligations to the firm once my son makes you pregnant. Call me old fashioned if you wish, but it seems that would be impossible," he said condescendingly.

Sidney felt her rage build inside herself once more. She knew she should just turn and walk away, but there were words building in her mind which wanted to come out. She knew she shouldn't say any of the things she was thinking, but in that moment, it just seemed impossible to resist... so she spoke.

"Actually, I'm thinking of getting your son pregnant. Then he can have the baby and it won't be a problem for me at work," said Sidney without a hint of emotion. "I've already picked out the maternity dress for him. He looks very cute in it. You should see him."

Henry's face turned bright red with embarrassment. "How dare she?" he thought. Obviously what she said was impossible, but the very suggestion that Henry Miller's son could in any way be put into a feminine role was too much for Henry to take. He ground his teeth as he glared at the young woman. He had no idea how to respond.

"Is there anything else?" asked Sidney

coldly.

Henry picked up his file again. Sidney took the opportunity to leave. Her face burned red with shame and anger. She didn't know how much longer she could take being treated this way. Even if Hunter Miller was the only good-sized law firm in town, and even if they had all the town's respectable clients, and even if she was marrying Henry Miller's son, she thought long and hard about turning in her resignation right then and there. She didn't though; she couldn't. Instead, she returned to her office and she began to cry. She picked up the phone to dial Eric's number, but then she saw Melanie's latest message. She stared at the name "Melanie Morgan." She knew she should never call this number ever again... but then she did.

Meanwhile, five offices down, Henry picked up his own phone. He called Tom Collins, the firm's personnel law specialist.

"Mr. Miller, what can I do for you?" asked Collins.

"Tom, I need to know what it takes to fire an employee... a lawyer... a *woman*."

—o—

Melanie sat in Dean Dyer's office. Dwyer had asked her to come give him an update. He had also invited the Mayor because there were rumors of this issue growing beyond being merely a school issue. Mayor Gabby Landsberg, known as "Mayor Gabby" to the voters, was a small woman with a big voice and a bigger smile. She became mayor five years prior when her husband, then-Mayor Tommy Landsberg, decided not to run again. The reason he chose not to run again was a secret shared only by a few, including Melanie, his psychiatrist.

Also in the room was Dwyer's assistant, Sondra Stern.

Melanie planned to tell them that the problem was getting worse, when it really wasn't. She intended to use that as a pretext for starting the next phase of her plan. None of them suspected a thing.

"Unfortunately, the situation is getting considerably worse," said Melanie.

"Really? I thought everything was going well," said Dwyer with a great deal of surprise. "Since we instituted the guardian system, we've had almost no problems. The girls seem happy, the boys seem safe, and outside of a few isolated incidents, everything seems to be running smoothly... given the circumstances."

Melanie shook her head. "You're only seeing one aspect of this. I've been meeting with dozens of local families and I've been closely monitoring the psychological impact of all of this on both the boys and the girls. We were hoping that making the girls act as guardians for the boys would trigger their nurture instincts, just as mothers experience with their own children. Simultaneously, we hoped the boys would learn to overcome their masculine egos and willingly accept their new positions."

"And that's not happening?" asked Dwyer.

"Of course it's not happening, you idiot! I made it up!" thought Melanie, but she instead said: "Sadly, no, it's not happening. The boys' egos are nearing a breaking point. Their latent masculine desires to control the women in their lives are causing them to feel the need to rebel, which is impossible because of their condition, and that's causing them deep psychological trauma. We need to resolve that trauma immediately to prevent psychotic breaks."

"Psychotic breaks?" asked Dwyer.

"Psychotic breaks," repeated Melanie.

"That's bad?"

"It's even worse than it sounds."

Dwyer swallowed hard. "How do we prevent that?"

Melanie took a deep breath and acted like she didn't want to say what she was about to say. This made Dwyer even more nervous. "You won't like this," she said before adding, "I don't like it either." She paused.

"What is it?" asked Dwyer nervously.

Melanie sighed. "We need to take away their masculinity."

Dwyer's jaw dropped. "You mean cut off their—!"

"No, no, not that," said Melanie, though on the inside she laughed. *"It always comes down to your penises, doesn't it?"* she thought to herself. *"Why can't you men ever understand that there's more to masculinity than the sausage hanging between your legs? We should cut them all off and see how you all act then."*

"So what do you mean?" asked Dwyer.

"I mean that we need to teach them that they can no longer be alpha males," said Melanie. "They must accept that they are now betas and that the women are now the alphas. To harmonize that with their views of men and women, so they no longer feel the stress of their egos screaming that they need to be in charge, we need to turn them into females."

"What exactly are you suggesting?" gasped Dwyer. Melanie would never forget the look of horror on Dwyer's face.

"To put it simply, we need to make them dress and act like girls."

"That's insane!" exclaimed Dwyer. "We can't do that!"

Sondra Stern, who had been sitting quietly in the back, suddenly burst out laughing. Melanie immediately recognized this laugh. She wasn't laughing at the idea, she was laughing at the possibilities that accompanied the idea. Melanie had found a fellow-traveler. Stern then went to work on browbeating Dwyer into accepting the idea. In the meantime, Melanie spoke quietly with the Mayor. The Mayor seemed to accept the need for Melanie's plan, though she remained cautious. She specifically noted that it would be a difficult sell to the parents of these boys.

"I believe I can make the case," said Melanie.

"All right, it's up to you," said Mayor Gabby. "If you can convince them, then I'll go along."

Melanie then turned back to Dwyer. He took a little longer to come around, but he eventually agreed as well... provided Melanie could convince the college's Board to adopt the plan. Melanie smiled. Her plan was one step closer to reality.

—o—

Melanie turned her car up the street which led to her office. She had just come from her meeting with Dwyer and Mayor Gabby. She was marveling at the ease of her victory. She would soon have her revenge. She smiled. But her smile faded the moment she pulled up before her office and saw Sidney's car. She knew Sidney wanted to meet, but she hadn't expected to find her here. Melanie felt a lump in her throat and her stomach tightened. When she had received Sidney's call, asking for a meeting, her heart skipped a beat. She was sure this would be her chance to win Sidney back... but now she wasn't so sure.

"I guess there's only one way to find out," she said.

Melanie looked at the flowers on the seat next to her. She had bought them to give them to Sidney when they met, but now that seemed like a bad idea somehow, so she left them and she stepped out of her car. Slowly, reluctantly, she made her way up the concrete steps to her office. She took a hold of the doorknob and she froze, afraid to go any further.

"You can do this," she told herself.

Melanie took a deep breath and she walked through the door. Inside, she found Sidney lying on the leather couch with her legs spread out over the arm of the couch. Her skirt was on the floor next to her high-heeled pumps. Her panties lay on top of her skirt. Her nipples were erect beneath her red bra, Melanie's favorite. Melanie's nipples responded in kind and she instantly became wet.

She was uncertain, however.

"I was at the school, working on something, when I got your call. I didn't... I wasn't... I, well," said Melanie, stumbling slightly over her words.

Sidney swung her feet to the floor and rose from the couch. Even without her heels on, Sidney was taller than Melanie. Her perfect breasts were much larger as well. Sidney placed her left hand on Melanie's breast and tickled her erect nipple through her blouse.

Melanie felt a tingle within her pussy. She was becoming very excited. But she remained pensive. Sidney had come to her before like this several times whenever her boss had been cruel to her; each time she had gone back to Eric. Melanie wondered if that was the case this time or if she had come back to her.

"Henry?" asked Melanie. Her mouth was dry.

Sidney seemed cringe and a tear appeared in her eye. She nodded her head.

Melanie hugged her tightly. "I'm sorry, baby. He can be so cruel."

"It's ok, I can take it," she said softly.

"I know you can, but sometimes you just need a shoulder and I'm here for you," said Melanie soothingly.

Sidney smiled through her tears and kissed

Melanie on the cheek. Then she ran her hand down Melanie's back and she squeezed Melanie's rear, pushing her fingers beneath Sidney's panties and tickling the bottom of her lips from behind.

Melanie smiled. This felt amazing. It felt so right too, and she wanted so badly to believe that Sidney had come back to her, but before she could fully accept that and let her broken heart believe, she needed to ask one more question. She dreaded asking it, but she had to know.

"Since you're here with me, rather than him, does this mean you've left him?" asked Melanie.

An image of her loyal and loving fiancé flashed through Sidney's mind and she froze. Her whole body went soft and all the tightness with which she had been holding Melanie vanished instantly. She became like deadweight in Melanie's arms. She shook her head.

"I can't," she said.

"Wait!" pleaded Melanie.

"I can't!" she repeated and she pushed Melanie away. "I want to so badly, but I can't. I shouldn't have come!"

"Wait! Don't go!"

Sidney shook her head and grabbed her panties. She pulled those up her legs. "I shouldn't have come. This was a mistake!"

"Wait, please don't go!" said Melanie and

she stepped closer to Sidney. Sidney, however, kept her away with her hand. She then grabbed her skirt and pulled that up her legs and zipped it.

"I can't. I shouldn't have come. I love, Eric. I can't do this."

"Don't you love me?" asked Melanie. A tear appeared in her eye. She felt sick that she was about to lose her lover again.

Sidney cringed. She shook her head. "It's different. I love him."

"You love me too!"

"It's... it's different. You're an addiction."

Melanie looked like she'd been slapped across the face. She folded her arms and balanced her right foot on the heel of her shoe, which she jabbed into the carpet three times. "'An addiction'?!" she repeated angrily. "That's what I am to you? Well, I hate to break this to you, Sid, but love fades. You'll tire of him. And the things you think are so great now are going to grate on you."

Sidney zipped her skirt. She couldn't look at Melanie. "No, I love him. That won't ever change."

"Really? Then why did you come to me instead of him? Tell me that!"

This shot seemed to make Sidney recoil. She shook her head and slipped her feet into her heels. Then she grabbed her purse and she started toward the door as quickly as she could.

Melanie laughed cynically and followed her. "So you think it won't change, do you? Ha! He's a man, Sid. I don't care what he tells you about his 'lifestyle,' he's still a man beneath the skirts. And men are all the same."

"Just because you had a horrible experience with Ri—"

"Don't you dare bring my ex-husband into this," growled Melanie. "I'm not the one with the problem. I'm not the one who can't decide what she wants. I'm not the one who won't admit she's a lesbian and then seeks the comfort of effeminate men to kid herself."

Sidney bit her lip and a tear ran down her face. "I'm sorry I came."

Melanie laughed cruelly. "I'm sorry I didn't!"

This caused Sidney to stop and spin around. She looked Melanie up and down. There was a look of disgust in her eyes which wounded Melanie deeply. Sidney shook her head as if to say, "I never knew you," and she turned and marched to the door.

Melanie instantly saw her mistake. "I'm sorry, I didn't mean it. I love you. I want to be with you. Please, don't go! I need you! Please stay!"

"We're not good for each other," said

Sidney.

"Please. I need you in my life," pleaded Melanie.

Sidney came to the door and opened it. She didn't respond. Before she could walk through the door, however, Melanie dropped to her knees and wrapped her arms around Sidney's legs. More tears appeared in Melanie's eyes.

"Please," she begged. "Please, don't go!"

Sidney pulled herself free and walked off. She never said another word.

Melanie broke down and cried into her hands as she watched her former lover walk down the concrete steps and out of her life... or had she? A moment later, Melanie had an idea of how she could force Sidney back into her life.

"She wants to be rid of me? Good luck. I know how to make you spend time with me," growled Melanie.

Melanie picked up her phone. She would make Sidney be with her. Then she would have a chance to win her back. And if she couldn't, well, whatever happened then would happen.

—o—

It was the following day.

Henry Miller sat behind his desk with the look in his eye of a hunter who had cornered his prey. He was trying to look bored, but instead he came across as malicious, and perhaps a little vicious. There were even hints of a smug smile at the corners of his lips which made it clear that he planned to enjoy what was about to happen. Next to him sat Tom Collins, the firm's personnel specialist. He showed no emotion.

Across from them sat Sidney. She knew exactly what was happening, and she had already come to terms with it during the short walk from the door, when she first realized Tom was in the room, to the chair where her career at the firm was about to be terminated. In fact, in a way, Sidney was even looking forward to this. Henry would fire her. Then she would be free of him. She would start her own firm and she would run rings around this stodgy old firm... even in four-inch heels. She crossed her legs and she waited to receive her freedom.

Henry jumped right in. "I've been examining your performance lately, and there are some problems that the firm simply cannot ignore."

"Oh," said Sidney.

"Yes," hissed Henry through his crooked smile. "I'm afraid that we're going to need to let you g—"

Riiiiiing!

Henry's phone rang. He stared at it for a

moment.

Riiiiiing!

Henry hit the speaker button. "I told you that I was not to be disturbed."

"Yes, sir, I understand," said his secretary Ruth in a tone which suggested that she was about to deliver news she knew her boss would hate. "But this is very important, sir. You'll want to hear this immediately."

"Whatever it is can wait until I'm finished with the present matter," growled Henry.

"This is about that matter, sir," said Ruth cautiously.

Henry furrowed his brow. Then he clicked the button to turn off the speaker and he picked up the receiver. He spun his chair around so that his back was turned to Sidney. "What is it?!" he demanded.

Ruth said something Sidney couldn't hear.

"You're kidding? Let me speak to them," said Henry.

There was a pause.

"Madame Mayor, how are you?" asked Henry.

He waited silently as the Mayor spoke, responding only occasionally with "yes, I understand" and "uh huh."

"But Madame Mayor, are you sure?"

Sidney heard a voice on the other end, but

could not understand what was said.

"But why her? We have bett—" He paused. "Well, yes, but—" He paused again. "I understand, but really—" Henry tapped the arm of his chair angrily with his fingers. "No, no, Madame Mayor, we don't want that. Yes, I'm sure they are a good law firm, but—"

Sidney could see Henry bending the pencil in his hand to the breaking point. He was clearly very unhappy.

"Yes, Madame Mayor," he finally said. "I'll be sure to tell her. Thank you, ma'am. I'll send her over tomorrow. Good night, Madame Mayor."

Henry hung up the phone. He rubbed his temples for a minute before turning around again. His expression had changed completely. The smug smile was gone and severe disappointment had replaced the expectation he had shown before. He took a deep breath.

"I've decided to put you on a matter we just received which relates to Satin Falls Academy," grumbled Henry. "You will report to Dean Dwyer tomorrow and the Mayor. They've got something going on over there about somebody having a virus or something and they want some help. Frankly, it sounds like a waste of time, so I think you will be the best person to handle it." He did not mention that the Mayor insisted that Sidney be given the matter, something he still did not understand.

Sidney ran her tongue over her teeth. She didn't fully understand what had just happened. She had been prepared to be fired, but instead, she was given a major assignment, and it sounded like the Mayor herself had forced Henry to give her the assignment.

"Why?" she asked herself.

She had no idea. Two things were clear, however. First, Henry was very, very unhappy about this. That made Sidney rather happy. Secondly, Henry was lying when he described this as "a waste of time." Sidney knew that the city was the firm's most important client; when the Mayor called, the firm jumped. So any assignment for the city was an important assignment. Not to mention, she knew from Amber that what was going on at the school was really serious. She just didn't know why she had been chosen for this yet.

"Fine," said Sidney.

Henry glared at her. "Let me provide one word of caution, however," he said. His voice was seething with contempt. "You will be reprosonting the firm, so lose the hooker shoos and the slutty skirts. Dress like a professional."

This comment seemed to make Tom Collins roll himself up into a ball and disappear into his chair. Sidney on the other hand bit her tongue. For a very brief moment, she considered quitting. But then she realized that if Henry had given her this assignment rather than fire her, then for some reason he needed her and that gave her power, and she planned to take advantage of that: *"The shoe's on the other foot this time, you old bastard,"* thought Sidney.

"Is that all?" asked Sidney.

Henry picked up a file from his desk, turned his back to her and started reading. This was the signal that she was dismissed and she happily took it. She left Henry's office both angry at her treatment, happy that she apparently had some power over Henry now, and intrigued as to how she got it.

She would find out soon enough.

Chapter 7: "The Submission Spreads"
—o—

Amber entered the kitchen as Sidney chopped up another carrot. She was making stew. Amber looked sad, despite her cheerful attire. She wore a short white skirt, a cute red and white-striped top with the word "LOVE" written across her chest in glitter, red and white tennis shoes, and a flower clip in her hair. She had come back from a date with Jason, who wore panties and a bra beneath his clothes and swore this has been his own choice and not Cindy's, even though they both knew better. Amber leaned against the counter, folded her arms and pouted.

"I know that look," said Sidney. "Trouble with Jason?"

"Sort of."

"What'd he do?"

"It's not him, it's this whole thing," said Amber. "His evil brat stepsister Cindy is totally taking advantage of this and I don't know what do about it. She's going way too far."

Sidney wasn't sure how to respond to this. She had learned generally about the issue with the virus at school though she didn't know the specifics and she hadn't quite grasped yet how vulnerable the boys really were; she had a meeting scheduled with Dwyer to discuss the legal aspects the following morning where she hoped to learn more about it. At this point, as she understood the virus, she still saw this more as the boys being deferential, but not entirely without will power. She equated it to her own happy relationship with Eric, who voluntarily followed her orders and seemed happy. She suspected the virus created something similar. Hence, when it came to the issue of Cindy and Jason, Sidney assumed that Amber just wasn't ready to accept yet that Jason was in reality a cross-dresser who was now more deferential to his stepsister than Amber liked because of this virus. She doubted that Cindy was the monster Amber made her out to be.

"It's a virus, it's beyond anyone's control—" said Sidney.

"I know that," said Amber, "but it's not beyond Cindy's control to not abuse Jason."

"Have you considered that this could just be an excuse?"

"What kind of excuse?"

"Maybe Jason really just does like to wear women's clothes, but he's ashamed to admit it. So he blames Cindy," said Melanie.

Amber glared at Sidney. She was starting to wonder if Sidney had listened to anything she had been telling her. "It's not like that," she said.

"Well, if that's the case, then maybe you

should approach his parents," suggested Sidney. She thought that calling Amber's bluff might be a good way to shake out the truth of what was happening. Unfortunately, Amber had an answer. "They're never there. She only does it when they aren't home. Besides, she'll punish him worse if she finds out that he turned her in," said Amber.

"Have you talked to anyone at the school?"

"Yeah, I talked to Dr. Morgan."

The mention of Melanie's name instantly tied Sidney's stomach in a knot. "What did she say?"

"It was kind of confusing, but it didn't seem to bother her. But honestly, she strikes me as a flake. I don't like her," said Amber and she paused. "You know, I'm not even sure she wants to cure this virus."

"What makes you say that?"

Amber shrugged her shoulders. "She just gives me a creepy feeling. And she doesn't seem to like boys much."

Sidney blushed. She was well aware that Melanie did not like males very much.

"So how is Eric?" asked Amber.

Sidney felt tremendous relief that Amber had changed the topic. "He's fine," she said. "He's putting together some secret gift for you, by the way. He won't tell me what it is, though. It's for the wedding."

Amber smiled. "I like Eric a lot."

"Yeah, he's quite a catch."

Amber folded her arms tightly and kicked the toe of her tennis shoe against the kitchen floor. "Can I ask you something really personal about you and Eric?"

Sidney raised an eyebrow. "That depends on what it is."

"He's kind of different, right?"

Sidney rinsed her hands, took a towel and turned to face Amber as she dried her hands. "In what way?"

"I mean, he's really sweet and he knows a lot about stuff."

"What kind of stuff?"

"Stuff stuff, girl stuff."

Sidney shrugged her shoulders. "What's your point?"

Amber blushed. "Like, I had this top, right, and I could never think what I should match it with. I mentioned this to Beth on the phone one day when he was here and he must have heard me, 'cause when I hung up, he told me exactly like what would match and stuff... like shoes and skirts and things. He's great with makeup tips too, and... and guys normally aren't," she added cautiously.

Sidney shrugged her shoulder again. "Eric

has an eye for a lot things and he's very attentive to people, that's one of the things I like about him."

"It's just that he's really good at this stuff and he's like really nice and gentle and everything."

"And, what's your point?"

Amber bit her lip. "I just thought... with everything going on. I'm sorry, I shouldn't have said anything. I just thought maybe he could help me understand what Jason is going through." Her face turned even redder.

So did Sidney's. She stayed very silent hoping that Amber's embarrassment took her off this topic.

It did.

"I'm sorry," said Amber with a red face. "I don't know what I'm saying. I don't really mean to say anything. I don't care if he is or isn't... well, anything. I think he's great and I just—"

Sidney smiled and hugged Amber. "It's ok, Amber."

—o—

Meanwhile, several blocks away, Greg Cole came home earlier from work than normal. The secretaries had been grousing about never getting a day off and, for reasons unknown, the boss decided to give everyone the rest of the day off once they started complaining. It seemed strange at the time, but Greg wasn't going to argue with it. He liked the idea of time off as much as the next guy.

In any event, that's how it started: Greg came home early. That was how he became witness to the strange scene going on at his house. As he walked through the door, he saw Jason busy dusting the living room as Cindy sat on the couch reading a magazine. That wasn't necessarily unusual. What was unusual, however, was what Jason wore. He wore a flowery sundress and flower-patterned open-toed slingbacks with four-inch heels. These belonged to Greg's wife Brenda, as did the dress. Jason's face also was made up with lipstick, eye shadow and blush. His fingernails and his toenails were painted pink.

"What the hell is going on?!" demanded Greg.

Both Jason and Cindy looked horrified to see him. Clearly, they weren't expecting him home so soon.

"I can explain—" began Jason.

"How the hell are you going to explain this?!" demanded Greg, waving his hands at his son. "You're wearing your stepmother's dress!"

"She made me do it!" spat out Jason and he pointed his pink fingernail at Cindy.

"Did not!" insisted Cindy.

"Yes, you did!"

"No, I didn't! Dad, I swear it wasn't me! It was her!" said Jason.

Cindy folded her arms. "That's not true. Tell him I didn't make you do this. Tell him you've been secretly wearing girl's clothes for years."

"She didn't make me do this," said Jason. "I've been secretly wearing girl's clothes for years." He then grimaced.

Greg's jaw dropped. "Is that true, Jason?"

"No, it's not true!" squealed Jason.

"Yes, it is!" said Cindy. "Tell him it's true, Jason!"

"Yes, it's true," said Jason. He looked like he wanted to explode.

"He swore me to secrecy," Cindy added.

"That's not true," countered Jason.

"Be quiet," commanded Cindy and Jason shut up.

Greg glared at the two of them. He felt sick and jittery that he had found his own son dressed like a sissy. This was his worst nightmare. It was time to put an end to this, whatever it took. "I don't know what's going on here," he growled, "but—"

Cindy could sense the anger within her stepfather. She knew they were in serious trouble. She decided to try for a long shot. "It's not what you think! Please, don't be upset!" pleaded Cindy.

Then something strange happened.

Cindy expected that her stepfather would explode, but he didn't. Instead, his face went entirely blank and then a strange sense of calm came over it. He looked confused. Then he scratched his head as if he had forgotten something and was trying to remember what it was.

"What was I saying?" he asked himself.

Cindy watched him carefully. She had seen this before... in Jason. "Are you upset?" she asked cautiously.

"Why would I be upset?" asked Greg.

"You're not upset that I dressed Jason up as a girl?"

Greg shook his head. "No, not at all. But it does need to stop now."

Cindy scratched her chin. She was certain that what she was seeing now in Greg was exactly the same thing that had afflicted Jason. She decided to test her theory. "This doesn't bother you and it doesn't need to stop. Don't you agree?"

Greg looked momentarily confused. Then he said, "You're right, there's no reason this needs to stop."

Jason stared at his father in shock. Was his

father really abandoning him to the mercy of the evil Cindy?

"You aren't going to tell my mom either... are you?" asked Cindy.

"No. I don't see any reason to tell your mother."

"In fact, you're just going to forget about this and not tell anyone about it."

Greg smiled. "Why don't we just forget about this whole thing? I'll be upstairs if you need me." He left the room and made his way upstairs.

Cindy watched him go. An evil smile crept across her face. Life just got even better for her. She returned her attention to her stepbrother. "Go change back into your boy clothes... but leave the panties on as a reminder."

—o—

Sidney walked through the hallway of the administration building at the college. She came to the Dean's office. It was a beautiful office which rivaled those at Hunter Miller. She walked up to the receptionist.

"Hi, I'm here to see Dean Dwyer," said Sidney.

The woman smiled at her and told her it would be a moment. She then disappeared into a back office.

Sidney stood at the counter looking around. As she stood there, she slid her feet out of her five-inch open-toed black slingbacks one at a time and flexed her toes. These were gorgeous shoes, but they weren't quite meant for the lengthy hike from the parking garage.

"It's old Henry's revenge for wearing 'hooker shoes'," she told herself with a laugh.

Of course, wearing the black and white pencil dress didn't help her mobility either. She never would have worn this dress or these shoes if she didn't feel that she suddenly had some mysterious benefactor protecting her from Henry. That gave her a stronger sense of freedom than she normally felt at work, and she wanted to make a statement; perhaps she should have waited another day.

"Can I help you?" asked Dean Dwyer a moment later.

"Hi, I'm Sidney Blake. I'm from Hunter Miller. Here's my card," she said and she handed him her card.

"Oh good," said Dwyer. "We have quite a strange issue going on and we'll need a lot of help. Why don't we go to my office to speak?"

Dwyer led Sidney to his office and offered her a seat. She took it. He then explained to her all that had happened. Sidney had heard some of this from Amber, but not all the behind-the-scene details. It was certainly a fascinating issue; though Sidney wasn't sure she believed Dwyer's characterization of the boys as "helpless." She had found in her practice that clients always overstate the problem and she assumed that was the case here as well. Not to mention, she just found it hard to believe that they were truly helpless. "He probably means they're subdued," she thought.

"So that's really our problem," said Dwyer when he finished explaining the issue. "We're working on various solutions and we need your firm to help us understand what our limits are in terms of what we can require and what we can't."

"I understand."

"To do that, you'll be working closely with our project lead," said Dwyer.

"That's fine," replied Sidney.

"She's actually the one who requested that you be added to the team," said Dwyer. "I believe you two know each other."

Sidney suddenly felt a chill race down her spine. "And who is that?" she asked cautiously.

Dwyer was just about to answer, when there was a knock on the open door behind Sidney. "What a coincidence, this is our project lead," said Dwyer and he rose from his desk and pointed to the woman standing in Dwyer's doorway. "Sidney, let me introduce Dr. Melanie Morgan."

Sidney's chill turned into a shudder. She kept her poker face, though. She stood up, smoothed her skirt, and turned to face Melanie.

"Hello, Sidney," said Melanie with a crooked smile.

Sidney bit her lip. "Hello, Dr. Morgan."

"I'm glad you're on the team. We'll be working very closely on this project," said Melanie. There was a creepy tone to what she said which made Sidney shudder again. This was not good.

—o—

A few days later, Melanie appeared before the Board again. Her new plan was meeting a good deal of skepticism and she had come to push it through the Board. So far, none of the Board members supported it. She intended to change that. Indeed, she had no doubt she would get the Board's permission to feminize the boys before she left today. Then she could use this as a springboard for feminizing the men when the virus finally affected them; her geneticist friend had assured her that it should eventually affect them just as much, though as far as she knew, it had not at this point. She found that frustrating actually as they were the real target of her plan. Still, she vowed to move ahead with her plan with the college to be ready when it did finally affect the rest of the men.

"It's simple," said Melanie authoritatively.

"How so?" asked the male Board member.

"Either we take this step or we risk serious psychological harm to these young men," said Melanie.

"I just don't understand this," replied the male Board member. "How can it help their 'masculine egos,' as you put it, to feminize them? That sounds like it would do the opposite."

Melanie gritted her teeth. She knew this would be difficult, but knowing that didn't make it any easier, and this man was proving to be quite an obstacle. "Their masculine egos are the problem," said Melanie with a hint of frustration. "These boys still think of themselves as normal males and they expect to control their environment. So every time they find themselves following an order, it runs contrary to their self-image and it causes feeling of inferiority and shame."

"Yes, you keep saying that, but that doesn't mean anything to me," said the man.

"Wouldn't making them dress like girls make this worse?" asked one of the women. The female Board members had been more receptive, but still not as receptive as Melanie had hoped, as they remained largely skeptical as well.

Melanie shook her head. "By making them dress like girls, we take away the possibility that they could be the alpha males. That's the key. Essentially, it removes the stress that is causing the psychotic breaks by taking away the thing they are defending which causes the stress when they can't defend it."

"I see," said the woman, though it was clear she still didn't fully understand.

Melanie continued with an example she had spent days crafting: "Think of it like this. A man is standing next to his wife. Two other men come by and mock him. They are large and strong and can probably hurt the man. But because his wife has seen him emasculated by the two men, his male ego tells him this will lessen him as a man in her eyes if he doesn't fight back. Thus, he chooses to challenge them, to save face. If he doesn't, he will feel shame for letting his manhood be challenged. Now, imagine if his wife had dressed him as a woman and treated him like a girlfriend. There would be no expectation either by him or by her that he will 'act like a man.' So when the two men mock him, there is no psychological need to defend his masculine ego, nor is there any shame if he simply walks away."

It was as if a light went on in the room.

This example made tremendous sense to the two women and they suddenly understood how Melanie's plan was supposed to work. They could see the purpose of her plan and precisely how it would work, *and why it would work*. Both now nodded their heads approvingly.

"That makes sense," said the one.

"Yes, I get it," said the other.

"It also gets around problems like those at the pep rally," said Melanie.

The Board had been fully briefed about the incident with the football team at the pep rally. That was actually the main reason they were at all receptive to Melanie's new plan in the first place, because clearly something was going on beneath the surface that needed to be understood. What they did not know, however, was that Gwen Wilson was one of Melanie's clients. Nor did they know that Melanie had suggested the idea to Gwen.

"Yes, that was quite worrying," said one of the women.

"Wait a minute!" said the male Board member. "How does that solve the prob—?"

"Honestly William, just be quiet," said one of the women. "Dr. Morgan has made an excellent point which we all see. Your objection is just your 'masculine ego' trying to defend itself from the idea. No harm will come to these boys from dressing like girls, and if Dr. Morgan is correct, this could help them adjust to their new reality."

Melanie smiled to herself upon hearing the woman parrot back her words.

Interestingly, the male Board member looked like he wanted to say something, but never opened his mouth. The others failed to notice.

"I am concerned about the parents though," said the other woman. "The fathers in particular will not like this at all. They will respond like William has responded. They will not like the idea of their sons being emasculated... for lack of a better word."

Melanie nodded her head. "It will be a challenge. But I can put together a presentation which explains everything to the parents. And with this Board voting this as a requirement, they won't have much choice other than to accept it."

The women nodded their heads.

The male member sat silently.

Melanie smiled. She was almost there. She added one more reassuring lie to sell them on the plan: "Also, we should absolutely stress that this is only a temporary measure. Once the boys demonstrate an ability to accept their new reality, we can always reverse this policy."

"Excellent point," said the first woman and she smiled. The second woman too was smiling.

"Let's vote," said the second woman.

The measure passed. Melanie's plan would be announced through a booklet sent to parents. Then a formal meeting would take place to discuss the booklet. After that, the plan would be implemented and anyone wishing to attend the school would need to comply with the plan.

—o—

About a week after Melanie got the Board's approval, Brenda Cole sat on her couch as her husband gave her a foot massage. Greg had volunteered to do this every night for a week now, as well as cooking her dinner. He'd even told her he wanted her to choose what to watch on television. Brenda didn't know why he'd turned over this new leaf, but she wasn't complaining. She assumed it had to do with how rudely he'd acted lately, but that wasn't it.

Cindy knew why this was happening.

So did Greg, but he wasn't allowed to say.

As Greg rubbed his wife's feet as he had been ordered by Cindy, Brenda took the opportunity to look through the mail. Among the bills and junk mail was a large envelope from the school. Inside was a twenty-page booklet. This booklet was prepared by the school, with a credit to Dr. Melanie Morgan, and it explained the new policies as well as the psychology behind those new policies. It also included several pages of suggestions.

"Wow!" said Brenda. "You should read this."

"What is it?" asked Greg.

"It's a booklet from the school. It describes what they want to do next and why."

"What's it say?"

Brenda scanned the first several pages. "Unbelievable."

"What does it say?"

"Shush, Greg. Let me read it first."

Greg went silent. He waited patiently for his wife to stop reading and address him. As he waited, he kept rubbing her feet.

"Wow," repeated Brenda a moment later, when she finished reading it. "This is their list of recommendations for how to treat the boys like Jason from now on."

Jason, by the way, was in his room at the moment doing his homework. He sat at his desk in a sweatshirt, jeans and three-inch high-heeled open-toed pumps. He wanted to take the heels off, but Cindy ordered him to leave them on, unless Brenda called him. Then he needed to switch into tennis shoes.

"What do they recommend?" asked Greg sourly. He didn't like the idea that his son had been put under the control of a girl, and it upset him greatly that Brenda bought into this. He worried that this pamphlet was more of the same.

"It's a list of clothes he should wear and the such... a full wardrobe really. First, they are introducing a school uniform for the boys," said Brenda. She flipped the page. "Oh, that's cute! It's like a little Catholic schoolgirl uniform."

Greg's jaw dropped. "A what?"

"A Catholic schoolgirl uniform. It's got a white blouse, a checkered skirt, and they have a variety of heels. Ooh, they're all very high."

Greg furrowed his brow. "That's ridiculous. And what, are the girls going to wear?"

Brenda scanned the page. "It says there won't be a dress code for the girls because 'allowing the girls the freedom to pick their own clothes emphasizes their new roles as independent authority figures.'"

Greg shook his head. "This is all feminist crap!" he growled.

"Oh be quiet, Greg. You don't know what you're talking about. This is all based on science."

Greg looked like he wanted to speak, but once more he couldn't.

Brenda continued. "It also suggests clothes for outside of school. They suggest dressing him like a girl 3-5 years younger than he is. They say, 'this will reset his worldview so he learns to view contemporary girls as more advanced and thus authority figures.' It says he should always wear high heels when wearing shoes because of the insecurity it brings to need to balance at all times, and it suggests minimum heel heights based on age and the height of the boy. For Jason, the minimum height should be three inches."

Greg really looked like he wanted to say something, but nothing came out.

"They also say, 'High heels will restrict the boy's movements and make him less sure on his feet. This will induce a sense of vulnerability as the women around him will be faster, more agile, and have greater balance, which will make him more comfortable accepting the authority of the women around him.' Interesting. Oh, there's a section here on choosing panties and one on corsets."

Greg shook his body nervously.

"What is it, Greg?" asked Brenda in a frustrated tone.

"This all sounds like a lot of crap to me!"

"You're just feeling insecure, Greg. This is for Jason's own good and no amount of wishing it weren't true will change that. If it helps him adjust to dress like a girl, then that is what he's going to do and we're going to support him. Honestly, Greg, he's your own son. Don't you care about him getting better?"

"But this whole thing is garbage!" he protested.

Brenda rolled her eyes. "Oh, just be quiet, dear," she said. Then, when Greg didn't respond, Brenda continued. "They suggest making him wear makeup 'to remove residual traces of masculinity' because 'this will help the boy come to terms with his need to overcome the remnants of his masculine ego.' They also suggest assigning him 'menial tasks around the house' so he learns to follow the orders of women, not to let him make decisions so he avoids feelings of responsibility and authority, and 'treating him as an inferior' for the time being. I wonder what that means."

Greg's face turned bright red.

Brenda ignored him and she skipped ahead in the pamphlet. "Ah, here it is. Let's see, they say to treat him 'as you would a young girl who is not ready to be an adult, because this will break his need to see himself as the alpha male.' Alternatively, they suggest treating him 'as one would a servant,' so he learns that he can no longer aspire to positions of management or leadership."

Greg looked exasperated and confused. He didn't understand why he was having such a problem speaking his mind. He knew what he wanted to say, but for some reason, he just couldn't say it.

Brenda kept looking over the booklet. "They also have a section in here on how to treat a daughter, like Cindy. It says she 'must be given leeway to issue orders to any affected male, with tolerance given for abuses of power as the young woman must find the proper boundaries herself.' That makes sense, I guess? It also says that we should encourage Cindy 'to embrace her new authoritative role and to aspire to positions of management and leadership.' It also says we should encourage her to dress more adult, give her greater responsibilities and greater freedom, such as giving her a later curfew and a later bedtime than the boy for whom she is a guardian."

Greg rolled his eyes.

"Oh Greg, really," said Brenda sourly. "I know she's a year younger than Jason, but this makes sense. If she's going to control Jason when we're not here, then she needs the authority to do that and we need to be seen as giving her that authority. We need to support her in this, not trying to micromanage her."

Greg shook his head.

"Don't shake your head at me, Greg," said Brenda. "We're going to follow the school's guidance and that's that. First, I'm going to put Cindy in charge of making sure all the chores are done around here. She can be the 'house manager' for lack of a better word. That should help teach her responsibility and will let Jason see her in an authoritative role as she will have the power to assign him chores. Then, this weekend, I'll take Cindy and Jason shopping and I'll let Cindy pick his wardrobe according to these new rules. That will let her demonstrate personal responsibility."

Greg grimaced. This was horrible... but he couldn't say anything about it, though Brenda hadn't noticed his silence.

—o—

Meanwhile, Sidney sat on Eric's couch. She was waiting to see what he would change into. He said he had picked up a surprise outfit he wanted to wear for her. She was feeling increasingly horny waiting.

Beep!

Her cell phone rang. It was Amber.

"Hey Amber, what's up?" asked Sidney.

"Can they do this?!" asked Amber. She sounded upset.

"Do what?"

"What it says in this book they sent."

Sidney shrugged her shoulders. "I have no idea what you're talking about. I haven't seen any book yet."

"I thought you were working on the school issue?" asked Amber.

"I am, but I just started and I haven't heard anything about a book."

Amber flipped the book open for reference even though she knew what it said, as she had read it cover to cover twice to make sure she hadn't misread any of it. "They're going to make the boys dress like girls!"

Sidney raised an eyebrow. "What?"

"This book. It says they're going to make the boys start dressing like girls. They even have a school uniform for them now," said Amber.

"Who said this?"

"This book."

"And where did the book come from?"

"The school sent it. That Dr. Morgan woman came up with the idea and now the school is requiring it. Can they do that?"

Sidney stared at the wall. She had no idea. Presumably a school had the power to establish its own dress code, even if the dress code was perverse. But why would they do this? And why hadn't they run this by her, seeing as how she was supposed to provide the legal work that backed up what they did. Something struck Sidney as very wrong suddenly.

"I want to see that book. I'll come home in

a few minutes. Then we can look at it together," said Sidney.

"Do you promise?"

"Yes, I promise." She paused. "Don't worry, Amber. We're going to look into this and, if something bad is happening, then we're going to stop it."

An hour of so later, Sidney finished reading the booklet. While it seemed strange to her, she couldn't think of anything legally wrong with it. And since she had no other way to challenge Melanie on this, all Sidney could do was recommend that she and Amber keep watching until they found proof of wrongdoing. Like Amber, she now believed that something wrong was indeed going on here, but she realized they just couldn't do anything about it yet.

Chapter 8: "Shopping For Sissies"
—o—

Despite all the chaos slowly enveloping the town, life went on as normal... at least for some. It was Saturday and Sidney and Eric were shopping for groceries and a few other things. Amber had come along as she'd been promised a new pair of shoes. The shoe shop was their next stop. Eric pushed the cart as Sidney and Amber walked ahead of him. Sidney wore white slacks and flats. Amber wore a red and yellow sundress and low-heeled brown sandals. Eric wore grey dress pants, a collared shirt and women's loafers. These were indistinguishable from men's loafers except the burgundy color was a little too effeminate to be men's shoes. Still, only Sidney and Eric knew what these really were.

"How are things at school, Amber?" asked Eric.

"They're interesting, that's for sure," said Amber and she chuckled.

Sidney let out a short, cynical laugh when she heard Amber chuckle. "I thought you were the crusader for boy's rights? Are you telling me you're getting a kick out of this?"

Amber bit her lip and blushed. "No," she said defensively.

"It sure sounded like it with you chuckling,"

said Sidney as she added a can of tomato paste to the cart.

Amber blushed even deeper. "I mean... well, it's kind of... uh, weird."

"Just weird?"

Amber blushed deeper yet. Another few degrees and her face would be redder than the tomato paste Sidney had just added to the cart. "I mean... it's kind of exciting... in a way," she admitted in an embarrassed tone and she hugged her shoulders. She also felt wetness building between her legs.

Sidney laughed. "So much for our social justice crusader!"

"No, I still don't think it's right," protested Amber. She then twisted her lips. "It's just funny to see all the boys acting so differently, especially the ones in dresses already." The wetness grew between her legs.

Eric raised an eyebrow. "Boys in dresses?"

Sidney nodded her head. "Yeah, that's what Melanie claims is the treatment. She says that making the boys dress and act like girls will prevent them from feeling the shame of being powerless to resist the girls. It all sounds a little... uh, *odd* to me, but I can't find anything improper about what she's doing, so we kind of have to accept it for now."

Eric furrowed his brow deeply. "Melanie?

Melanie Morgan? As in the woman you—"

"Yes, Eric, *that Melanie*," said Sidney ominously.

Eric immediately stopped talking. He realized that she did not want him saying another word about their relationship in front of Amber. When she was sure that Eric had gotten the message, Sidney continued.

"They've put Melanie in charge because she's the only psychiatrist in town."

"But don't they know she's... uh, *angry*?" asked Eric.

Sidney shrugged her shoulders.

"Angry about what?" asked Amber.

Eric bit his tongue. He decided not to say what was on his mind. Instead, he said, "I don't know if that's the right word. I've just heard that she's not a very nice person. I'm sure it will be ok, though."

"I don't know," said Amber. "It just seems like everything she says feels wrong. She should be trying to teach the boys independence, not dependence. And this command to make them all into girls just feels backwards."

Eric snickered. "I don't know. It might do them all some good to spend some time as girls."

Amber blushed and the wetness between her legs increased even more.

Sidney snickered now too. "I don't know

dear, would you want me to make you dress as a girl?" she asked and she winked at her fiancé.

Eric blushed. He was hard as a rock. "Anything you say, Miss!"

Both giggled.

"You guys are weird," said Amber.

This caused both Sidney and Eric to burst out laughing.

"Seriously though, it's kind of a strange and exciting feeling to know you have that much power, but I don't think it's right. I think this whole thing is wrong. They should be finding a way to make sure the boys are protected from the girls, not putting them in the girls' power," said Amber.

"The world is never that clear, sweetheart," said Eric and he started down the next aisle.

Amber turned to Eric. "Seriously, how would you like to be in Sidney's power and have to do anything she says?!"

Eric laughed. "It might not be so bad. Sidney's a great woman and I would trust her completely. What do you think, honey? Want to order me around?"

"I already do," said Sidney.

"I'm being serious," protested Amber.

"So am I," purred Eric and he kissed Sidney.

Amber rolled her eyes. "Fine, assume it

was someone else. You wouldn't want to be in my power, would you?"

"Amber, I trust you even more than your sister. You have a kind heart."

Amber blushed. "You get my point though, right? You still wouldn't want to have to do anything I tell you, right?"

Eric laughed. "Amber, if anyone on this planet could handle having absolute power over another, it would be you, sweetie."

Amber furrowed her brow. She wasn't so sure anyone could handle having that kind of power. Even she had caught herself taking advantage of her newfound powers in weak moments in little ways, like getting through the hallway quicker. She was also fighting hard against this strange desire she had been feeling for weeks now to see what Jason looked like as a girl. She knew she could make him do it at any time, but she felt that would be wrong... but she couldn't shake the desire from her mind either and she feared it was only a matter of time before she used the power to make it happen.

—o—

As Eric, Amber and Sidney shopped for groceries, Jason Cole found himself in the backseat of his stepmother's car as they pulled up next door. Life wasn't great for Jason at the moment. Not only did he face the same daily humiliations all the other boys faced at school, but he also had to deal with Cindy. Cindy seemed to get off on humiliating him now that he could not resist her. Today, they were shopping for new clothes for Jason in accordance with the instructions they had received from the school's booklet. This was going to be a nightmare.

Jason blushed as he stepped out of the car. He wore a white pleated skirt, a pink sweater and pink pumps with a three-inch heel. He carried an oversized brown purse, which contained his makeup. He would have thought he would be used to this by now, seeing as how Cindy had dressed him as a girl for weeks at home and how several of the other boys in town had also been forced to start dressing like girls publicly already – the official start was not until Monday – but Jason still found himself terrified of being seeing dressed the way he was.

He kept his head down and followed Cindy and Brenda into the store; this store sold only women's clothes. Jason felt the cool wind race up his skirt and tickle his erect penis inside his panties. His high heels echoed humiliatingly off the cement as they made their way across the sidewalk and then across the tile floor as they entered: *CLICK CLICK CLICK!*

"I'm going to have such fun," whispered Cindy to Jason as they entered the store.

Jason turned to face Brenda. "Do we really have to do this?" he asked.

"This is what the school wants," said Brenda.

Jason swallowed hard. "Can I at least pick out my own clothes? Please?!" he pleaded.

Brenda shook her head. "No. Cindy will do it."

"Why does Cindy get to do it?" He sounded exasperated.

"Because Cindy is in charge of you now. I explained that. That's what Dr. Morgan recommends. So Cindy will be your boss and you will follow her orders. You need to learn to respect her authority because you will always be compelled to obey her and other girls from now on."

"But I don't want to!" he protested.

"This is for your own good, Jason. And the fact you can't recognize that tells me how badly this is needed. Dr. Morgan is clearly right that you young men can't accept the new reality the way you are. Now go with Cindy and do what she tells you. Obey her!" growled Brenda.

"Yes, Ma'am," said Jason. He had no choice as she had phrased this as a command.

Cindy led Jason to a rack of dresses. These

looked like something a little girl might wear, not a young woman. As she flipped through these, Jason looked around. He realized that there were several other boys in the shop, each being led around by a woman or women. Those boys didn't look any less embarrassed to be there than he did; that didn't provide him with any comfort. After scanning the shop, Jason looked at the dresses Cindy was examining.

"Wait a minute," protested Jason, "those look like little girl dresses!"

"Yeah, so?" asked Cindy coldly.

"I'm a college student! I'll be twenty soon. I should at least be allowed to dress like—" he cringed before continuing, "—other girls my age," he said.

Cindy snickered. "I never in my wildest dreams thought I would ever hear you begging to dress like 'other girls your age'!"

"I didn't beg!"

"Yeah, well, don't push your luck or I might make you."

"Not with your mother here."

"Wanna try me?" asked Cindy.

Jason swallowed hard. He decided that backing down would be the smartest policy at this point. "I'm sorry, Ma'am," he said humiliatingly. This was what Cindy required him to say at home whenever she felt he owed her an apology.

"That's better."

"Seriously though, I am not a child."

"Well, you're going to be my *little* sister from now on," said Cindy.

Jason's jaw dropped. "You can't do that!"

Cindy chuckled. "I can do anything I want."

"But Cindy!"

"Cindy?! Is that what I want to hear?"

"I'm sorry... *Miss*... 'but Miss!'" pleaded Jason.

Cindy shook her head. "It's happening, so you better just accept it."

Jason stood there in shock as Cindy pulled out several dresses that looked like things young girls might wear. They were pastel and frilly and lacey and very, very short. He would feel like a fool wearing them. But that seemed to be what Cindy wanted. Her goal seemed to be to humiliate him as much as possible.

"Here, try this one on first," said Cindy and she pointed to the dressing room.

Jason took the dress and made his way to the dressing room. On the one hand, this should not have embarrassed him. He was already wearing a skirt and pumps, so changing into a dress should not have changed anything. What's more, other boys were starting to dress like this too, so it's not like he was alone. Plus, everyone knew this wasn't his idea. But that didn't change the fact he felt utterly utterly humiliated. This dress, which was white and covered in lace, was so much more sissy-ish than the skirt he was wearing and everyone would be looking at him. And even though they knew this wasn't his idea, that didn't mean they weren't still laughing at him.

Still, he did as he was told. He had no choice.

A few moments later, Jason shuddered as he examined himself in the mirror. He looked like a sissy. The dress was so loose and so frilly, and it stopped just below his panties. It did nothing to hide his erection either.

"Why am I hard at all?" he asked himself.

This brought him even more shame, and he had no doubt that it would become a topic of conversation if Cindy saw it; which, of course, she would.

"Come along, *little sister*," called Cindy to Jason mockingly.

Jason cringed, but he walked out of the dressing room. Cindy immediately burst out laughing, which made Jason burn bright red with shame.

"Oh my God! You look like such a sissy!" said Cindy between laughs.

"Can I go change please?" asked Jason.

"Hardly," said Cindy. She looked the

helpless, feminized young man up and down once more, before adding, "But we do need to get you more appropriate shoes, sissy boy."

Jason breathed a sigh of relief. If Cindy was determined to make him look like a little girl, then he assumed that at least he could finally get out of the heels. These were killing his feet. Indeed, all week she had him walking around the house in pumps with three and even three-and-a-half-inch heels, and they hurt his feet. Plus, they made him feel particularly effeminate. But little girls wore things like flat Mary-Janes, so Jason was at least happy about that.

He shouldn't have been.

"These look good," said Cindy when they reached the shoe section and she picked up a pair of white sandals with a massive five-inch heel. These had a one-inch platform, but that still meant the heel itself and the effective heel were both at least one inch higher than anything he had worn before. These would also show off his painted toenails, which his pumps had not.

"You want me to wear those?!" asked Jason in shock.

"Yes. They match your sissy dress perfectly."

"But I thought I was supposed to be your *little* sister?" he asked.

"You are," said Cindy with a giggle and she

patted his cheek. "You'll just be my little sister in heels. Besides, I want you in heels. I like seeing you struggle and I like knowing that you're uncomfortable."

Jason strangely felt his erection grow at her words. He tried to ignore it.

"Now put these on and let's go show my mother," said Cindy.

Jason didn't want to wear these shoes, but without the slightest thought of resistance, he took them, set them down, stepped out of his pumps, slipped his feet into these heels and then crouched down and strapped them to his feet. A moment later, Cindy took his hand and pulled him through the store to her mother.

Brenda gasped when she saw Jason. She covered her mouth to hide her uncontrollable smile. "If only Greg were here to see his son right now," thought Brenda and she giggled at the image of her overly-macho husband's reaction to seeing his son sissified. She had married Greg because she thought she loved him, but she was learning that he was hard to live with, particularly because of his sexist attitude, which seemed to get worse all the time. It had become so bad that she genuinely had come to like the idea of anything that humiliated him and brought him down a notch.

Jason was better, but Brenda worried he

would become like his father. One of the benefits of what was going on with the virus, she thought, was that at least it had reduced the chances of that.

Cindy pushed Jason right up to Brenda and held out her hands toward him as if to present him to her. "Tah dah!" she sang.

"That's quite a dress," said Brenda and she snickered.

"It fits him perfectly," said Cindy.

Brenda looked down and saw his erection sticking up beneath the dress, which did nothing to hide it. She laughed inwardly at how Greg would react to seeing his son erect because he was wearing a dress. Still, this was likely too much to allow.

"Uh, it doesn't fit all of him," said Brenda and she pointed toward his crotch.

Cindy looked down at Jason's erection. "Oh, that?"

"Yes, that."

Cindy reached for Jason's erection. Jason tried to jump away.

"Stand still and be quiet," ordered Cindy.

Jason froze.

Cindy then grabbed his erection and tried to push it back between his legs. It didn't want to stay there, however.

"Here, let me try," said Brenda and she took

his erection and tried the same thing Cindy did. Again, it didn't want to stay hidden. The moment she let go of it, it slipped right back out and stood up tall beneath his dress.

Jason was dying with shame as the two women played with his erection.

"I don't know, honey," said Brenda and she pushed it again.

"I don't either," said Cindy. "Maybe with tighter panties."

"No, I don't think this is going to work," added Brenda and she reached out and pushed his erection to one side, which made it swing from side to side beneath the short frilly dress.

Just then, Eric, Sidney and Amber walked into the store. They were here to buy Amber new shoes for school. Sidney and Eric immediately saw Jason and the other boys trying on dresses and they looked at each other uneasily. Amber, however, saw only one boy: Jason. She saw the sissy dress he wore. She saw the amazing heels she wouldn't even dare to try to wear herself. She knew what Cindy was doing to Jason in terms of dressing him as a girl at home, but she had never seen it yet. Now she had. And she became instantly wet.

Indeed, she didn't feel the horror she expected and wanted to feel at all. Instead, her nipples popped up and her pussy filled with her juices to such a degree that they soaked her panties and even made her inner thighs wet. She felt a tremor deep inside her and her pussy lips tingled. There was no doubt that she was intensely turned on seeing what she saw... probably more so by this than by anything ever in her life.

"Oh my God!" she thought.

Jason saw her at the same time. Their eyes met. He saw a smirk appear on her lips and he felt like he shrank instantly to the size of a bug. He had never felt smaller, weaker, or more humiliated in his entire life. He would have started crying right then and there except that Cindy's hand was back on his erection and that was turning him on despite himself.

"It's just not going to work," said Brenda.

"I think I can find a way," said Cindy.

At this point, Amber saw Cindy and Brenda trying to manipulating his erection to try to hide it. Her jaw dropped. She looked for Sidney to point this out to her as proof of how Cindy had been acting, but Sidney had disappeared across the store. Amber turned back to Jason to watch these events. She was transfixed as her thighs got slipperier and slipperier.

"How?" asked Brenda in the meantime.

"They must make something that can hold it in place. I'll find something. Can we get the dress?" asked Cindy hopefully.

Brenda raised an eyebrow and looked over Jason once more. He looked like such a sissy. She knew she shouldn't allow this, even though the thought of seeing Greg's face when his son came waltzing into the house in this dress was just overwhelming. She would love to see that and how it brought Greg's machismo attitude down a notch.

"It might even make him easier to live with," she thought.

Still, it wasn't right and she wasn't going to allow it. She was just about to tell Cindy that too when she remembered the booklet she had received. The booklet made the point that the more humiliating the clothes, the better it would be for the young man. It also made the point that parents needed to trust the young female guardians to make their own decisions even if they seemed excessive or humiliating.

"I guess this is what they wanted?" thought Brenda cautiously.

She considered this for a moment and then decided to trust the experts. After all, the school had the best trained experts working on this and they wouldn't lead her wrong, would they?

"Ok, we can buy it," said Brenda.

Cindy felt like she would explode in a flaming ball of happiness when she heard those words. Jason, on the other hand, felt shocked and utterly humiliated. He looked over his shoulder at Amber once more, but she was still looking at him strangely, with a kinky sort of look in her eyes. Jason realized he would find no help there today.

In fact, it wouldn't just be Jason who would find no help today. Melanie had won a complete victory up to now and the boys would all face the same fate because of it. One after another would be dragged into this store or others like it and feminized, and there was nothing they could do to stop it.

What's more, with the virus starting to spread to all the men of Satin Falls, Melanie's plan was about to expand. Soon, she would manage to have every man in Satin Falls feminized, and there was no one who could stop her... no one except Sidney and Amber. But the desire of both Amber and Sidney to stop the virus was about to be severely tested and there was no guarantee which way they would go. The men of Satin Falls were in for a wild ride... in high heels.

The End of Part One.

Part Two:
Feminized And Humiliated

"Second Prologue"

—o—

Things were spinning out of control in Satin Falls. All the younger males in town had fallen prey to the virus. Not one of them could resist any command given by any female. The girls, naturally, were taking full advantage of this to make the boys do the things the girls wanted. Sometimes, this was simply getting a boy to move aside as the girl passed him in the hallway, but more often than not it involved humiliating paybacks by ex-girlfriends or little sisters, attempts by the girls to mold their boyfriends into their image of perfection, or the abuses that come naturally when one person receives unlimited power over another.

Making matter worse, Melanie Morgan's plan to feminize the boys was going into effect starting Monday morning. That meant the girls would be required to feminize the boys and they would be encouraged to humiliate them to help suppress the "male ego," which Melanie assured everyone was causing the boys trauma. Once that plan took effect, the girls would effectively have a license to toy with the boys.

What's more, there was no escape for the boys. Every boy needed to comply with Melanie's plan if he wanted to continue at the college. Nor couldn't they leave the town either to escape the plan because the outside world was even less safe for them. Even those not at the college quickly found their mothers and girlfriends making them comply with the plan because everyone believed this was necessary to cure them.

Actually, not *everyone* believed this. Most of the women did, but few of the men accepted this. The men didn't see how feminizing a man could help him accept being powerless and submissive to women. The men, however, were unable to stop the women from implementing Melanie's plan, because they too were finally succumbing to the virus. It had taken longer with them, and most still didn't know yet that they had been infected, but they were increasingly following in the boys' high-heeled footsteps into submission to the women in their lives.

By this critical point, only two people in town could stop Melanie's plan, Sidney and Amber. However, they didn't know yet what her plan was exactly or even that there was an ulterior motive. They just knew that something seemed wrong with Melanie's ideas. Even worse, both Amber and Sidney were about to have their desire to stop the virus tested by temptation.

Things looked bad for the males in Satin Falls.

Chapter 9: "Temptation"

—o—

It was Monday morning. Satin Falls Academy was teeming with activity. The university Board was here. Dean Dwyer was here. Melanie was here, as was Sidney. The Mayor was here too. She had brought several local journalists in an attempt to convince them to maintain the news blackout of what was going on in the town until they could get a handle on it; outside attention could be very bad right now. Quite a few mothers, older sisters and girlfriends were here too. Additionally, many of the female students were here already. They had gotten here early to watch events play out and, ominously, most brought cameras with them.

The bell rang. It was eight o'clock. Classes would begin soon.

The doors opened and all the girls rushed inside to wait for the boys.

The first boy arrived a few minutes later.

"Woot woot!" cheered a group of girls as the boy walked through the door. This young man wore the new uniform required for the boys. This uniform consisted of a short black plaid skirt, a white blouse with pearl inlaid trim, a short black feminine jacket with three-quarter length sleeves, one button and hot pink trim, tan stockings, and black or pink high-heeled sandals with heels between three and five inches. The boys also were required to wear pink nail polish, full makeup, and a feminine hair style. The dress code even required pink or black panties. Cleverly, it also stated, "corsets are not forbidden," which encouraged most of the women to add a corset to the uniform even without seeming to require it. All in all, this was a humiliating uniform for the boys, but it was what they would all wear from now on because the Board thought that requiring a uniform would help ease the parents' concerns and would avoid chaos because it would prevent school from turning into a drag show of sorts where the girls competed to turn the males in their charge into the most outrageously feminine or sissyish creatures they could. Still, the uniform was quite feminine and sexy because that is what Melanie demanded; in truth, she would have preferred the drag show, but she accepted the uniform to placate the Board.

The girls, on the other hand, had no uniform and no dress code. Consequently, they seized on this opportunity to wear pants and low-heeled or wedge-heeled shoes today. They wouldn't dress like that regularly, especially the more girly ones, but today felt like the day to make sure they were less feminine in dress than their hapless male classmates.

"Come on now, girls! Remember your obligations to protect these boys," pleaded Dwyer, when the girls cheered the first boy.

Unfortunately, no one listened.

A moment later, a second boy arrived. He came with his girlfriend. She wore blue shorts and wedges. He wore the uniform with pink heels. Once again, the girls raised a cheer and took pictures.

"Woot woot!" they cheered.

"Nice heels, *girlfriend!*" came a mocking cry.

"Just ignore them," said the boy's girlfriend.

Then another arrived... and another. Soon enough, a great many of the male students had arrived and were wandering the halls. To a one, they all looked humiliated and intimidated. They spoke softly and got out of the girls' ways... any girl. They held their arms closely to their bodies, took delicate steps in their unfamiliar high heels, and worried that some random girl would come by and flip up their skirts, exposing their panties.

The girls, on the other hand, looked like they were firmly in charge. They laughed and spoke loudly and roamed the halls with broad shoulders and wide strides, and they loved to ogle the boys. Everywhere the boys went there were photo flashes and whistles as the girls admired them... and, of course, emasculating comments.

"You've got amazing legs for a boy, Tommy!"

"You're a natural in skirts, Kent!"

"You look like you've been wearing skirts your whole life!"

"Whoops, I can see your little pee pee beneath your skirt. Why are you hard? Does this turn you on?"

And so on. The girls even started telling the boys to act more femininely and most gave instructions on how to walk more seductively, instructions on ways to talk more femininely, and suggestions for more feminine posture. With all of these commands, the girls were quickly emasculating the boys at full speed and turning them into sissies in appearance and in how they carried and handled themselves.

Dwyer's face burned red as he witnessed this. This struck him as wrong. He stepped into the main hall to put an end to this. Specifically, he approached a group of girls to order them to stop flipping up the boys' skirts. They would walk up behind some unsuspecting boy, flip up his skirt, and then call out "pink" or "black" depending on the color of his panties. When they found a boy without panties, they ordered him to hold up his skirt and go march through the hall letting everyone see his erection. All of this brought Dwyer's wrath.

Only, it didn't work out the way Dwyer expected.

"You girls, stop that! Leave that boy alone and stop flipping up boys' skirts!" demanded Dwyer.

Normally, the girls would have panicked at being caught misbehaving by the Dean and would have immediately complied with his orders. But recent events had made one of them very bold and she turned to face Dwyer.

"Leave us alone," said the bold young woman. "*We're* in charge now."

The others froze.

But then a strange thing happened. Without any idea that he was following a command given by the young woman, Dwyer stopped, turned and started back toward his office. He decided that it would be best to leave these particular girls alone to whatever they were doing. All three girls saw this and instantly realized what this meant... they had seen similar reactions from the young men around them for days now.

"Oh my God!" squealed the second girl. "Did you see what just happened?"

"Wait! Come back here," commanded the bold, first girl. Her tone was firm and strong, but she also sounded almost giddy.

Dwyer turned around and returned to the three girls.

"What do we do now?" asked the second girl.

"I say we make him go sit naked in his office," said the third girl.

"We should put makeup on him first!" said the first. "Like the other boys!"

"Yeah!" agreed the third.

The first immediately whipped out her makeup kit and began applying makeup to the helpless Dean as he stood there frozen. Fortunately for him, Sondra Stern saw what was going on and she raced over. By the time she got there, however, Dwyer already wore red lipstick and brown eye shadow.

"You girls get to class, *NOW!*" growled Stern.

The three girls scattered and raced away from her as quickly as they could. Sondra then looked Dwyer up and down and shook her head as she observed the makeup on his face. A smug smile appeared in the corner of her mouth and she chuckled. She then took Dwyer's hand and led him to the office, where she had him sit at his desk. It was time to speak to the Board about who should run the school now.

—o—

Amber walked Jason home after class. They walked slowly because he wore five-inch high-heeled sandals; they were hot pink. Amber wore tennis shoes. Jason wore the heels because Cindy had ordered it. Amber could have countered that order, but she hadn't. Nor was she entirely sure why she hadn't. The truth, however, was that Amber was deeply torn about the entire situation.

On the one hand, Amber felt badly that Jason was unable to resist any command given by any female. That struck her as incredibly unfair and she wished it wasn't so. It just didn't seem right that one person should be forced to obey the will of another, especially when that person was the evil Cindy who thrived on humiliating Jason. What was worse, though, was that Melanie's plan gave Cindy the green light to be as nasty as she wanted to be to Jason and no one would try to stop her because they all thought this would cure Jason. This frustrated Amber and made her want to put an end to Melanie's plan and save Jason with every fiber of her being.

Well, not *every* fiber... and that was the problem.

For while Amber saw this as an outrage, her desire to end all of this ran into a singular problem: Amber was finding herself intensely turned on by Jason's feminization. She never expected this, but it was proving to be absolutely true. And this wasn't just some ephemeral turn on like she felt at seeing a hot actor in a movie and having a brief fantasy of what it would be like to be with him. No, this was much, much more than that.

Whenever Amber saw Jason in some article of feminine clothing, such as the uniform he wore right now, her heart fluttered. She became short of breath and her entire body trembled and burned. It felt like a need personified through her body. Her nipples became painfully hard, her pussy lips tingled and the muscles within contracted like they wanted to grab his penis and hold it inside her. Wetness filled her pussy and soaked her panties and even began to run down her thighs to the point where she worried that it could be seen if her skirt was short enough.

Beyond the physical changes, Amber found her mind instantly obsessed too. Just as her pussy flooded with her juices, her mind flooded with images of Jason looking like a woman, dressed seductively, and Amber taking him like a man might take a woman... though she didn't fully understand the mechanics of how that might work as she wasn't particularly knowledgeable about the ways of sex.

This happened every time, and it made it so very, very hard for her to remember that she was opposed as a matter of principle to what was happening to the boys and that she wanted it stopped. Right now, for example, as they walked and Jason complained about how the boys were treated on this first day, all Amber could think about was the sound of Jason's high heels striking the cement as they walked along the sidewalk: *CLICK! CLICK! CLICK! CLICK! CLICK! CLICK!*

And each step...

CLICK! CLICK! CLICK! CLICK!

...each wonderfully feminine step...

CLICK! CLICK! CLICK! CLICK!

...made her burn hot within...

CLICK! CLICK! CLICK! CLICK!

...and made her want to throw her boyfriend to the ground...

CLICK! CLICK! CLICK! CLICK!

...and take him sexually.

"It just isn't fair," said Jason.

CLICK! CLICK! CLICK! CLICK!

Amber barely heard Jason's voice. She was hearing only his heels and that sound made her wither. "Uh, um, yeah," she said absently in response to whatever Jason had said to her.

CLICK! CLICK! CLICK! CLICK!

"Somebody needs to do something," said

Jason.

"Good God, I'm turned on!" she thought. The juices between her thighs had made them slick and she felt them slide together as she walked.

"Don't you think so?" asked Jason.

CLICK! CLICK! CLICK! CLICK!

Amber realized Jason had asked a question, but she didn't know what it was. Her mind was lost in images of Jason lying on a bed in lingerie and high heels. Amber felt a tremor deep within her pussy. Her lips curled and her face flushed in an explosion of redness. "Uh, yeah, you're right," said Amber between difficult breaths; she was breathing hard and irregularly now.

CLICK! CLICK! CLICK! CLICK!

"And that woman, Morgan, isn't doing anything to help," said Jason.

CLICK! CLICK! CLICK! CLICK!

Amber's chest heaved. She felt her pussy tighten. "Yeah, she's a problem," she agreed between breaths.

CLICK! CLICK!

Jason stopped walking and turned to Amber. "She's more than *a* problem. She *is* the problem!" he exclaimed.

"Uh, yeah, I agree," said Amber. She took this moment to suck in as much wind as she could. She had been struggling to breathe with her pounding heart and because she kept holding her breath every time her pussy muscles contracted.

"Are you ok?" asked Jason. "You seem winded."

"Uh, yeah. I, uh, just worked out really hard and my legs are tired."

Jason looked down at his girlfriend's legs. He shook his head. "At least you aren't wearing heels. You should try walking in these," he said and he turned his foot to show her his high-heeled shoe.

Amber took the opportunity to stare at his pretty feet within their high heels and his hot-pink painted toenails; she imagined touching them right now and she felt more juices run down her thigh. "Yeah, I know. I wear them a lot, remember. You do get used to them."

"I guess," he said. "Well, fortunately, we're almost home."

Amber looked up and realized that they were about a house away from Jason's home. She hadn't noticed how far they'd come because she had been in her own world inside her head for the whole walk. But now they were here, so they went inside and went to Jason's room. He started stripping off his uniform.

"Cindy's not here," he said. "So I can wear whatever I want. Of course, that's going to change the moment she gets home. She loves enforcing the dress code in that stupid book written by Dr. Morgan and making me dress like a sissy." Jason grabbed some shorts and a t-shirt after he stripped down to only his corset, his panties and his stockings; he wasn't allowed to remove the corset and he saw no point in changing the panties or stockings with Cindy coming home soon. Naturally, he still wore make up and earrings as well.

Amber watched this and felt a quiver within her pussy. She blushed.

"Cindy seems to have a thing for frilly dresses," complained Jason as he pulled the shorts up his shaved legs.

Amber listened, but her thoughts were elsewhere. Indeed, her mind was fixed on something she wanted very much, but dared not ask for because she knew that Jason would never agree to what she wanted and he would probably be offended just by her asking. Imagine her surprise, however, when a moment later, before she even realized what was happening, she suddenly found herself asking: "Uh, Jason, can you do something for me?"

"What?"

She blushed. She never meant to ask him for this but now that she had started, she felt like she had trapped herself. Really, the only choice she had was to press ahead. Her stomach twisted into knots. "It's... well," she said and she paused. She felt highly embarrassed by the whole thing.

Jason raised an eyebrow. "What?" he repeated.

Amber twisted her lips. Then she blurted it out: "Would you dress like a girl for me?!"

Jason's jaw dropped.

"I know it's humiliating and I'm sorry, but please, I really really want to see it, and I can't explain it, it's just something that I like feel like it's important to me and I don't know why I want it, but I do," added Amber so quickly that it sounded like one long word.

"Are you kidding?" asked Jason. He was shocked.

Amber looked down at the floor. She felt a deep sense of shame pass over her as if she had just confessed her deepest secret and been rejected. "I... I'm sorry. I just... I don't know why." A thought occurred to her in that instant: she could use her control over Jason to make him forget that she asked. Should she do it, however? She had told herself before that she never wanted to use the power on Jason, but maybe this was an exception. Maybe, this was one time where the power could be used for good. She weighed this very heavily in her mind.

"You're serious, aren't you?" asked Jason.

He blushed.

Amber nodded her head. "I'm sorry, Jason. It's just that seeing you in these girl's clothes has been super exciting for me. I don't know why. I can't explain it. I never thought it would turn me on at all, but it did and now I can't get it out of my mind. I know I'm a freak or something, but it's just eating me up." As she said this, she struggled with whether or not to use her power. She was leaning toward it, even though she knew that was wrong.

"Amber," said Jason. He paused. He looked utterly confused.

"It's all right if you don't want to," she said. Her mouth had gone dry and her face burned with shame. "I won't force you. I know how unfair that is and how hard this all is for you. I really am sorry, but it just came up and I didn't know what to do. I wish I'd never mentioned it."

Amber was now fighting incredibly hard not to utter the words: "Forget everything I just said." That seemed like the best way out of this horrible, humiliating mistake she had made, and Jason would never know. Still, it wasn't right, she told herself. It just seemed wrong... but it might be best. She was so torn.

"Well, I'm glad you won't force me," said Jason.

Amber shook her head. "I would never do

that," she said, even as she struggled to decide whether or not to erase his memory. She continued. "I mean, that's really unfair. Seriously, how fair is it that all I have to say is, 'Jason go dress in your girl's clothes,' and you would need to do it, right?"

Jason immediately turned and started toward his closet.

Amber hadn't noticed yet as she was still looking at the floor. She finished her thought: "How can you build a relationship with that kind of power? It wipes out trust," she said. She kicked the floor and bit her lip. "I'm sorry. I never should have even mentioned it. I hope you can forgive me." She looked up.

Jason was gone.

He now stood at his closet collecting clothes. She walked over to him and watched as he grabbed the white lace babydoll dress, the most sissyish thing he owned, and some brown leather sandals with a very high heel. He grabbed various items of lingerie as well.

"Jason? What are you doing?" asked Amber softly.

"I'm changing," said Jason.

"I thought you didn't want to put on girl's clothes?" asked Amber.

Jason didn't answer. Amber instantly realized that this was how the boys acted when they were under a command. They ignored whatever contradictions existed in their minds to carry out the command.

"Did I cause this?" she asked. She bit her lip.

Meanwhile, Jason walked to his bathroom with his arms full of female clothing. Amber watched him go. She thought back on their conversation and what she had said. That's when it hit her

"Oh no! I did cause this!" she gasped as she suddenly realized that she had inadvertently given Jason a command to go change into his feminine clothes, and that was exactly what he was doing now. She rubbed her throat. "I can undo the command," she thought. "I need to undo it."

But she didn't.

Instead, Amber stood there as her boyfriend locked himself in the bathroom and began to change. She knew what was happening was wrong. She had told herself repeatedly that it was just morally wrong to use this power nature had given the girls. What's more, she knew that she was more than just using the power, she was abusing it. She wasn't doing something for Jason's own good or because of some pressing need, she was doing this to satisfy her own sexual curiosity. She had turned her boyfriend into a sex toy and that was just wrong.

Yet, she couldn't bring herself to stop him.

"It was an accident," she told herself, by way of justification. "I didn't mean to do it." But did that really mean it wasn't her fault? She wanted to believe that, but she knew better.

In the bathroom, Amber heard Jason strip out of the shorts he wore. They fell to the floor, where she heard the metal button that closed the shorts hit the tile floor. He was down to his panties and his stockings and his corset now. The image excited her and she felt a shudder run down her spine, though she told herself she didn't know what that shudder meant; she still wasn't sure she wanted to believe she felt the way she obviously felt.

"What if I just wait until he comes out to make him change back?" she asked herself. "That's reasonable, right?"

Amber heard the rustling of clothes in the bathroom; Jason was getting dressed now in his girly clothes. That thought made her pussy tingle again. The prospect of seeing Jason all dressed like a girl in something other than his relatively boring uniform and to get to touch him was so exciting that wetness flooded out of her once more and again ran down her thighs.

It troubled her too though. "This... this is wrong," she said.

Still, she didn't stop him.

Meanwhile, a few feet away, behind the bathroom door, Jason had stripped himself of his shorts and t-shirt. He'd removed all the underwear he wore as well, as those didn't match the dress he intended to wear. Only his corset remained from earlier, and of course the pink polish on his fingernails and his toenails and the makeup on his face.

His penis was hard as a rock.

Jason pulled the white silk panties up his legs and tucked his erection inside them as best he could; they really did nothing to hide it. Then he pulled the tan stockings up his legs. Next, he slipped the short white lacey dress over his head and pulled it down his body. The dress looked almost like a nightie. Its hem hung loosely to just below the bottom of his panties and, like the panties, it also did nothing to hide his erection. In the back, the dress plunged to near the middle of his back; it stopped just above his corset. This showed off a hint of his sissy tan lines. He looked very demure and sexy in the dress.

He then stepped into the tan leather high-heeled sandals. These had five-inch heels atop a one-inch wooden platform. They were open-toed, open-backed, and had a thick strap that came across the front of his foot, just above the arch. They were intensely sexy.

Back in Jason's bedroom, Amber now

heard the sound of his high heels striking against the tile floor as he slipped into them. She knew he would be out any second. She was still struggling with what to do at this point. What she wanted to do and what she needed to do were two very different things.

"I can have him change back when he comes out," she said again. She nodded to herself as if agreeing with herself would make her actions right. At the same time, however, a deep sense of shame arose within her. She knew how wrong this was. "If I do this, then I'm no better than Melanie," she told herself.

Amber sighed.

She knew what she wanted; she just knew she had no right to take it... even if she could and even if she made it so that Jason never knew. Then she heard more movement of Jason's high heels against the floor. That sound made her pussy burn. She was so desperate to see him in those heels... so, so desperate. She *needed* to see that.

"I—" she started, but never finished the thought.

Suddenly, something arose within her and reminded her that if she truly saw herself as a good person, then she couldn't allow herself this liberty with her boyfriend. She needed to stop this.

"No!" she said firmly. "I can't do this."

Amber marched over to the bathroom door. She knocked.

"Jason, honey. I can't do this to you. I'm sorry, baby. I accidentally gave you the order to put on your girl's clothes. I wanted to see it, because what I said about it turning me on was true, but I never wanted to force you to do it. I really am sorry. I'm giving you a new order, so listen closely: disregard my prior order. Wear whatever you want. You don't have to wear anything you don't want to. I'm sorry," she repeated sadly. "I'm going to leave now so you have some privacy. Please forgive me."

With that, she turned and started to walk away from the bathroom toward the stairs that would lead to the front door. Behind her, however, the bathroom door opened and Jason emerged.

"Wait!" he called out.

Amber stopped but didn't turn around because she knew how Jason would be dressed and seeing him would not be fair to him. She had no right to see him dressed as he was.

There was a moment of silence.

"I am dressed the way I want to be dressed," he said.

"What do you mean?" asked Amber over her shoulder.

"I want to wear this for you."

"Really?"

"Yes."

Amber felt a warm, happy feeling pass over her. She turned to see her boyfriend. He looked hot in his white dress and brown sandals. All the exciting feelings returned instantly and she rushed over to hug him. She was super wet.

They kissed.

—o—

Sidney had come home early from work. Things were rather chaotic at the office and they decided to close for the day as they sorted everything out. There was some big meeting of the partners planned to discuss the problem that had arisen, though associates like Sidney were not invited. Hence, she decided to come home and spend the afternoon with Eric. He had more wedding selections for her to look through.

They sat on the couch as Sidney flipped through several pages of ideas Eric had gathered. Eric wore his favorite red housedress. Unfortunately, he also wore these old, worn out red platform sandals which Sidney despised. They were the only thing in his wardrobe which she couldn't stand, but he was attached to them for some reason and he kept wearing them. She had thought at one time about demanding that he get rid of them, but she realized that would only cause problems, so she accepted them very, very grudgingly... but she still hated them.

Sidney, by the way, still wore the tan pencil skirt and neutral open-toed pumps she wore to the office.

Eric handed her a set of images of dresses he had collected.

"Ooh, I like this one," said Sidney. She pointed to the dress with the rose-shaped bodice.

"That's my favorite," said Eric.

"It's fantastic."

"I would kill to wear that at the wedding."

Sidney smiled. She would love to let Eric wear the dress too, but alas, that was impossible. They had to keep his secret femininity hidden from his family. So Sidney set her hand on his thigh and she squeezed it as a show of support. Eric then handed her a set of photos involving shoes. Sidney began flipping through them. They were all gorgeous. Eric had an amazing eye for women's clothes.

"These are pretty too," said Sidney.

Eric smiled. "Thank you."

Sidney kept flipping through the photos.

Eric waited a few seconds before cautiously asking Sidney a question: "Can I ask you a question?"

"Of course, dear," said Sidney.

"There's a rumor going around... whispers really, that something is going on in town."

Sidney nodded her head. "That's true."

"I know a little bit about what's been going on at the school from what you and Amber have told me, but I don't know much. They've managed to keep that out of the newspaper," said Eric.

"With good reason. Would you want it getting around that every young man in Satin Falls is completely at the mercy of any woman or girl who wants to take advantage of them?" asked Sidney.

Eric shook his head. "No, definitely not. And I agree with keeping it out of the news, *but* that does make it hard to separate fact from rumor," said Eric.

"True."

"But that's not what concerns me."

"Ok. What's bothering you?" asked Sidney.

Eric looked pensive.

In the meantime, Sidney pointed to a pair of sandals with a single strap over the toes, an ankle strap, and a one-inch platform. They were silver. "These are really beautiful."

"Yes, I like those too," said Eric. He paused again and ran his tongue over his teeth.

"Go on, dear. I'm listening," said Sidney.

"What bothers me is that I'm hearing rumors... rumors that the same thing that affected the boys is now affecting all the men in town. Have you heard anything about that?"

Sidney took a deep breath and set down the photos. She knew more than most people because of her legal position and the briefings she had received. She wasn't sure what she could say at this point, however. Additionally, she didn't want to worry her fiancé, especially over something he could do nothing about. She pursed her lips as she considered what to tell him, but she took too long to respond and Eric realized she was weighing how to respond, which told him there was something she didn't want to tell him.

"So there is something," said Eric.

Sidney nodded her head. "Yeah, there is," she admitted. "It started with the boys, but now it seems to be spreading to the men."

"All of us?"

"I don't know."

"And this is that same loss of will power thing?"

Sidney nodded her head.

Eric bit his lip. He looked nervous. "Would you make me do things I don't want to do?" he asked suddenly.

Sidney felt taken aback by his question for the simple reason that in all this time she had been dealing with the issue, she had never once considered what would happen if the virus affected Eric. He already followed her orders, though he did so by choice, so would it really change anything if he now needed to follow her orders regardless of how he felt about them? She thought not. In any event though, she was sure she would never make him do anything against his will because, like Amber, she saw this power as immoral, so the answer to his question was easy.

"I would never make you do anything against your will, honey," said Sidney.

Eric smiled softly. "I'm glad." Then his worried expression returned. "Can you tell if I'm already affected?" he asked.

Sidney shrugged her shoulders. "I don't know. I guess we could test it."

"How do we do that?" asked Eric nervously.

"I'll give you an order and you resist it, and we'll see if you do it or not."

Eric nodded his head. "Ok," he said cautiously. "I suppose that would work."

Sidney looked around for some order she could give. She thought of something a moment later. "Got one."

Eric suddenly placed his hands on her wrist. "Wait," he said. He took a deep breath.

"Are you ok?" asked Sidney.

"I'm nervous. To tell the truth, I'm not even sure I want to know," he said.

"Why is that?"

He sighed. "I just don't like the idea of this at all. I'm happy to follow your orders, but I want to do so because I choose to do so. That makes me feel special that I get to follow your orders. I don't want to lose that by losing my choice in whether or not to submit." He twisted his lips. "I don't think it would be the same. It wouldn't feel special."

Sidney hadn't thought of that and she considered this for a moment. She wondered if she would feel the same if he lost his choice in which orders to follow. Would it make her as happy knowing that Eric had no choice but to submit rather than knowing that he was submitting because he wanted to belong to her? It was an interesting question and she wasn't sure. But it would never come up, she told herself, because she swore to herself she would never use that power over Eric. She would always let him decide if he wanted to submit.

"Ok... let's find out," said Eric, snapping Sidney out of her thoughts.

Sidney smiled at her fiancé. "Ready?"

"Yes, Miss," he said and he closed his eyes.

"Remember to resist my command," she said.

"Yes, Miss."

"Ok," said Sidney. "Open your eyes." He did and she pointed to a vase on the bookshelf across the room. "Go pick up that vase."

Without a word, Eric rose to his feet. He walked over to the bookshelf and picked up the vase. He turned around to face Sidney. He said nothing.

"I asked you to resist my order," she said.

"What order?" he asked.

"You don't remember me giving you an order?" asked Sidney.

"No, Miss."

Sidney raised an eyebrow. "Put the vase down and come sit next to me."

"Yes, Miss," said Eric. "He returned the vase to the bookshelf and sat down next to his fiancée again.

"Did you try to resist my order?" asked Sidney.

"What order did you give?"

"You seriously don't remember an order?"

"No, Miss."

"Why did you pick up the vase?"

"Because you asked me too," said Eric in a matter-of-fact tone of voice.

In his response in that instant, Sidney realized the full extent of the power she now held over her fiancé. This was way beyond anything she had expected. Not only could she issue an order which he would obey without question, but he didn't even seem to recognize her order as an order. To him, it was just something she said which he did because she asked him to do it. That realization raised another question: could she make him forget she had given the order entirely? She decided to test it.

"I want you to forget that we had this conversation about the virus," said Sidney.

Eric's face went blank. Then he smiled.

"What were we talking about?" asked Sidney.

"We were talking about the wedding," said Eric.

"What about the virus?"

Eric cocked his head to one side. "What about the virus?" He sounded completely confused.

Sidney gasped. She now realized she could make Eric do *anything she wanted* and she could do it without him ever even realizing she had done it. The feeling of power that gave her was beyond amazing, it was like being on fire with power. There was no other feeling she could compare this too. Even the first time she watched Eric obey one of her orders paled in comparison. She had not expected this incredible feeling of power welling up inside her. It felt like an intense drug only a million times stronger. She felt a rush of blood race throughout her body; her pussy became very wet and it tingled. Her mind was overwhelmed with joyous sensations.

"My God, I had no idea it would be like this!" she thought. She gasped for air and she struggled to process what she was feeling.

"What about the virus, Miss?" asked Eric again. He was still confused.

Sidney shook her head. "Nothing," she said.

"Yes, Miss," said Eric and he returned to the photos as Sidney tried to wrap her mind around what she had just experienced. She had no idea how to deal with what she just felt. One thing was for sure though, she knew she wanted more!

"Whoa!" she said when it hit her what she was considering. "I can't do this. It's immoral!"

She bit her lip, but at the same time, she felt a tremor deep within her pussy and she suddenly felt weak all over. Her pussy became wetter as cum dripped out of her. She began breathing heavily and she trembled.

"Can I really give this up?" she asked herself.

She felt her pussy lips tingle and she let herself sink into the warm, exciting feeling. But a moment later, she tried to shake that off.

"No! I have to give it up," she told herself. "I can't use this power. It's immoral. It would be so wrong to use it. Eric is not a toy, he's a human being!"

Then she remembered the feeling of power and another tremor raced through her pussy as images of Eric on his knees flooded her mind, overwhelming her again.

"Oh my God!" she thought.

Her pussy tightened and filled with more wetness.

"Maybe there's some way I can use the power in good faith," she suggested to herself.

Eric, meanwhile, sat next to Sidney looking through wedding pictures. He had no idea what was going through his fiancée's mind or why. He did, however, realize that she was breathing strangely and she had clutched her chest.

"Are you ok?" asked Eric.

"Yes... I just uh, felt hot for a moment," she lied.

"Should I get you some water?"

Sidney shook her head. "No... no, I'm fine."

Eric smiled and returned to the wedding pictures once more. Sidney's mind, however, continued down its dangerous course.

"What if I just use it for good?" she asked herself.

Sidney knew right away that this was just a

pretext to justify her desire to keep this power, but that didn't stop her from pretending that wasn't the case; in effect, she lied to herself. Yet, that didn't seem to bother her. Instead, as she told herself this lie, she felt a wave of relief pass over her and lift her high as she began to believe she had found a loophole which would let her use this power "from time to time" without feeling like she was a bad person. It felt like absolution.

"That would be acceptable. I'll only use the power for good, or if it's absolutely necessary for some reason," she told herself a moment later, and she desperately wanted to believe this was true.

She let out a long, slow breath to exhale all the tension she felt from reaching that decision. She had reached an acceptable compromise in her mind. The power was evil; it was wrong, and she would never use it... *unless* she had a good cause to use it to help Eric or if it was absolutely necessary. That's how it would be. She looked her wonderful fiancé in the eyes and swore to herself that she would only ever use the power to protect him.

"Yes, that's acceptable," she said beneath her breath. Then she "inexplicably" began to giggle involuntarily, though it was only inexplicable if she ignored the nagging sense deep within her that she was deceiving herself.

"Are you sure you're all right?" asked Eric.

Sidney took a deep breath and nodded her head. She told herself she wasn't sure why she had giggled, but it had passed now. Everything was all right again. She felt calm again.

"Yes, dear. I'm fine," she said.

Eric returned to his photos again and Sidney stroked his hair with her hand. She looked her fiancé up and down from head to toe. She was about to tell him she loved him, but then her gaze stopped on those ugly red sandals.

An idea came to her.

She smirked. "One little indulgence won't hurt, will it?" she asked herself. She nodded her head to convince herself that this was allowed under her new rules. "Besides, he'll never know."

She smiled at her fiancé. He was still flipping through the wedding pictures, blissfully unaware of what had happened or what his fiancée was thinking.

"Eric," she said.

"Yes, Miss?" asked Eric.

"Those red sandals of yours," said Sidney.

"My red sandals?" repeated Eric suspiciously.

"Yes, those," she said and she pointed at his feet. "The ones I hate."

Eric nodded his head. "I know, but I love th—"

"You will throw those away right now. Then you will forget that you ever owned them and you will forget that I said this," said Sidney. A cold chill came over her and it made her shiver as she said this.

Eric unbuckled the sandals and removed them from his feet. A moment later, Eric rose from his seat without another word and he walked off to the garbage can with the sandals. Sidney watched him go and then heard the red heels landing inside the can with a thud. As she heard this, a sense of power began to fill Sidney and her whole body tingled. This made her intensely horny, but it also seemed to bring with it just a hint of shame.

"It's only one little indulgence... I won't do it again," she assured herself. "Besides, he'll never know."

Her pussy tingled. The hated shoes were gone.

—o—

Meanwhile, Jason's room had become quite the mess. Amber and Jason had discovered that they were just about the same size, which meant, ironically, that Jason's clothes fit Amber. Because of this, Jason and Amber decided to play dress up. Amber now wore the white lace dress and the brown high-heeled sandals Jason had worn when he left the bathroom. Jason wore a similar dress in pink along with some open-toed white platform pumps. His penis had remained erect the whole time since he emerged from the bathroom.

Amber looked at his penis. "Can I ask you a question?" she asked.

"Sure," said Jason as he brushed back her hair.

"Your, uh, thingy has been hard since you stepped out of the bathroom," she said and she blushed.

Jason looked at his erection and blushed. "Yeah."

"Does that mean that this turns you on too?" she asked.

Jason blushed even deeper. The answer to that struck him as obvious; still he didn't really feel too comfortable saying it. He wasn't supposed to be turned on by wearing women's clothes, though it apparently did turn him on.

It was interesting to Jason that he never knew this about himself before. It just never occurred to him that this might be a possibility until he was forced to try on his first dress. The moment he did, he felt funny all over and his penis instantly became hard. He wasn't sure why, but he did. Indeed, he wasn't even sure if it was the dress that excited him at all. It could just as easily have been being under Cindy's control or even something else he didn't recognize at that point. Or it could all just have been a coincidence.

As the days passed, however, he started to realize that he truly disliked the sense of powerlessness he felt from being under Cindy's thumb. What's more, he definitely wasn't turned on either whenever some random girl accosted him in the hallway with some humiliating demand. So it wasn't being dominated that turned him on. But every time Cindy put him into women's clothes, he found himself feeling that tingle again and getting hard. And he stayed hard the whole time he was dressed. So eventually, he realized that this is what it had to be; he had to be turned on by being feminized.

Surprisingly, this realization actually made things worse for him. For one thing, he suddenly began to wonder if he was the only boy who felt this way. It felt shameful that he might be secretly enjoying part of this when all the others kept saying that being a man required hating every moment of their feminization. It also made him worry that Cindy might somehow gain this insight. It was bad enough that she had all this power over his mind already, to have the knowledge of what turned him on would feel like the ultimate invasion of his privacy and it felt like it would make her power over him even stronger.

What's more, it worried him that he would lose Amber if she found out that this turned him on, especially after Cindy started using his feminization as a means to taunt Amber. Amber seemed very upset by this and made strange faces whenever she saw him feminized. Jason took these looks to mean disgust or something similar. Hence, he decided he needed to keep this secret.

That said, once he realized that this excited him, he found himself fascinated with the idea and eager to explore it. So whenever Cindy went to bed, Jason would sneak out of bed and into his closet, or his mother's closet initially, and explore the clothes he found there; he would always need to masturbate while dressed or shortly thereafter. What he learned was that wearing these clothes turned him on something fierce. There was no doubt about it. He was just terrified to be discovered.

Then came this day with Amber walking him home and asking him to dress as a woman. He never expected that. And when it first happened, he thought she might be joking or pulling some trick. He recalled her look at the store when he and Cindy and Brenda went shopping for his new wardrobe and he mistook her look for contempt. After that, he vowed he would never tell her the truth. And so when she asked him to dress like a girl today, he instantly recalled that look and he thought she must be looking to humiliate him in some way for some reason.

But then she confessed to being turned on by the idea and she seemed so desperate to know that she wasn't alone in this. That shook him and he realized that she was being genuine and that this was finally his opportunity to open this secret to another person who would understand and share it with him.

"Can I really do this?" he thought.

He told himself that he could.

Jason was just about to confess his feelings when he suddenly felt compelled to go to the bathroom to change into his girl's clothes. That took the confession entirely out of his mind, and it wasn't until Amber released the order that he regained his free will on the issue and could tell her the truth.

When he told her that dressing like a woman turned him on, that had been the happiest moment of his life.

Now he lay on the bed in a pink dress with white platform heels with his erection sticking straight up in the air as Amber lay on her side next to him in *his* white lace dress and brown high-heeled sandals. She had asked him to share his secret and he told her everything... and it made her even wetter. By the time Jason finished his confession, Amber could take it no more. She kissed Jason on the lips and she slid her hand beneath his skirt and inside his panties. This was the first time she had ever touched a male before and it felt amazing as she wrapped her warm, soft hand around his shaft. She stroked him several times.

"Does that feel good?" she asked.

Jason smiled. "It feels fantastic." He kissed her.

Amber kept stroking and stroking. She watched Jason's chest heave up and down and his eyes slowly close. A huge smile crossed his face.

"Can I see it?" she asked.

Jason reached down and pulled back his skirt. Then Amber pulled down his panties so his testicles and shaft stood free.

"It's very pretty," she said. She kept stroking.

"Go faster," he said.

She did.

"Oh yeah, baby," said Jason. He felt his erection throb. He felt the pressure building inside his testicles. He knew he would cum soon. "Keep going, baby. We're almost there."

Amber felt intensely excited. She was amazingly turned on too. Not only did it excite her to hold Jason's penis and to see what was about to happen, but seeing him feminized still kept her very wet all on its own. She couldn't imagine a better way to experience this for the first time.

A moment later, Jason pulled air through his nostrils roughly. Then he held his breath. His back arched and his muscles tightened. His penis throbbed in Amber's hand. Then he exhaled and he thrust his hips forward. As he did, hot white fluid shot out of the end of his penis, up into the air, and came crashing down on his dress, his panties, and Amber's hand.

She giggled. "That was really exciting!"

Chapter 10: "Melanie Pushes Further"

—o—

Within a few days, it had become obvious that the virus had spread to the men. Every male in Satin Falls was now infected. Mayor Gabby no longer had any choice but to become involved. Before she spoke to the city council, however, she wanted to have a lengthy discussion with Melanie to determine what exactly was going on.

Mayor Gabby and Melanie's relationship went back to when Melanie first arrived in town. It began when Melanie started treating Gabby's husband, then-Mayor Tommy Landsberg. Tommy Landsberg was Melanie's first client when she moved to Satin Falls. At the time, Melanie was angry and depressed following her failed marriage. What's more, she felt humiliated by her ex-husband who seemed to get everything he wanted from the male divorce judge. Because of this, she had developed a real hatred for men and she had even begun to question her own sexuality. That's when Tommy walked through her door.

Tommy had been mayor for eight years and he was becoming increasingly less sure of his decisions. He was struggling with feelings of inadequacy and the pressure of needing to constantly be in control. He was also finding it difficult to cope with a wife with a very strong personality, who made it clear that she wanted very much to rule the roost.

The standard treatment most psychiatrists would have employed in those circumstances would have been for Melanie to build up Tommy's confidence again so that he could function. But no sooner had she begun treating Tommy than Gabby walked through her door.

Gabby was gorgeous. She had long, flowing red hair, an hourglass shape and legs that didn't quit. She dressed to kill too. She was also funny and smart and her personality lit up the room. Melanie instantly felt a strong sexual attraction to her, and she sensed that Gabby might be interested in her as well. At Melanie's urging, they met for drinks. That's when Melanie discovered that Gabby had a powerful desire to be mayor instead of her husband. Melanie instantly saw this as an opportunity to win over the strong and beautiful woman.

Consequently, the following day, rather than continue the standard treatment, Melanie did something a little different. She recommended to Tommy that he give himself a break from command by swapping roles with his wife for a week. During that week, Gabby would make all the decisions and would act as the dominant partner, whereas Tommy would follow her orders.

Tommy agreed.

The week went well for Tommy and his stress reduced. So she waited another week as his stress built up again and then she recommended that Tommy and Gabby swap places once more. Once again, Tommy agreed and he felt stress free the entire week. Two weeks later, this repeated itself again. Slowly, in this manner, Melanie taught Tommy to associate submission with freedom from stress. At the same time, these weeks in charge also gave Gabby a chance to see what she needed to do to seize control of their household.

Over the course of the next six months, Melanie slowly pushed Tommy further and further into submission with each session. First, it was swapping a week. Then it became two weeks. Then three. Similarly, at first, it was just swapping roles. Then she suggested that Tommy address his wife as a superior when they swapped. Then she suggested that Tommy wear some of Gabby's clothes. At the same time, she told Gabby to give Tommy total freedom, but then she took away the freedoms until Tommy spent more of his time catering to Gabby's needs than his own.

Eventually, the idea took hold.

Shortly thereafter, with significant encouragement from Melanie and Gabby, Tommy decided to step down as mayor. He would retire and become a househusband as Gabby found some minor job to provide the little bit of income they still needed to support their lifestyles.

"You really don't mind working?" asked Tommy.

"Not at all, dear. You've done so much, it's time to let me take the burden from you," said Gabby.

Tommy smiled. He felt happy.

All of that changed a week later, however. Tommy was shocked, when Gabby announced that she intended to run for mayor in his place. Tommy couldn't believe it. But by that point, it was too late for him to back out or to do anything else about it. This was how it would be and he could do nothing to change it. Naturally, Gabby won the election, and Tommy became her househusband. With the help of Melanie, Gabby then tightened her hold over Tommy. Soon, he would find himself spending all of his time catering to her needs and desires. Interestingly, he eventually found himself to be quite happy and content doing this. Gabby was thrilled as well.

A grateful Gabby then had a brief affair with Melanie, which turned into a close long-term friendship which continued right up to this very moment; Melanie's next relationship would be with Sidney, by the way.

Melanie now visited Gabby, per her

request.

"Come in," said Mayor Gabby to Melanie, who stood at the door. She motioned for Melanie to close the door and have a seat. "Thank you for coming."

"No problem, Gabby. I was going to see you anyways," said Melanie. "Our problem is growing."

"I know," said Mayor Gabby. "It's happening all over town now to the men."

"That's what I've seen too."

Mayor Gabby looked worried. "This is really bad, Melanie. You should see the reports I've gotten in the past twenty-four hours. The manager of the bank handed a woman ten thousand dollars this morning 'because she asked for it.' It was only a quick thinking teller who kept the woman from getting away. An hour later, two police officers nearly shot a woman's husband because she claimed he was fooling around on her and she told them they should shoot him. A bus driver broke his route to take a woman to her house. He ran several red lights in the process. I've had reports like this all day. You see the scope of the problem, right?" asked Mayor Gabby.

"Yes, I do. Basically, no man can be trusted with any position of authority anymore. Not to mention, they all need to be protected from unscrupulous women and even errant comments," said Melanie.

Mayor Gabby nodded her head. "This is bad."

"Yes, it is."

Mayor Gabby rose from her chair and came around to the front of her desk, where she took Melanie's hand while leaning against the arm of the chair next to Melanie. "We're in trouble, girlfriend. We need your help. *I* need your help. I need a solution to this problem."

Melanie nodded her head. "Unfortunately, there is no solution yet. There is no cure. That said, however, my work at the college has taught me how to handle this and how to minimize its effects."

Mayor Gabby patted Melanie on the knee through her slacks. "I knew you could help."

"Thank you, Gabb—"

"*But*," said Mayor Gabby cautiously, interrupting Melanie, and she let go of Melanie's hand. She walked over to the window. She turned to face Melanie again and she folded her arms. "There's one problem."

"What's that?"

"Your plan from the school will never fly. There's no way we can tell the women of Satin Falls to feminize their husbands and their fathers like you did at the school."

"It's necessary," said Melanie bluntly.

"It can't be done. The women will never accept it."

"If we don't do it, then the male ego can't stand being under the control of women and you risk a psychotic break." So far, that phrase had scared everyone who heard it, but it didn't seem to sway Mayor Gabby. Melanie felt a twinge of worry. She saw her plan failing and that shook her.

"Here's the thing, Melanie," said Mayor Gabby and she twisted her lips. "The women of this town are going to freak out if I tell them, 'all your husbands need to be demoted and from now on you need to watch them, control them... oh, and dress them like women'. I won't last a week as mayor."

"It is necessary," repeated Melanie.

Mayor Gabby stared straight into Melanie's eyes as if she were trying to read her very thoughts. "Is it?" she asked flatly.

Melanie froze. She hadn't expected to be questioned by Gabby.

The Mayor continued: "Or is this something you want to see happen? I've known you a long time, Melanie, pretty intimately too, and I know how you feel about men. I also know that this sounds exactly like the sort of thing you would dream up as a way to get a little revenge on the men around here."

Melanie furrowed her brow. "Gabby... I'm hurt."

"That could be, but are you being truthful with me?"

Melanie rose to her feet. "Yes, I admit that I am not a fan of men, but I am a professional and I would never do what you're suggesting. Ask anyone at the school. I've been resisting feminization for as long as possible at the school. We simply had no choice. And now that we've done it, it truly is working."

"You're telling me the truth?" asked the Mayor cautiously.

"I've never lied to you, Gabby," said Melanie. This was true, at least as far as Mayor Gabby knew. Melanie sensed that she was close to turning this particular table, so she mustered a tear, which she quickly wiped away. "Honestly, I feel shocked that you would think that about me."

Mayor Gabby instantly felt ashamed that she had questioned her friend and former lover, even if she felt her concerns had been legitimate at the time she raised them. She hugged Melanie tightly. "I'm sorry, sweetie. As Mayor, I often need to ask unpleasant questions. I never meant to hurt you. Please forgive me."

Melanie let out a long, cynical laugh inside her head. *"You idiot!"* she thought. But on the outside, she pretended to wipe away another tear and she sadly said, "It's ok, Gabby. I understand. You're just doing your job."

"I'm sorry," repeated Gabby.

"I forgive you," said Melanie as she wiped away another fake tear.

Gabby suddenly felt a deep sense of relief. She had not ruined her friendship with Melanie after all. Interestingly, she would find it much harder to follow up on her doubts about Melanie after this. In the meantime, however, Gabby nodded her head in thanks to Melanie. She then returned to the issue at hand.

"So tell me, Melanie. What do we need to do? And how do I sell the idea to just over a thousand women that they should feminize their husbands?"

Melanie smiled. "I have some ideas."

—o—

Melanie looked around the City Hall auditorium. The room was packed; this was the largest town hall meeting in city history. Almost every adult woman who lived in Satin Falls was present, as were around a quarter of the men. Joining Melanie on stage were the Mayor, the five members of the town council, including three men and two women, the Chief of Police and several other representatives of the city's workers.

The local media was here in force as well.

Mayor Gabby stepped up to the podium.

"Good evening, citizen of Satin Falls," said Gabby. She spoke in a serious tone. "Friends, we have a problem. Many of you already have some idea of what that problem is, either because you have students at the local college or because you've witnessed what has been going on first hand over the past couple days."

A general murmur raced through the crowd.

Mayor Gabby shuffled her notes as she waited for the crowd to calm down again. When they did, she spoke. "What we know is this," she said.

She then described how the virus was created and how it works. She explained that it attacks only the Y chromosome, which means the women are immune, and that so far they have no cure. She then explained how this had affected the town's males. As she explained this, the room exploded in a burst of voice that sounded like a riot at first. Once again, she waited for calm.

"Naturally," continued Mayor Gabby, "this presents us with a tremendous problem. If the men are unable to resist any command given by any woman, then the men are vulnerable to all sorts of manipulation and potential dangers. I won't offer specific examples, but we've already had several incidents."

The room exploded again as the gathered women shared examples they had seen. The men around them sat blushing as they tended to be the objects of those rather humiliating examples. It took a moment for them to calm down again.

"The city has retained Dr. Melanie Morgan to advise us on how she thinks we should handle this," continued Mayor Gabby, being careful not to offer approval of Melanie's plan just yet. "Let me introduce Dr. Morgan to explain her thoughts. She has been working with the college to solve the problem there and has made tremendous headway."

With that, Mayor Gabby stepped aside and Melanie took her place. The room was tense as each person waited intently to hear what Melanie would offer.

"I will say this bluntly, because you need to hear the truth without sugarcoating," said Melanie.

The room went completely silent.

Melanie continued: "No man in Satin Falls can be trusted any longer with managerial positions or jobs with decision-making authority. The only jobs they are currently fit for are menial jobs, working under the direct control and supervision of women."

When Melanie finished this sentence, she

stopped speaking to gage the audience's reaction. They sat in stunned silent. Then, like a damn bursting, hundreds of voices poured forth into the silence. It was like a waterfall of thought being unleashed until it became deafening. Melanie realized right away that she could not fight the crowd, so she followed Mayor Gabby's lead and she let the voices die down on their own before she continued. It took several minutes.

"We recommend that all female managers immediately reassign male employees away from jobs where they could be influenced by female customers, clients or staff. Female owners of businesses should replace any male managers or officers with females. For businesses owned and run by males, we recommend that the wives of the owners or partners get together and agree on a new female management team to oversee the business. If you are a single male with no female friends to help you, we have set up a hotline where you can get help in this regard," said Melanie.

She then paused for the expected outburst of voices, but it didn't happen. At first, Melanie thought this was a sign of rejection, that she had gone too far and the crowd had become skeptical. But then she realized this was a sign that the truth had set in and the women in the audience were already processing how they would act according to her plan.

She continued.

"We also beg each of you to maintain this as a secret. We have asked the newspapers and the local news not to cover this story, except in a special edition to be delivered tomorrow *locally only*. We ask that no one mention this on the web or that anyone contact people outside of Satin Falls about these issues."

"Why not?" called someone from the audience. "Maybe they can help!"

"If this information got out, Satin Falls would become a target for every dishonest conman and woman in the country. They would descend upon this town, knowing that its men are utterly helpless to resist and we would lose everything we have built here," said Melanie.

A murmur raced through the crowd. This point struck home.

"But how are we going to fix this if we don't get help?" asked the same woman.

This raised a second murmur, which now seemed to sway the crowd in the other direction.

Mayor Gabby rose and came to the microphone. "We're working on a solution. We have retained a preeminent geneticist from a top university who is conducting research into a cure. We hope all of this will prove to be temporary."

This seemed to settle the crowd.

Melanie returned to the microphone and took a deep breath. "There is one more thing, however, and this will be very difficult to hear and even harder to understand." She paused.

The room waited silently for her. The tension was very high.

"We found at the college that the males had an extremely hard time accepting their new status as second class citizens. Because of their egos, they kept wanting to wrest control from the girls. This caused significant problems for the girls as it would cause problems for each of you," said Melanie. She paused to let this sink in. She saw a great many sideways glances from the women at the men sitting next to them. Melanie could see them all thinking about the problems the men had already caused them and imagining more. She had scored a direct hit. "It also caused psychological problems for the males." Now she saw the women nodding their heads at the message that what was about to come could be excused as being for the good of the males, even as they saw it mainly as a means to avoid the men causing more problems. "We have found only one way to prevent this, and we're going to recommend that each of you follow this guidance."

"What is it?" came another voice from the crowd.

Melanie looked around the room. Then she spoke.

—o—

"I can't believe this is really happening," said Amber. She had accompanied Sidney to the meeting at City Hall and now Sidney was driving them home.

"It is," said Sidney.

"I know. I just can't believe it. There was hardly a word spoken against the plan by any of the women there," said Amber.

"Melanie put on a convincing show."

"I don't know. I don't trust her," said Amber.

"I don't either, but that doesn't mean she wasn't convincing."

"What do we do now?"

"What do you mean?" asked Sidney.

"Well, obviously, we need to stop her, right?" asked Amber.

Sidney bit her lip. "Uh, yeah," she said. She was finding herself very conflicted lately. She knew intellectually that what was happening was wrong, but she was also enjoying the new power she had over Eric more and more. It gave her a true thrill to feel that powerful. What's more, it made life easier. It made it easy to get him to help out as needed and it gave her the option of avoiding certain issues where they had never agreed in the past.

"You don't sound to sure," said Amber.

"I'm just really busy," said Sidney, dodging the issue.

"Have you seen anything that could help us?" asked Amber.

"What do you mean?"

"Like when you work with her. Has she done anything that we could use against her?"

Sidney shook her head. "Not really. It's not like she's a movie villain who is going to explain her evil plan to me right before she shoots her henchmen. She just keeps saying the same things about ego and psychotic breaks." Sidney didn't mention that while Melanie had called her in for advice, she kept Sidney's knowledge of what was going on rather limited. She also tended to waste a good deal of time hitting on Sidney and trying to convince her to return to her.

"What about some notes?" asked Amber.

"What kind of notes?" asked Sidney.

"I don't know. Maybe some notes where she talks about what's going on."

"I've never seen her notes. She keeps them in a brown folder, but she's never let me near it. I doubt there's anything there anyways. You might need to face the fact that there's just nothing we can do."

Amber raised an eyebrow. She wondered if Sidney had changed her mind. Amber didn't want to believe that, but it sounded like it. They rode in silence for several streets until they turned up the road toward the apartment.

"You do want to put an end to this, right?" asked Amber suddenly.

Sidney pulled up before their apartment. "I'm going to stay with Eric tonight. Sleep tight, kiddo. But to answer your question, yes, I want to put an end to this," said Sidney, though she wasn't truly sure she believed this anymore.

Amber wasn't convinced.

—o—

"I can't believe this is really happening!" exclaimed Melanie with a maniacal laugh as she drove herself home. She thought about all the confused and scared faces that followed her every word during her speech and she laughed again. "I can't believe how easy this was too! They bought every single word... *every single word!* Not one of them had the slightest idea what was going on!"

She turned up the street toward her house.

"Tomorrow will be an amazing day! Every one of them is going to get what they deserve. And within a few days, all the men will be feminized, and they'll know how it feels to be humiliated."

She smirked.

"One small step for woman, one huge step for womankind!"

She laughed maniacally again.

—o—

Sidney kicked off her heels and unzipped her slacks. Eric picked up her shoes and took them to the closet, where he placed them with her other shoes. He then returned to Sidney and picked up her slacks as well. These would be washed and ironed in the morning.

"How did the meeting go, Miss?" asked Eric.

"It went about how you would expect. It took the women a while to accept what was going on, but they were actually more receptive to all of it than I expected. Melanie gave a surprisingly good presentation," said Sidney.

"She can be quite convincing, or so I'm told."

"It's too bad they don't know her like I know her. They might not have trusted her."

"Did you raise that?" asked Eric.

Sidney shook her head. "No. I don't have any proof to back up whatever I would say, so it would just sound like a personal grudge. I need proof before I can say anything," she said.

Eric heard hesitation in her voice. "You are planning to stop her, aren't you?"

Sidney paused. She was still somewhat torn by the whole thing, though her mind was clearing. She had been enticed initially by the power she had over Eric and that had excited her, but she knew it was wrong and her rational mind was slowly overcoming her sexual urges. She would do the right thing, she assured herself. So she nodded to her fiancé.

"Yes, I am," she said. "I will stop her."

That seemed to assure him. Eric hung up Sidney's pants and returned from the closet with a nightie. "This one, Miss?"

"Yes, thank you, dear. That one is lovely." She kissed Eric on the cheek.

"I've set out your clothes for the morning already, Miss."

As Eric said this, Sidney was reminded of work, something she hadn't thought about as she had been focused so intensely on Melanie. The moment that thought hit her, she had a vision of Henry Miller, Eric's father, on his knees in a dress and high heels begging Sidney not to humiliate him. The thought made her pussy swell with excitement and it positively filled with her juices.

"Oh my God! I can't wait for tomorrow!"

she exclaimed and she giggled uncontrollably.

"Why is that, Miss?" asked Eric.

Sidney instantly snapped back to reality. Her face turned bright red with embarrassment and she stared at Eric. She had no idea what to say.

Riiiing!

Her phone rang. Sidney felt tremendous relief that she could avoid answering Eric's question for the moment. She answered the phone, even as Eric kept staring at her curiously.

"Hello," she said and she turned her back on Eric.

"Sidney Blake please," said the woman.

"This is her."

"Sidney, this is Mona Hunter... John Hunter's wife... from the firm."

"Yes, Ms. Hunter. What can I do for you?"

"I need to speak to you about the firm..." They spoke for twenty minutes. By the time Sidney hung up, she was beaming. She also looked like she couldn't believe what she had heard was true.

"Who was that, Miss?" asked Eric. The curiosity was killing him.

"It was the wife of Henry's partner," said Sidney.

Eric raised an eyebrow. "What did she want?"

Sidney sat down, crossed her legs, and swung her leg excitedly. She couldn't stop smiling and she periodically giggled. "Get this. The wives of the partners got together after Melanie's briefing and had a little meeting at the coffee shop down the street from city hall. They agreed that the men could no longer be trusted to run the firm." She paused to giggle. Her smile grew and her leg shook faster. "As the only female lawyer in the firm, the wives of the partners decided that I should be put in charge of running the firm! I'm going to be Henry's boss starting tomorrow!" she squealed.

Eric's jaw dropped. "Really?"

"Yes!!" she exclaimed.

Eric shook his head. "Wow!"

"Wow is right! This is going to kill him! I swear it will positively kill him!" Sidney kissed her fiancé on his painted lips. "Oh my God, I can't wait for tomorrow!" she said.

A look of concern crossed Eric's face.

Sidney didn't notice. She was too busy planning her revenge. Her promise to stop Melanie seemed forgotten once more.

Chapter 11: "Henry Miller... Changed"
—o—

When the light changed, the group of secretaries swished their way across the street in their high-heeled shoes and tight skirts. They were in a hurry today. In a few minutes, they would learn just how much their office would be turned upside down and they didn't want to miss a minute of it. Who would run the office? Was it true the men could not resist their commands? Would the men still be in charge? What would the men be wearing? None of the women knew the answers to any of these questions, but they were looking forward to finding out.

A few minutes later, every woman at Hunter Miller was called into the main conference room. All the secretaries were there. All the wives of the partners were there, except Henry's wife Violet. Sidney was there too. The room was awash with female voices.

"Settle down, ladies," said an older woman who had been appointed by the partners' wives to speak for the group.

The room grew silent.

"As you all know, there been some 'issues' that have arisen regarding the men of Satin Falls. Those issues have affected us here as well now. Consequently, the wives of the partners have gotten together and we have decided that, for the good of the firm, we will hand over control of the firm to the only female attorney on staff. Sidney Blake will be managing the firm from now on."

The crowd gasped collectively and all the women looked around at each other.

"You will all answer to her, as will every attorney in this office, and nothing leaves this office without her approval," added the woman.

A significant murmur passed over the crowd.

The woman raised her hand to quiet the room and then she continued: "Now, as you know, Dr. Melanie Morgan has made certain recommendations for the treatment of the men. We're going to comply with those because we want to do our part to make the men better. Hence, we ask that you do your parts as well."

An even louder murmur passed through the crowd.

"Quiet down, quiet down," said the woman. "That means, of course, that the men will be dressed as woman in the office—"

This brought the loudest murmur yet.

"—and each of you is encouraged to treat them accordingly. Do not let your actions reflect poorly on the firm or interfere with the work they must do, but within those limits, please do your part to help out." The woman looked around the room at the excited, confused and pensive faces. "Are there any questions?"

"Are you saying we won't get into trouble if we... uh, I'm not even sure how to put it," asked one of the secretaries.

"Let me have Sidney answer that as she'll be running the firm day to day."

With that, the older woman stepped aside and let Sidney take her place. Sidney could barely contain her excitement. The irony of all of this was absolutely delicious to her that Henry had been on the verge of firing her and now she was running *his* firm and she would be *his* boss. She couldn't wait to see him once the men joined them. She was going to rub this in before everyone.

"The short answer is no," said Sidney.

"'No, we won't get in trouble'?" asked the secretary.

"Exactly. No, you will not get in trouble," said Sidney. "The treatment calls for feminization and humiliation to break down the male ego, so you will not be punished for participating in either of those activities, provided your actions do not reflect poorly on the firm."

Smiles slowly appeared on every face in the crowd.

Sidney continued. "As was said before, you

will all report to me from now on. If you have any questions, my door will always be open for each of you. Remember that we are in charge now and we need to make this firm work. So keep that in mind as we get back to work. Before we return you to work, however, let me introduce the men to you again."

As Sidney said this, her secretary opened the door to the conference room and called out to the men, who had been gathered in the hallway. They entered the conference room one at a time. The first through the door was Wilson Owens, one of the partners. Wilson typically wore grey suits and he was very, very proper. Today was different. Today, Wilson wore a bright red dress which hung loosely around his knees. His hair had been dyed blonde. His face was covered in makeup. And on his feet were red high-heeled sandals.

The room gasped.

Then the giggling began.

Before anyone could say much about Wilson, however, the next man appeared. This was a junior partner named James Castle. James wore a black sequined gown and matching high-heeled sandals with diamond encrusted straps. His somewhat longish hair had been curled and trimmed into a feminine cut. He also wore dangling earrings which jingled as he walked. His erection showed beneath his dress; this brought a good deal more giggling.

Another appeared a moment after that. He wore a white miniskirt, a black top, and black and white high-heeled shoes. Then came the next. He wore a dark blue bandage dress and silver sandals. Then came one in a green dress and another in a black leather miniskirt.

As they came in, one after another, the room erupted in cheers, followed by emasculating comments from the women. And as the room filled with the feminized men, the women began to separate and make their way to whichever man they preferred, either because they worked for him or just because they had some interest in that particular man, and they began giving them tips on how they wanted that man to act. There was no doubt the women had taken over and the men would not escape with their masculinities intact.

Interestingly, all the women were super excited, with only one exception. That exception was Sidney. Certainly, she enjoyed seeing all the male attorneys emasculated. They had not been kind to her and she enjoyed seeing them reduced to the playthings of the women they previously ordered around. And she absolutely loved her moment of triumph and the sense of power she felt being given total control over the firm. Those things made her very, very happy. But something was missing from her victory and that sat like a gaping hole in the middle of her joy. Without that, her triumph was nothing. And that something was a feminized, terrified, sniveling Henry Miller.

"Where is Henry?" she wanted to know.

No one seemed to know.

Sidney looked all over the room, but couldn't see him. She looked around the firm, but he didn't seem to be hiding anywhere either. Even the light in his office had not been turned on.

"He's not here!" she growled.

So as the women took the men back to their offices and got them set for how things would run, Sidney returned to her own office. She called Violet Miller, Henry's wife.

"Violet, this is Sidney," said Sidney.

"Hello Sidney," said Violet.

"I'm at the office and I wanted to call you to see if you knew where Henry was."

"Oh yes, he's in his study."

Sidney paused. She gritted her teeth. She wanted him here, on his knees before her futilely begging her to be kind to him. "Why isn't he at the office?" she asked as calmly as she could.

"He didn't want to go. Is it important that he be there?" asked Violet.

"Very," said Sidney.

"I can ask him to go, if you like."

"You don't need to ask. *Just tell him,* Violet."

Violet paused. "I'm not sure that's a good idea."

Sidney bit her lip. She wasn't sure what to say at this point.

"Are you and Eric coming over tonight for dinner?" asked Violet.

"We can," said Sidney.

"Oh good. Why don't you come over and we can discuss it then? Maybe you can talk to him."

"All right," said Sidney. "We'll be there."

—o—

Amber sat down next to her friend Beth. Beth was rather cute, despite being what some would consider "chubby." Unfortunately, her weight had always bothered her, even if most people considered her attractive, and that made her feel self-conscious around boys. With the virus, however, that had all changed now. Knowing that she no longer needed to fear rejection from the boys, Beth had blossomed and her confidence was growing. She had even found a boyfriend.

"Hey Beth," said Amber. "Can I borrow

your computer?"

Beth nodded her head and handed her friend her tablet. "What are you working on?"

"I'm doing some research," said Amber, "but I can't use my computer at home because my sister and her fiancé are using it to plan their wedding and they took it back to his apartment."

"What kind of research?" asked Beth.

"I'm worried about what this Dr. Morgan is telling people," said Amber.

Beth cocked her head to one side. "In what way?"

"This whole idea of turning the boys into girls just sounds really wrong to me. So I wrote down the big words she used and I want to look them up." Amber noticed Beth furrow her brow. "What? What's the problem?" asked Amber.

Beth twisted her lips. "You know me; I don't like people being mean or lying or anything like that, right? I mean, I'm not the type to want anyone to be mean to anybody, right? But why are you looking into this? Don't you like it?"

"Do I like it that she wants us to dress the boys as girls?"

"Yeah," said Beth nervously.

For a brief moment, Amber wondered if she had found another girl like herself who was turned on by seeing a male feminized. Perhaps this was more common than she thought.

Unfortunately, that wasn't what Beth meant.

"Yeah," repeated Beth, "that and the rest. Like having control over the boys."

"You like having control?" asked Amber.

"I mean, so many of them are jerks, right? And they kind of deserve it. I mean, girls are nice and we should be in charge, right? Girls don't abuse power like boys do. I read that in one of my classes on the differences between the genders."

"Do you really believe that?" asked Amber cautiously. She couldn't believe her friend would want to see other people made powerless. This was so unlike her and it scared Amber that this power had changed her so significantly.

"Yeah, I do."

Amber bit her tongue and stared at the floor.

Suddenly, Beth uncomfortably blurted out: "Honestly, I just like the boys having to do whatever we tell them."

"Why is that?"

Beth blushed. "I don't know. I guess because I don't feel weak or insignificant anymore."

"Beth, you've never been weak or insignificant—"

"I know," replied Beth in a way which suggested that she disagreed with the sentiment.

"What you're feeling now has always been

inside you, you just didn't trust yourself to use it. It has nothing to do with having this power over the boys. It's all you," said Amber.

Beth shrugged her shoulders doubtfully. "I don't know. I don't want to lose it."

"You won't!"

"How do I know? I mean, right now things are great for me. I don't want that changing."

"But think about the cost," said Amber.

"What cost? It's not like the girls are going to be nasty to the boys like they would be to us!" said Beth.

Amber frowned. This discussion worried her. If Beth wasn't willing to give up this power then it struck her that few others would be willing to give up the power either. Putting an end to this could be harder than she expected. Amber needed to speak with Sidney right away. She needed Sidney's help. Unfortunately, Sidney's mind was elsewhere at the moment.

—o—

Eric felt intensely nervous. He stood in his parents' living room wearing a dress. Specifically, he wore a purple cocktail dress and black open-toed slingback pumps. His nails and makeup were exquisite. He'd never worn a single feminine item in front of his mother or his father before, and he wouldn't have done so tonight except that Sidney insisted.

"This is your chance to finally do it," said Sidney as they dressed to go to Eric's parents' house. She held up the purple cocktail dress she wanted him to wear to dinner tonight.

"How do you figure?" asked Eric.

"Because they'll think that the only reason you're wearing it is because of Melanie's silly plan. So they won't know that you really want to wear dresses and heels."

"How does that help?"

"Because it will give them a chance to see you dressed and to get used to the idea," said Sidney. "Who knows? They might even like it."

Eric snickered. "There's no chance of that."

"Probably not," admitted Sidney. "But you *are* wearing it." She tossed him the dress and pointed to the heels she had set on the bed for him to wear. These were black, open-toed slingbacks with a five-inch heel.

"I'd rather not," said Eric nervously.

Sidney put her hands on her hips and furrowed her brow. She didn't say a word, but her position was clear.

"Please, honey," said Eric. "This isn't something I want to do."

"It's going to happen, Eric. One way or another."

Eric bit his lip.

"Eric, I can make you do this, but I'd rather you did this voluntarily," said Sidney. "Trust me, honey, this is for the best. Besides, it would look weird if you didn't wear a dress because every other man in town has been feminized."

Eric hung his head. He had no choice, but that didn't make him any more comfortable about it. He had never dressed before his parents, nor had he told them about his desires. And while they would clearly assume that Sidney had forced him to do this, it still terrified him that he might be giving away his dark secret. He felt sick as he slipped into the pretty dress.

An hour later, they were at Eric's parents' house. Eric's mother Violet looked him up and down. She frowned and shook her head. Eric's little sister Kayleigh stood quietly in the background snickering.

"Your father is not going to like this," said Violet.

"Well, Eric had no choice," said Sidney. "I made Eric dress this way. So Henry should blame me, not Eric."

Eric took a deep breath. "Hold on," he said suddenly.

Everyone froze and looked at him.

"This wasn't Sidney's doing," said Eric softly.

"What are you talking about?" asked his mother.

"This is the real me. This is how I want to dress," said Eric. "I've always been drawn to women's clothes and feeling submissive." He hadn't planned to tell his family about his cross-dressing, but Sidney had backed him into a corner and he felt he had no choice. If they were going to see him in a dress, then he wanted it to be on his terms, not under the cover of the virus.

His mother gasped. Her jaw dropped. Sidney's jaw dropped as well.

"Are you sure?" asked Violet.

"Yes, I am."

Violet looked around nervously for a moment. "Your father isn't going to like this at all." She paused and bit her lip. "But if it's what you want, then I just have to accept it, don't I?" She walked over to Eric and hugged him. "I guess I'll just have to get used to having a second daughter!"

Eric was surprised, but happy. Sidney was shocked, both that Eric said anything and that his mother was so calm about it.

"So how do we tell your father?" asked Violet.

"About that," said Sidney. "Violet, as you know, I've taken over the firm. But with Henry staying away, it's undermining my authority. I honestly need him to come to the office and submit to me, just like all the other partners have done."

Violet shook her head. "I asked him, but he refused."

"I know," said Sidney. "But you do know that you can order him, right Violet?"

"Henry never listens to me."

"Violet, do you understand what has happened?" asked Sidney.

"What do you mean?"

"The men can't resist orders from women anymore... any orders. You have complete control over him."

Violet looked doubtfully at Sidney. "I've heard that, but Henry told me he wasn't affected."

"Henry lied to you. He's affected."

Violet raised an eyebrow. "Do you think so?"

"Trust me. All the men were affected. None of them could overcome the virus."

Violet looked at Eric, who nodded his head in agreement with Sidney's comment. "What should I do?" she asked.

Eric smiled at his mother. Before he could speak, however, Sidney said, "Let me handle this, Violet. I'll speak to Henry. I know how to handle this."

Violet considered all she had heard. She

took a deep breath. Then she nodded her head. "He's in the study," she said.

Sidney smiled. "I'll be back."

Violet and Eric waited for nearly twenty minutes in the living room as Sidney went to "have a talk" with Henry. Violet kept looking at her son and would at times comment on how much she liked some aspect of his clothing. She clearly was not ready yet to accept his cross-dressing, but she was trying; it helped that he was feminine and pretty when he was dressed. The biggest issue for her at the moment seemed to be how Henry would respond to him being a cross-dresser. That had her very worried.

"All right," said Sidney as she reappeared from the bedroom. "I think we're ready."

"Ready for what?" asked Violet.

"You're about to see," said Sidney. She pointed down the hallway. "I give you, the *new* Henry Miller!"

CLICK CLICK CLICK CLICK!

The sound of high heels echoed down the hallway. They announced the coming of something shocking. A moment later, Henry appeared. He wore one of Violet's pink house dresses, which was way too small, and some ill-fitting silver mules. He looked like a fool. Unfortunately, this was all Sidney could find that would fit. Still, it made the point quite nicely.

"Oh my God!" gasped Violet. "Henry!"

Henry blushed, but kept walking until he reached the living room, just as Sidney had ordered. When Henry reached the living room, he curtseyed to his wife, then to Sidney and finally to his son.

"Please command me, Violet. I am your toy. Feminize me, humiliate me, take control of me. I want you to dominate me and make me into your servant," said Henry. His face was bright red.

Violet's jaw dropped. She looked her formerly dominant, sexist husband up and down. Then she laughed. She laughed long and hard, and this laugh cut deeply into Henry's ego and made this so much worse for him. Finally, when she stopped laughing, she shook her head and said, "You look a fright Henry."

"It's this damn woman!" he growled.

"Language, Henry," said Sidney.

Henry looked sheepish the moment Sidney admonished him. He understood the power she had over him because she had made it very clear to him in the bedroom; she wanted him to know in no uncertain terms just how powerless he was. So she taught him this in a lesson he would never forget.

It began with Henry stripping himself naked in his bedroom as Sidney laughed. Then, seemingly without any thought on his part, he found himself stepping into his wife's high-heeled shoes. Next, he dropped to his knees and began kissing Sidney's feet and begging:

"Please humiliate me! Make me pay for all that I have done," he pleaded.

As he did this, he suddenly realized that *Sidney had made him do all of this.*

"How are you doing that?!" he demanded.

Sidney just smiled. Then she made him wrap his fingers around his penis and begin stroking. He had never felt more humiliated in his life than he felt right then and there, on his knees, in his wife's shoes, as he stroked himself to orgasm.

"Keep stroking, sissy boy," said Sidney.

"Let me go! Let me stop!"

"Ha! Never, Henry!" said Sidney. "I'm going to strip away your masculinity until nothing is left, and in its place, I'm going to add helpless, submissive femininity. I'm going to turn you into a sissy, and there is nothing you can do about it. Now just stay silent and keep stroking."

For some reason, Henry couldn't respond.

A moment later, Henry felt his penis grow as large as it could. It throbbed in rhythm. It *needed* to explode. Then, it spurted forth its treasure, all over the floor between Henry and Sidney.

"Lick it up, sissy," said Sidney.

Without a word, Henry leaned over and licked up his own cum from the floor. It was sticky and salty and disgusting. And it was super humiliating to find himself doing this, especially with Sidney standing over him. In fact, as he licked his cum from the floor, all he could see were her toes sticking out the fronts of her shoes inches from his face. And all he could hear was Sidney mocking him.

"That was your first taste of cum, wasn't it, Henry? Well, get used to it. There will be so much more in your future because from now on, you are my little bitch, Henry. That's right. I'm going to dress you as a woman, Henry. But not just any woman. No, I'm going to dress you as a slut. Then I'm going to make you live and act like a woman... a slutty woman... a bimbo. And just when you think it can't get any worse, I'm going to be there to make it worse. Before everything is done, you'll be so feminized that you won't ever be able to go back. And best of all, *I'm going to command you to want me to do that.* Yes, I'm going to command you to crave humiliation and feminization, sissy boy!"

As Sidney said this, she had no idea if she could even do that, nor did she care. All she wanted right now was to torture the man who had nearly broken her. She wanted payback.

"So get ready, Henry... there's nothing you can do to stop it."

She then dressed Henry.

A few minutes later, Henry found himself standing before his wife and his femininely dressed son, whom he could only assume had been similarly treated by Sidney. He burned red with shame as he performed the curtseys. Finally, after the curtseys Sidney's "programming" ended and he felt a moment of freedom. He used that moment to try to enlist Violet to help set him free now. It was now or never!

"Help me, Violet! This woman is crazy! She dressed me this way!" he pleaded.

Violet looked at Sidney and shook her head disapprovingly. "And she was wrong to do so," said Violet firmly.

Henry raised an eyebrow. It had worked. He suddenly felt extremely confident that his humiliation had come to an end, because Violet would protect him from Sidney and return to her own submissive ways... but he was wrong.

"She should have found clothes that fit," concluded Violet.

Henry felt like he'd been neutered. He nearly collapsed to the floor. "Violet! How could you abandon me?!"

"Oh Henry, be quiet. Being submissive to a nice young woman like Sidney won't be the end of the world. It will do you some good." She then turned to face Sidney. "Henry would like to come back to the office and follow your orders. Would you like to go with Henry and me tomorrow to buy Henry a new wardrobe?"

Sidney snickered. "Yes... yes, I would."

—o—

The following morning, Sidney, Violet and Henry went to a local clothing store which shared a common space with the wedding shop Eric had been using. This would let them kill two birds with one stone by getting Henry both a new wardrobe and a dress for the wedding... it had been decided by Sidney that all the men would wear dresses to the wedding and the women would wear either dresses or pants, depending on their preference. Eric didn't really like the idea, but Sidney made him agree.

"What about this?" asked Violet and she held up a gray dress.

Sidney cringed. It was rather frumpy. "Why don't we look for something a little more exciting?" suggested Sidney. She walked Violet over to a different part of the store and showed her a collection of rather sexy dresses.

"I'm not sure Henry will want to wear anything that revealing," said Violet.

Sidney smirked. "Violet, Henry has no choice."

"Are you sure?"

"Yes, I'm sure."

"He keeps saying that this is only temporary," said Violet.

"It's not."

Violet ran her tongue over her teeth. "So I *really* can choose anything I want?"

"Yes, you can."

Violet smiled. She turned to Henry, who stood in the corner with his arms folded. He had been pouting. "Henry, come here, dear."

Henry walked over to his wife.

Violet took a gorgeous red sequin gown from a rack and handed it to Henry. It had a side slit that would run from his ankle to the middle of this thigh. "Put this on," she said.

Henry took the dress and started toward the dressing room. He had no choice.

"Hold it!" said Violet and Henry stopped. She then picked up a pair of strappy red high-heeled sandals with very high heels and handed those to Henry as well. "These too. Now go."

Henry went to the dressing room.

Violet watched him go. A strange look appeared in her eye. "He really can't resist, can he?"

"No, he can't."

"So I can make him stop doing all the things he does which annoy me?" asked Violet.

"Yes," said Sidney.

"And he can't stop me from doing anything?"

"No, he can't."

"And this Dr. Morgan says I should do my best to embarrass him too?"

"Yes, you should."

Violet giggled.

For the next few minutes, Violet and Sidney looked through the selection of clothing. Sidney noticed that Violet now completely lost interest in the more conservative dresses and instead started looking at tighter and lower cut dresses. She also added at least an inch to all the high heels she examined. This made Sidney smile.

Finally, Henry returned wearing the red sequin dress and the heels. He struggled in the heels as he'd never really worn anything like these shoes before. It made Sidney burn with a feeling of vengeance to see him dressed this way and struggling.

"You need some serious practice, Henry!" said Sidney.

"Don't worry, he'll get plenty of practice from now on," said Violet. She then ordered Henry to come stand in the mirror so they could examine him. He looked very feminine and very embarrassed in the dress. The women walked around him in circles, adjusting the dress and admiring the way he looked in an overly dramatic feminine manner. This was not anything Henry ever expected to happen in his life and he felt a burning sense of shame with each comment. Even worse, Sidney's touch, *of all people*, made him hard, which brought him even more shame.

"Oh look. Henry's hard. He must like wearing dresses," said Sidney. "Do you Henry? Do you like wearing dresses?"

"Oh Henry, behave," said Violet in a droll manner.

The two women then burst out laughing.

Next, they drifted over to the wedding section. Violet stepped away to check on several possible bridesmaid dresses for Henry. Meanwhile, Sidney took the opportunity to look through the wedding dresses. She came upon the one Eric had showed her with the rose-shaped bosom. It was even prettier in person than it had been online. She remembered how Eric had told her several times how much he would love to wear this dress, and it suddenly dawned on her that she could now give him that chance, now that she could pretend to force him. He would never wear it on his own, even with his confession to his mother, but she could make him. She decided to lay the groundwork for this... and to tweak Henry in the process.

"Oh look at this beautiful dress! I'll bet Eric would look a dream in this!" exclaimed Sidney.

"Don't you dare dress my son in a wedding dress!" growled Henry. Images of his son in the purple cocktail dress flashed through his mind and made him cringe. He had always worried that Eric wasn't quite man enough for his taste in sons, and seeing him looking so feminine startled Henry; he had not been told about Eric's confession.

"I'll dress him in whatever I want, Henry," said Sidney.

"Don't you dare!"

"In fact, I think I'm going to systematically feminize you both. By the time I'm finished, you'll both be women forever. And do you know what's even better? I'm going to make you both believe you want to be feminized. Think about that Henry, you and your son living out your lives as simpering sissies."

"I was right about you! You don't care about Eric. You're the type of woman who gets off on emasculating men. That's all you are, an emasculator!" exclaimed Henry angrily. "I understand your type."

Sidney leaned in close, still holding the dress. "Well, guess what," she whispered to Henry. "I'm going to make your son wear this dress, just as you will wear a dress to the wedding. Then I'm going to marry him and turn him into my housewife as I become our sole provider."

Henry was cringing and visibly balling his fists, but this was obviously all just impotent rage. He could do nothing about it and he knew it. Sidney decided to push him even harder.

"And there's one more thing you should know, Henry. When Eric and I get married, Eric is going to take my name. *Eric Blake...* it has a nice ring to it, doesn't it?" she asked.

Henry visibly ground his teeth.

"Oh, and don't you dare say a word of this to anyone," whispered Sidney. "This is our secret." She laughed.

Henry looked like he might pass out from shock. This made Sidney feel warm and happy on the inside. She recalled all the days he had all but destroyed her emotionally and she was happy to get some payback. Everything she said was things Eric actually wanted, but Sidney loved the idea of portraying them as things she planned to force upon Eric because she knew that it would eat Henry up on the inside and crush his masculinity that he couldn't stop her from feminizing his son. Telling him to keep this secret was her master stroke, in her opinion, as it would keep Henry anxious the entire time until the wedding because he couldn't say a word about what he thought he had discovered.

Just then, Violet returned with an arm full of dresses. "Oh Henry, we have a lot to try on!" she said.

Henry glared at her, unable to say what he wanted.

It was going to be a long afternoon for Henry.

—o—

Sidney hugged her fiancé tightly. They were in the living room at Eric's apartment. Both wore matching pink nighties and wedge-heeled slippers. They had just finished painting each other's nails as Sidney regaled Eric with their adventure in finding Henry an appropriate wardrobe.

"Did you really buy my father a dress?" asked Eric.

"Not just *a* dress, but many dresses: dresses for the office, dresses for home. We even bought him a dress for the wedding," said Sidney.

Eric's jaw dropped. "You didn't!" he gasped.

Sidney smirked. "Yes, we did."

"He's going to go insane."

"He's going to learn a little respect. He needs to learn that women are people too and they deserve respect. And I don't want him hassling you about wearing a dress at our wedding."

Eric raised an eyebrow. "I'm wearing a dress?" he asked incredulously.

Sidney smiled. "Yep."

"Are you serious?"

"Absolutely. I know it's always been a dream of yours and I want you to have it."

"It won't embarrass you?" he asked.

"First of all, all the men in town are wearing dresses, remember?" asked Sidney. "So you're going to blend right in. Secondly, no, it doesn't embarrass me. That is what you want and I want you to be happy. I will accept whatever it takes for my little househubby to be happy."

Eric blushed. "My father is going to flip—"

"Your father isn't going to say anything. Don't forget, he's wearing a dress too."

Eric chuckled. "I can't believe you bought him a dress! Heels too?"

"Of course, heels... nice and high. How can he wear a dress without heels? They're pretty too. They have pretty straps and they're open-toed because I thought he would like showing off his pretty painted toenails. Violet is going to make him practice until he can walk in them like a real woman."

"He has painted toenails?"

"Yep. Violet had them done when he got his mani-pedi."

"He got a mani-pedi?" asked Eric.

"Yep."

"He's going to go crazy!"

Sidney shrugged her shoulders.

"Can I see his dress?" asked Eric.

"Not until the wedding. It's my surprise to you."

"When can I try on my dress?" asked Eric.

"How about this weekend?"

"Do you have a picture?"

"No, not yet. But it's gorgeous. You'll love it. You're going to be the most beautiful groom ever!" Sidney wrapped her arms tighter around her fiancé and kissed him. "And you're all mine."

Eric smiled. Then his mind drifted to something that bothered him and he frowned. "Did you mean it when you said you would do whatever it took to make me happy?"

"Absolutely," she said and she kissed him. "What did you have in mind?"

Eric bit his lip. "I want you to join Amber again in fighting Melanie."

Now Sidney bit her lip. She was enjoying having this power far too much to stop now. "Why?" she asked reflexively.

"Because it's wrong. And because it makes me less special."

Sidney cocked her head to one side. "How so?"

"I cross-dress. I'm submissive too. I don't know why I do these things, but I do. It sets me apart. And when every other man in town is forced to do the same things I do on my own... things that make me so very different from other men, things that make me feel like I have a special relationship with gender and like I have something unique to share with you, I feel that it lessens me to be surrounded by other men who are going through the motions."

Sidney raised an eyebrow. Eric often presented her with interesting perspectives on events and this was one she had, admittedly, never considered.

He continued.

"I don't want to be dramatic, but the times I've dared to wear panties or women's loafers out of the house have been traumatic. It was like a drug. You wouldn't believe how high I felt, how it seemed I had done something courageous." He paused. "Today, I went to the store wearing a complete feminine outfit: a dress, high heels and my most feminine lingerie, and *I didn't feel a thing*. There was no naughtiness, no sexiness... nothing. As I looked around, so many men were dressed the same that I honestly felt like I looked normal, as if I were wearing jeans and sneakers.

And not a single woman looked at me with the slightest care that I might be wearing something I should not have been wearing. As strange as it may sound, I felt like I had lost something truly special about myself."

Sidney considered this for a moment. She wasn't sure she understood, but she got his point generally. Unfortunately, she wasn't sure she was willing to help him. Sure, she *wanted* to help him, but she was having far too much fun with Henry to stop right now.

"I'll do what I can," she said without committing to anything.

Chapter 12: "Henry Miller Reports To Work"

—o—

When Sidney took over the firm, she claimed Henry's office and bumped him to a cubicle down the hall. She didn't do that to any other attorney. She now sat behind his old desk as Henry sat across from her waiting nervously. He wore a hot-pink A-line dress that hung to his calves and high-heeled hot-pink slingbacks with a four-inch heel and a wide open toe. He looked feminine, uncomfortable and embarrassed, but Sidney wanted more... much more.

"Oh Henry, I'm going to enjoy this," said Sidney.

"You better watch yourself," warned Henry. "Dr. Morgan may find a cure for this condition any day. And when that happens, you'll be sorry."

Sidney smirked. She knew she had nothing to fear. Indeed, she was pretty sure that Melanie was in no rush to find a cure, if she was even looking for one. "I guess I'll just have to take that chance, Henry."

"You're making a big mistake!"

Sidney laughed. "No, Henry, you made the mistake. Now it's time to pay for it. And do you know what, Henry? You can't stop me and no one is going to protect you from what's about to happen."

With that, Sidney picked up a folder and pretended to look through it. She shook her head as she did. As she did, Henry looked increasingly nervous. He had no idea what was coming next, but he wasn't happy about it.

"Hmm. Well, Henry, I've been looking at your recent performance and I am sad to say that there have been problems the firm just cannot accept. I think we're going to need to demote you," said Sidney with a sense of glee.

"Demote me?!"

"Yes. It's clear that you aren't up to the very high standards of this firm. You need something easier... something simpler." As Sidney said this, her pussy flooded with her juices. She was unbelievably horny. Watching Henry's horror at being so humiliated was like drinking the nectar of the gods and she wanted so much more.

"This is an outrage!" growled Henry.

Sidney laughed. "Do you know what, Henry?"

He didn't answer.

"I can make you accept this. I can order you to think this is all just happy and wonderful and to completely accept whatever I want. But I won't. Do you know why, Henry? Because I don't want you to accept any of this. I want you to writhe in intense humiliation every time you need to follow some order given to you by a woman," said Sidney. *"And let's be clear, every woman here is your boss."*

"What do you want?" demanded Henry.

"Oh, I have what I want, Henry. I'm demoting you to be the most junior secretary on staff... a mere office girl! You're going to run around taking orders from every woman at the firm because that is your new place, beneath the heels of every woman around you. Let me repeat, *every woman is now your boss*, Henry."

Henry shook with humiliation.

Sidney saw this and just laughed. "Oh Henry, you're going to have a hard time at Miller Hunter! And I'm not even finished yet."

"What do you mean? There's more?"

"Oh yes."

"What?"

Sidney looked at Henry's shoes. They were hot and sexy. If she had worn them, Henry would be calling them "slut shoes." She wanted a little payback and then some on this account.

"I have to say that I don't like your high heels, Henry. I don't think they're appropriate for the office," she said.

Henry furrowed his brow. "You and Violet picked them out!" he protested, before adding, "Fine, I'll take them off."

Sidney laughed. "Oh no, you won't. You will never be out of your heels for even a second in this office, sissy."

"Then what do you want?"

"I want you to go home and ask Violet to buy you new shoes with heels that are least five-inches high. And you better get a pair of six-inch heels for Fridays. Any day that you wear less than five-inch heels, six on Friday, you will be punished for being out of uniform."

"Punished? How?!" demanded Henry.

Sidney smirked. "Stand up."

Henry stood up.

"Step forward and bend over the desk."

Henry stepped forward and bent over the desk.

"Spread your legs." He did. "Now brace yourself against the desk." He did that too. "Now stay like that."

"What are you doing?" he growled.

"What does it look like?" asked Sidney. She then clicked on the intercom and called in two secretaries. These were two of the younger women. They had both had significant problems with Henry over the past few months, with him accusing both of dressing like sluts. They had jumped at the chance for some payback when Sidney approached them.

"Yes, Ma'am," they said when they entered

the room. They knew what was coming as Sidney had told them before she met with Henry, but both still giggled when they saw the feminized Henry bent over the desk, ready for his paddling.

"Ladies, Henry needs to be punished. Twenty strokes each, please."

"You're kidding!" gasped Henry.

The two secretaries giggled. Then Henry heard the first woman smack a yardstick she was holding against her palm.

SMACK!!

He looked around nervously. "You can't be ser—"

"Be silent, Henry... except to thank the young ladies for each stroke," said Sidney and she nodded to the young lady.

The first young lady gave the yardstick a test swing. It cut through the air as she did. Then she raised it high in the air, aimed it at Henry's rear and let it fly.

CRACK!!

It slammed against his rear with intense force; the force was enough to make him lunge forward against the desk, especially as the unfamiliar heels gave him precious little balance. It stung too when it hit, both his rear and his ego. He felt incredibly humiliated to be hit this way. Even worse, a moment later, he heard himself speak.

"Thank you," said Henry.

The women all giggled. At the same time, Sidney felt her pussy fill with her fluids. This was an amazing turn on for her.

CRACK!!

The next blow came quickly. Everything repeated itself. Sidney felt even more horny.

"Thank you."

CRACK!!

"Thank you."

CRACK!!

"Thank you."

CRACK!!

"Thank you."

The young woman landed a total of twenty blows before the other young woman took over. By the time she finished, Henry's rear was enflamed. It was bright red, super hot, and it stung. His ego was deeply bruised too. This was an humiliation he would never live down... ever.

"All right, ladies," said Sidney when they finished. "Henry's ready for his new assignment now. Remember that he is the lowest person in the office and everyone else can give him any order they want. Now take him away."

The two women smirked.

"Yes, Ma'am," said one.

"Come with us," said the other to Henry.

Henry turned and started toward the door

and his new assignment as an office girl. When he reached the door, however, Sidney called him to stop.

"One more thing, Henry. If you misbehave in any way, I've given these young ladies the power to punish you further. So you better behave. Acknowledge my command."

Henry cringed. "Fine," he said.

"Try again," growled Sidney.

Henry felt a genuine shudder race down his spine. "Yes, Ma'am," he said sheepishly.

"Good girl. Now go enjoy your first day as our new office girl."

Sidney had never felt so satisfied in her life as when she watched the paddled, feminized, humiliated and defeated Henry slink from her office under the control of the two young ladies. The only downside was that she felt an intense need to masturbate, but there was nowhere she could do it.

—o—

Sidney leaned back against the couch. Eric curled up next to her in a retro-housedress. His red candies sat on the floor before the couch, as did Sidney's designer pumps. Amber stood before them. She had just arrived and she looked like she was about to explode.

"I need to talk to you," said Amber in a determined voice. She tried to ignore the fact that Eric was dressed as a woman and that it was turning her on something fierce; her thoughts kept turning to Jason.

"Can't it wait? It's been a long day," said Sidney, rubbing her forehead.

Amber shook her head. "I've been trying to talk to you about this for several days now and you keep blowing me off."

"I'm not blowing you off, Amber."

"You have too been blowing me off on this," said Amber angrily.

Sidney pursed her lips. "Amber, I'm not blowing you off. I've just been really busy lately, between the wedding and work. I'm running the firm now, you know. I want to be there for you, but I just don't have much time right now." As she said this, she realized just how bad this sounded to Amber and she understood that she had been blowing Amber off. She sighed. "All right, tell me what's on your mind."

Amber smiled. Then her expression became more serious. "I've been doing a lot of research and nothing Dr. Morgan has said is adding up."

"Amber, she's a trained psychiatrist, you aren't."

"I know that. But I can prove it."

"How?" asked Sidney.

"I got a transcript of the town hall meeting and the city council report," said Amber. "They don't have those on the website for some reason—"

"That's so no one from outside Satin Falls can find them," explained Sidney.

Amber ignored her and continued her thought: "—but I was able to get copies in person. Then I went through them and I looked at every phrase she used and every big psychological term she uses. I wrote all of those down and what she claimed they meant. Then I looked them up."

"Sounds like we have another lawyer in the family," said Eric.

Amber smiled. She always liked Eric's compliments. "Thank you," she said and she took the opportunity to glance at his dress and heels. Then she continued: "I looked up each word and each term online." She paused. "Most of them aren't real words, or if they are, she's misused them. A couple of them are even officially considered 'discredited.' And I can't find anything at all to support anything she's been telling everyone."

"What do you mean?" asked Sidney.

"I mean that everything she's been saying is nonsense."

"You mean—"

"She's making it all up. None of the words she's using mean what she claims."

Sidney bit her tongue. Amber had certainly found something problematic if this was true. Sidney would need to look into this, even if she didn't really want to. Quite frankly, she was rather happy with how things were going right now and she had no desire to change them, not with the power she had over Henry. But this couldn't be ignored.

"What are you going to do with the information?" asked Sidney.

"I'm going to confront her with it," said Amber.

Sidney pursed her lips. That was probably the worst thing Amber could do, and even though Sidney didn't want to deal with this, she couldn't let Amber blunder her way into trouble. She took a deep breath.

"All right. Forget that idea. You need to stay away from Melanie. I'll talk to her," said Sidney. "I'll confront her with this."

"Why don't we do it together?" asked Amber.

"No, I need to do this alone."

Amber pursed her lips. She wasn't sure if she could trust Sidney to handle this or if Sidney would just blow it off. At this point, however, she decided to trust Sidney and to see where this headed, for now.

—o—

Sidney took a deep breath and entered Melanie's office. As Sidney entered the reception area, Melanie rose from her desk and walked to the door of her office. They stared at each other in silence for several seconds. Sidney had come to discuss the concerns Amber had raised with her about Melanie... *and that was it*; she wasn't here to rekindle their relationship. Melanie had different ideas.

"I wanted to talk to you about the advice you gave the Mayor about the treatment," said Sidney.

"Is that really why you're here?" asked Melanie.

Sidney nodded. "Yes, it is."

Melanie backed against her desk and fondled a string of pearls around her neck with one hand. She wrapped them around her pointer finger. "Is that the only reason?" she asked.

"Yes, it is," insisted Sidney.

Without warning, Melanie stepped up to Sidney and jammed her lips against Sidney's. She spun Sidney and pushed her against her desk; her notes, pens, papers and other affects scattered to the floor. Then she grabbed Sidney's right breast with her hand and began pushing it and squeezing it. At the same time, she thrust her left hand under Sidney's skirt and tried to force it up toward her crotch as she kissed Sidney's neck and wrapped her hands around Sidney's rear and squeezed her butt cheeks.

"God I've missed you!" exclaimed Melanie.

Sidney pushed Melanie away again. "That's not why I'm here!"

Melanie stumbled backwards from the push. "You've got to be kidding me," she said sourly. "You are such a tease!"

"I'm here to talk about your plan and some concerns I've discovered," said Sidney. She decided to plow ahead and ignore Melanie's attempt to seduce her. She also thought it best to leave Amber's name out of this.

Melanie stepped back and folded her arms. There was true anger in her eyes. "What do you want?"

"What you told the Mayor, this whole treatment... it doesn't make any sense. How can men get over an ego-problem by having women strike at their egos? And I looked up a lot of what you said. You're misusing words and concepts," said Sidney harshly.

Melanie glared at her former lover. "Oh, so now you're a psychiatrist? I suppose you even looked all of this up in a textbook too, didn't you?

And now you think you're qualified to tell me my job. Is that it?"

"No, but I am concerned that something isn't right here. After your husband—"

Melanie instantly let out a single derisive laugh. It sent an ice cold chill down Sidney's spine.

"Oh, I see, and you think that's affected my judgment?" Melanie asked angrily.

"Yes, I know that was difficult for you," said Sidney cautiously.

"Don't you mean humiliating? Don't you mean, how stupid and inadequate could I be that the most famous psychiatrist in one of the biggest cities in the country never knew that her own husband was fooling around behind her back? Don't you mean how pathetic I am to only learn this when the newspaper got wind of his last affair and exposed him? Or maybe you mean how the judge still gave him everything he wanted?" she snarled.

Sidney didn't respond. She realized that Melanie was on the edge of an emotional chasm right now and anything she said would inflame the situation. She had to wait this out to see where Melanie headed. Sidney hoped that Melanie would begin to realize that she was doing this for all the wrong reasons.

Melanie's nostrils flared. She slowly walked

back behind her desk.

"Well, my dear cold-hearted tease, you are right," said Sidney with a laugh. "My plan is total bull. I have decided to feminize all the men in this town and turn them into the slaves of their wives *because that is what I want.*"

Sidney's jaw dropped. "So none of this is meant to help—"

"Ha! Of course not. Don't tell me you're as stupid as the Mayor or the others and you actually believe this was meant to help? Come on, Sidney, you're smarter than that. This is my gift to women, a town where men learn their place as the feminized toys of their wives, their girlfriends and their sisters."

Sidney was shocked at Melanie's brazenness. "I can't believe you!"

Melanie shrugged her shoulders indifferently. "What are you going to do about it?" asked Melanie smugly.

"I'm going to call the Mayor and tell her."

Melanie snickered. She picked up the phone and moved it across the desk toward Sidney. "Be my guest."

Sidney raised an eyebrow. "What's the catch?" she asked cautiously.

Melanie slowly pulled out her chair and sat down. She folded her arms and crossed her legs. "The catch, dear Sid, is that if you call the Mayor, all of this will end, and I don't think you want that. Do you really want that chauvinist pig boss of yours to take back his firm and then to get even with you for humiliating him? How do you think that will play out?"

"That won't stop me," said Sidney even though she still felt conflicted.

"Then make the call."

A lengthy silence passed in which both women stared at each other.

"Of course, even if you do find the strength to actually make the call, I doubt you can change anything. I'm going to deny everything and when it comes down to your word against mine, I'll win. What's more even if you can somehow sway the Mayor into thinking that you are right, do you really think the Mayor will admit her mistake and tell the voters? 'Oops, do you remember how we told you to feminize your husband, your sons, your boyfriend? Well, that was just a twisted prank.' Frankly, I can't see her doing that."

Sidney bit her lip. What Melanie said was all true and she knew it. Still, she needed to give it a try, even if it was hopeless. "I need to tell the mayor," she said without conviction.

"I'm sure you do," said Melanie dismissively. "Now if you'll excuse me, I have work to do."

With that, she sat down at her desk and

picked up a file. She began reading. She did this to intentionally remind Sidney of how Henry Miller contemptuously dismissed her, something Sidney had often told Melanie annoyed her to no end.

Sidney glared at her and left.

Chapter 13: "Greg & Brenda Cole"
—o—

It had been three weeks since Melanie's plan had gone into full effect. Things were not going well for the males. Indeed, the feminization process had been difficult for both the boys and the men. Not only were the males having problems adjusting to the sheer humiliation of what they were experiencing, but they were finding it difficult to dress like females even as a practical matter.

The high heels they all wore were uncomfortable, and there wasn't a male in town who didn't complain about his sore feet or calves. They weren't used to the restrictions imposed by pencil skirts or dresses either, or the almost straightjacket like nature of corsets, and they constantly felt like prisoners because of it; each quickly learned that he could not run or move quickly in these clothes and that every moment he spent on his feet required him to pay special attention to his balance.

Because of these things, the males wasted vast amounts of energy learning to balance, learning to sit without showing their panties, learning not to smear their makeup and learning to reapply it when needed – something the girls actively encouraged. It took tremendous concentration to remember their purses whenever they rose from a table or desk as well. There was a significant new focus on their hair. Their grooming rituals went from five minutes to forty minutes and now happened at night as well as in the morning.

In effect, being women had become their full-time occupation and it left them little time to do much of anything else. And always there was a woman watching to make sure they did what they were told, to make sure they remained feminine, and to humiliate and emasculate them constantly.

There were other problems too. The males discovered that skirts and panties just weren't meant to hide erections, and the women again took advantage of this situation. For many girls, it became a game to try to cause erections and then to guess how far out they could make the young man's skirt tent. Some young women even began carrying rulers or tape measures with them for this very purpose; the tape measure became the latest feminine accessory. The women tended to play slightly different games, but with similar results and of a similar humiliating nature.

All of this, of course, reinforced the idea within the males of their new status. They were no longer masters of their worlds, they were now mere amusements, toys for the women who had supplanted them. This was their present and their future and they needed to accept it.

To say that Melanie was pleased by all of this was an understatement. Everything seemed to be going according to plan and the men were now completely under the control of the women and were quickly being feminized.

Melanie sat on the bench on 4th Street. This area had been turned into a pedestrian mall with small restaurants, shops and two theaters some years back. As with every other Saturday, the street was packed with the residents of Satin Falls enjoying themselves. Only today, the women were enjoying themselves much more than the men. Indeed, everywhere Melanie looked, she saw women happily leading femininely-dressed men around. This gave Melanie a strong tingle, the kind of tingle which made her panties wet.

"What a perfect world," thought Melanie.

As she watched the crowd, Melanie chuckled at the revealing aspect of what she saw. This wasn't just a crowd of people, it was a genuine showcase for how differently women interpreted femininity. Some women dressed their men quite professionally or in a sophisticated manner: pencil skirts, tailored blouses and jackets, expensive pumps with sturdy, thick heels or sleek stilettos. Other women dressed their men more casually, in simple dresses, sandals in all heel heights, and accessories like oversized hats or purses. Some women seemed to prefer the slutty look, with body-hugging minidresses or miniskirts and high-heeled slides or even stripper heels. A handful even chose demure outfits, such as long loose dresses and heavy sweaters.

She laughed at what this must be doing to the egos of the men.

"Serves you all right," she thought.

She then focused on the women again. Each of the choices they made in terms of how they dressed their men told Melanie something about the woman who had made the choice. Specifically, it told her how that woman defined "feminine." Interestingly, however, most of these women then failed to conform to their idealized image of femininity themselves. Indeed, most of the women chose to dress themselves more conservatively than they dressed their males. Many wore pants or shorts or simple dresses, though some chose more racy outfits. Many wore flats or mid-heeled shoes. Some wore high heels, with the majority of those wearing wedges.

"I wonder what that means?" she asked herself. "There's an interesting psychological paper there, if I ever choose to write it. Why would a woman dress herself less femininely than she dresses her man?"

She didn't know.

One thing she did know, however, was that the women were enjoying being in control. It was obvious from the smiles and the jovial manner of each of these women as they moved around the pedestrian zone that they all were immensely satisfied to be in charge of their males.

Melanie smiled at her achievement.

"Hopefully, they will never willingly give this back no matter what happens," said Melanie.

—o—

One person who took the changes especially hard was Greg Cole.

It was a strange scene at the Cole household the day after the meeting. Brenda Cole stood in the living room, wearing the olive-green pantsuit and tan kidskin pumps she'd worn to work earlier in the day. Her husband Greg sat in the recliner behind her. He wore a black and white-checkered pencil skirt, a pink blouse and black high-heeled sandals. His nails were painted and his face was made up. He looked absolutely humiliated.

Across from Greg, on the couch, sat his son Jason. Jason wore a denim miniskirt, a yellow top with a rainbow printed on it, tan stockings, and yellow open-toed high-heeled mules. Like Greg, his face also was made up and his nails were painted too. Next to him sat Brenda's daughter Cindy, who wore brown slacks, brown pumps, a white blouse and a leather jacket.

"I've called this meeting to explain how things will work around the house from now on," said Brenda.

Jason looked nervously at his father, who kept staring at the floor.

Brenda continued. "Obviously, from now on I will be in charge. My power will be absolute in this house. No decision gets made without my approval, so don't try to get away with getting Greg's approval. That's not how things work anymore. Greg no longer has any decision-making authority."

Greg cringed.

"Because we can't trust how either of you will react because of this virus, from now on, if you need to buy something or you need to go somewhere, you will need to get me or Cindy to do it for you," said Brenda. She had already collected their driver's licenses and credit cards.

Both Greg and Jason cringed this time. It was humiliating to be made to ask the women if they could be taken somewhere or if they could buy something. Greg didn't really believe this was necessary either, but Brenda told him that his views didn't matter anymore.

"Since I'll be at work most of the day, when

I'm not here, Cindy will be in charge. Obey her," continued Brenda.

Greg furrowed his brow and looked up at his wife. "Me too?!" he asked incredulously. "That wasn't what we agreed."

"Yes, you too."

"You want *me* to obey *her*?! But she's your daughter!" exclaimed Greg.

"Yes, she is, Greg. But you are in no position to be left unsupervised."

Cindy snickered.

"But that's going to be incredibly humiliating if I have to follow her orders!" whined Greg.

"You'll just have to deal with it," said Brenda coldly.

"But... but—"

"What did I say, Greg?"

By this point, Cindy was openly laughing. This sent waves of humiliation racing down Greg's spine. He glared at her and then his wife. This was a nightmare from which he could not wake. To be feminized was bad enough. To now need to take orders from Cindy was just too much.

"Can I please speak to you in private about this?" asked Greg.

"No, I've made up my mind," said Brenda dismissively.

"Brenda!"

"Stop it, Greg! This is how it's going to be from now on. You've lost your position as head of household because you are no longer suited for it. You and Jason are simply incapable of being given any responsibility or even any degree of freedom. Hence, from now on, you will both follow orders and do as you're told. When I'm home, those orders will be mine. When I'm at work, those orders will be Cindy's. What's more, you will be courteous and helpful and neither of you will talk back," growled Brenda aggressively.

Greg's jaw dropped.

"And to make sure you do exactly as you're told, I've given Cindy the authority to punish either of you in any way she thinks necessary if you misbehave or show her disrespect," added Cindy.

"*Punish*?!" blurted out Greg.

"*Punish.*"

"Don't worry. If you behave, then I'll be fair," said Cindy with a huge smirk on her face. Greg and Jason looked at each other nervously. They knew that Cindy had no intention of being fair. She was enjoying humiliating them too much.

They were in trouble.

—o—

A few days later, Greg and Jason found themselves sitting in the back seat of Brenda's car as they pulled up to a store Jason knew all too well. This was going to be a nightmare. Greg and Jason both kept their heads down and followed Cindy and Brenda into the store. Greg felt the cool wind race up his skirt and tickle his erect penis inside his panties. His high heels echoed humiliatingly off the cement as they made their way across the sidewalk and then across the tile floor as they entered: **CLICK CLICK CLICK!** With all the experience he was getting, Greg was getting better at walking in heels every day. On the one hand, he saw this as a good thing because it meant less pain and discomfort. But on the other, getting good at walking in heels didn't mean he felt any less humiliated about wearing them.

"Do we really have to do this?" Greg asked his wife nervously. His mouth was dry and he trembled at being seen trying on women's clothes.

"Of course we do," said Brenda.

Greg swallowed hard. "Can I at least pick out my own clothes?"

Brenda shook her head. "No. Cindy and I will do it."

"Why does Cindy get a say in this?!" He sounded exasperated.

"Because Cindy is in charge of you now too.

I've explained that to you several times. When I'm not home, Cindy will be your boss and you will follow her orders, just as you would mine. You need to learn to respect her authority."

"But she's your daughter!"

"Don't start, Greg," growled Brenda. "We've been over this; my mind is made up. Now I want you on your best behavior this afternoon or I will make this extremely unpleasant for you... extremely unpleasant. Do you understand?"

"Yes, Ma'am," said Greg.

Brenda and Cindy led Greg to a rack of dresses. As they did, they let Jason wander the rest of the store; today, he wore a hot pink babydoll dress, frilly white panties, and very tall white high-heeled sandals. He had enough sissy clothes to satisfy Cindy and, hence, Cindy had no desire to buy him more at the moment; Greg was her target today.

"Oh, look at this, mom," said Cindy. She held up a pink babydoll dress similar to the one Jason wore. "He and Jason can be twins!"

Brenda stifled a giggle at the thought of dressing Greg and his son like twin girls... or sissies. She decided to check out the rest of the dresses first. "Let's see what else they have first."

Cindy frowned. "Ok, mom."

For the next several minutes, Brenda and Cindy looked through all the dresses on the rack to a great deal of "oohing" and "ahhing" and giggling. They found short bouncy dresses, tight minidresses, babydoll dresses, dresses that looked like maid costumes or "Alice in Wonderland" dresses. In another section, they found a set of little black dresses. They found A-line dresses. They found housedresses and summer dresses. All in all, they had a massive selection to choose from, and they looked at all of it. What's more, Cindy insisted that Greg try it all on. So he did.

"I think we'll take these," said Brenda and she patted the pile of dresses they had both liked on Greg.

"He's going to have an amazing wardrobe!" gushed Cindy.

"That he will," said Brenda with a chuckle. "Let's look at lingerie and high heels next."

"Oooh, yes!" exclaimed Cindy.

Greg cringed.

As before, Cindy and Brenda made Greg try it all on... pumps, sandals, stilettos, wedges, kitten heels and the rest. Greg hated it all; he had never felt more humiliated in his life than he felt during this trip and somehow the heels were worse than the dresses. Indeed, every shoe felt more humiliating than the last.

But it got worse.

As Greg tried on a black teddie and a particularly saucy pair of stiletto sandals, he suddenly found himself getting hard. This was the first time this had happened since Brenda had started dressing him in women's clothes and it was utterly humiliating, but his humiliation was only just beginning.

"Look what's happening," said Cindy and she pointed to Greg's crotch.

Brenda looked down and blushed. "Oh Greg!"

Greg blushed.

Brenda reached down and tried to tuck his erection back between his legs so it didn't stick up beneath the teddie. It didn't work. It popped right back into view. "Well, that's a problem."

"Yes, it is," agreed Cindy.

"Jason had the same problem. What did you find to help him?" asked Brenda.

"It's a sort of girdle that holds it in place. I found it online. But it won't really work here because it would look strange under the teddie. It would work under a normal skirt though."

Greg turned bright red as these two discussed his penis dispassionately as if it were a piece of furniture that needed to be moved. This was made even worse by the way they discussed it as if he wasn't even there or didn't need to be acknowledged. It made him feel irrelevant.

"That's ok, I suppose," said Brenda. "It can stick up under a teddie, just so it doesn't show under a skirt."

"A lot of boys are showing their dicks under their skirts."

"I know. A lot of women are doing the same with their men, but I don't want to ruin the illusion. It's hard enough to make Greg even close to passable as a woman and it doesn't help to have that thing poking up his skirt."

Cindy nodded her head. She understood what her mother was saying, though she didn't share her desire for Greg or Jason to be passable. She wanted it to be obvious to everyone that they were cross-dressed men, because it prevented them from becoming comfortable dressed as women... and the more uncomfortable they were in being dressed that way, the better in her mind.

Suddenly, things took a turn for the worse for Greg.

"Brenda! How are you?!" asked a voice which made Greg shudder. The voice belonged to Caroline Cotton, Greg's girlfriend before he started dating Brenda. She and Brenda had been causal friends, but hadn't seen each other since then because Caroline avoided Greg; their relationship hadn't ended well.

"Caroline!" squealed Brenda and they hugged each other.

"Oh, and this little sissy girl must be Greg!" said Caroline with an enormous grin on her face.

Clearly, her aversion to Greg had changed. She laughed as she looked him up and down. "My, my, Greg, how you've changed!"

Greg blushed and tried to disappear behind Brenda. She didn't let him.

"Aren't you going to say hello to Caroline, Greg?" asked Brenda. She pushed him forward toward Caroline.

"Hello," he said softly with his eyes down. He burned red with shame.

"Honestly, Greg, what kind of greeting is that?"

"It's ok, Brenda. I'm sure *she* is too embarrassed to be courteous," said Caroline.

"It's no excuse, though!" said Brenda. She put her hands on her hips. "Greg, I want to see an enthusiastic girly greeting right now or I'll make you drop to your knees right here and beg her forgiveness!"

Greg swallowed hard. That was the last thing he wanted.

"Now, Greg!" growled Brenda.

Caroline folded her arms and tapped her foot against the floor.

Greg took a deep breath, forced a fake smile on his face, and did his best to greet Caroline in a happy way. It wasn't enough. It wasn't nearly enough. Brenda immediately began glaring at him.

"All right, Greg," said Brenda.

"Please, don't!" he said.

Brenda ignored him. "You asked for this. Now give Caroline a greeting like you think a big, old sissy would."

Without missing a beat, Greg's wrist went limp, his lips formed into a pout, he shook his rear, and he giggled. "Hewwo, Miss Carowine!" giggled Greg and he curtseyed to Caroline.

Caroline's jaw dropped, as did Brenda's. Cindy doubled over laughing.

"I'm so happy to see you!" squealed Greg and he bounced up and down. Then he hugged Caroline around the waist and he puckered his lips and waited for Caroline to kiss him.

"Where the heck did you learn that?" asked Brenda rhetorically.

Caroline smirked. "I don't know, but somehow it was fitting." She then bent over and pecked him on the lips.

Greg blushed and held himself tightly. As he did, he twisted his ankle in front of him as if to show off his high-heeled shoe. The women laughed. Then they spoke for several minutes about getting together over drinks at some point in the future. After that, they discussed the wardrobe Brenda was buying Greg. Much to Greg's horror, Caroline offered to help pick things out and Brenda accepted.

So they started picking out clothes.

"Oh look at these gorgeous heels!" exclaimed Caroline. She picked up a pair of brown platform sandals with an intricate set of straps over the foot which formed an infinity symbol. They had six-inch heels.

"Those are amazing!" exclaimed Brenda.

"I am not wearing those!" growled Greg. "I'm putting my foot down."

Brenda raised an eyebrow. "Oh really?"

"Yes, really."

"Put them on Greg," she said simply and without emotion.

Greg immediately crouched down and removed his current heels and then stepped into the sandals with the massive heels. He could barely stand in them, much less walk in them. What's more, wearing high heels picked out by Caroline proved to be intensely humiliating, even more so than wearing clothes picked out by Brenda or Cindy.

"So much for putting your foot down, dear," said Brenda.

"Well, he put it right in the shoe," said Caroline with a laugh. Brenda and Cindy laughed at this too. Greg bit his tongue.

"Now sashay back and forth," said Brenda.

Greg struck a feminine pose and sashayed his was across the floor and back in the heels. He felt like a fool. Even worse, his erection returned.

"Oh, look at that," said Caroline. "He's hard!"

"Yes, he seems to have a problem with getting erect today. I can only assume that dressing in women's clothes must turn him on. I never would have guessed," said Brenda.

Greg wanted to deny it, but he knew better than to speak. As the old saying went, it is better to be thought a sissy than to open your mouth and have your wife force you to remove all doubt. So he waited tensely for whatever humiliation came next.

"I think we'll take the shoes," said Brenda. "He looks cute in them, even if he is struggling in them."

"I think the struggling is hilarious," said Caroline. "And I can't help but chuckle at the idea of Greg tottering around in those intense heels all day just because I thought he would look cute in them!"

Greg burned with shame and felt sick realizing that he would think of this from now on... every time he wore the heels: he was wearing these high heels because his ex-girlfriend picked them out to humiliate him! Greg hung his head in shame.

Finally, Caroline took her leave of them and said goodbye. "Well, Greg, it's certainly been...

uh, interesting," said Caroline. She chuckled. "Think of me when you wear those heels."

He would. He would remember her and the mocking looks she gave him every time he wore those heels. He burned with shame. This whole trip had been intensely humiliating.

Chapter 14: "Amber Saves The Day"

—o—

It was time to stop Melanie.

Amber leaned against the brick wall in the shadows. It was dark. She wore black yoga pants, a black jacket, and black sneakers. Across the road was Melanie Morgan's office. Amber looked at her watch. Sidney had asked Melanie to meet her at a restaurant across town. To be sure Melanie agreed to the meeting, Sidney had dangled the possibility of a reconciliation with Melanie, but Melanie hadn't left yet. Amber didn't know what Sidney had promised, and since Melanie hadn't left yet, she began to worry that the bait wasn't strong enough.

Suddenly, Melanie emerged from the building.

"Finally!" said Amber to herself.

Melanie wore a black dress and heels. She looked simultaneously anxious and yet hopeful. She walked down her steps to her car and slipped inside. A moment later, she sped off across town.

"There she goes," said Amber.

Amber waited for the car to disappear around the corner. Then she raced across the street and up Melanie's steps. She reached behind the wooden mailbox that hung on the wall and felt for a key. It was exactly where Sidney said it would be. She took the key and opened the door. She stepped inside.

"So far, so good," thought Amber.

It was dark and quiet. Amber made her way through the reception area to Melanie's main office. When she entered the office, she turned on the desk lamp and began looking for the mysterious brown folder. It wasn't on the desk or in the desk's drawers. Then she spotted it.

"Found it!" she exclaimed.

Amber pulled the folder off a shelf that stood next to the desk. She sat down in Melanie's desk and opened the folder. She prayed that it contained something they could use; this would all be for naught if her notes were just normal notes.

"Oh my!" exclaimed Amber as she flipped through page after page.

Her prayers had been more than answered. The folder appeared to be a sort of journal and it was packed with notes detailing how Melanie had warped and distorted everything so she could sell the city and the school on the result she wanted. What's more, almost every page included a running commentary mocking everyone else involved and all but bragging about how she had fooled them. She had particularly nasty words for the Mayor, and she really seemed obsessed with Sidney.

"Boy was Sidney wrong when she said Dr. Morgan wasn't a movie villain! Morgan just writes soliloquies rather than giving speeches! I need to get this to Sidney! This will totally expose her!"

Amber sent a text telling Sidney that she had found "the item" and it was "packed with smoking guns, on page after page." Then she closed the folder and she raced back outside with it. When she reached the cold night air, Jason drove up before the office and Amber dove into the car.

A moment later, they were racing away.

"Did you find it?" asked Jason hopefully.

"Like you won't believe. This folder will destroy her!"

Meanwhile, across town, Sidney saw Melanie pull up before the restaurant and get out of her car. She simultaneously got the first text from Amber. This seemed to be excellent news. Unfortunately, she didn't know yet if what Amber said was true or if that was just wishful thinking. Thus, she couldn't just leave; she needed to maintain her relationship with Melanie in case they needed to try again. That wasn't something she wanted, however.

"I'm glad you called," said Melanie as she sat down.

"I'm glad you came," said Sidney as calmly

as she could. She felt deeply conflicted. She had grown to truly despise Melanie. Yet, another part of her still saw Melanie as her lover.

Melanie reached her hand across the table. She expected Sidney to take her it.

Sidney considered taking it. But just then Amber followed up her texts with photos of ten or so pages from the journal. She did this so Sidney could read them for herself. Sidney flipped open the first image and began reading. Melanie tapped her fingers against the table to signal her impatience waiting for Sidney to take her hand, but Sidney kept reading. She finished scanning the first page and opened the second.

"Sidney," said Melanie to get her attention.

Sidney ignored her and kept reading. Her jaw dropped at what she read. Amber had been right.

"Sidney, I'm talking to you. *You* invited *me* here, remember?" said Melanie.

Sidney finished scanning that page and turned to the next. It just got more and more incriminating as she went. She couldn't believe what she was reading. She also couldn't believe how obsessed Melanie was with her.

Across the table, Melanie was getting angry at Sidney now. "Look, Sid. I'm not going to sit here and have you ignore me. So either you tell me why you asked me to come here or I'm leaving," growled Melanie.

Sidney reached the last page Amber had sent. These were more than enough to bring down Melanie. She glanced at Melanie; she couldn't believe the things this woman had written in the journal. Then she rose to her feet. She tossed money on the table for her drink and she walked out. She offered no explanation.

—o—

Amber and Sidney went together to see Mayor Gabby that very night. They weren't sure what to expect, but they were ready for a fight. Much to their surprise, however, Mayor Gabby was quite willing to listen. Then they showed her the journal. She read the first several pages. They braced themselves for some sort of outburst. The worried that she might condemn them to save her friend Melanie, but that never happened. Instead, Mayor Gabby calmly called her acting Chief of Police, Erica Carter, and ordered that Melanie be arrested immediately.

Melanie's reign of terror had come to an end.

Unfortunately, Melanie discovered that something was up. After the strange way Sidney had acted, Melanie began to wonder if Sidney's invite hadn't been some sort of trick. But what kind of trick?

"She was clearly working with someone," said Melanie as she drove back to her home. "She was working with whoever sent her the texts she kept reading. But why? What could they gain by getting me to go to that restaurant?"

Then it hit her.

Melanie bit her tongue. She knew immediately who the accomplice had to be – Sidney's do-gooder sister Amber – and she realized that the only purpose that made sense was that Sidney was supposed to distract her while Amber did something! Her mind instantly went to her journal.

"Dammit!" she growled.

Melanie changed directions and drove straight to her office. She felt a sense of panic as she pulled up before the office. She jumped out of her car and raced inside to her office. She made a direct line to her journal. Sure enough, the journal was gone.

"That little tramp!" growled Melanie.

Melanie knocked everything off her desk. Then she returned to her car and started home. She was going to confront Sidney and Amber, but first, she wanted to collect some letters and things Sidney had sent her. She needed something to stop Sidney and she intended to threaten to tell Eric that Sidney had continued their affair until recently; that would ruin her marriage before it started if Sidney didn't give in to her demands. The letters would be proof of that.

"Sidney's not going to win that easily!" growled Melanie.

As she turned the corner onto her street, however, she saw two police officers walking up to her front door. She knew right away what this meant. She returned to her car and fled the city.

—o—

A few hours later, it was obvious that Melanie was gone. No sign of her could be found anywhere in the town. Mayor Gabby, Sidney and Amber now turned to what to do next. Whether Melanie was found or not, they still faced the problem that the town's males could be controlled by any woman.

"So what do we do?" asked Sidney.

"The first thing we do is call in outside experts. I've got some names in mind and I'll make the calls as soon as we're finished here," said Gabby. "Don't worry, they're discreet. The bigger problem is how do we back out of the advice Melanie got everyone to follow about feminizing their males without the entire town freaking out?"

The three women looked at each other and

then looked at the floor.

"Honesty is the best policy," said Amber.

Gabby and Sidney glanced at each other. Neither seemed comfortable. A lengthy silence passed between them. Finally, Mayor Gabby smiled.

"Do you know what?" asked Gabby.

"What?" asked Sidney.

"Amber might be right. This may just be one of those moments where we tell the truth, the whole truth, and we trust the women of this town to make the right decision," said Gabby.

And so they did.

An emergency town hall meeting was called the following day, and the results were surprising. With the exception of only a couple women, who quickly quieted down, the women all praised Gabby for her courage in admitting the truth. They didn't blame her for relying on Melanie, nor did they hold a grudge for what her advice had made them do. Instead, a civil and complex discussion took place about what they should do about this. In the process, they learned that many of the women had very different views about how to handle this problem. Some actually felt that Melanie's advice had made things better. Others felt their men could handle being under the women's control, but not the feminization. Some felt that they could teach their husbands to resist the orders given to them, or at least prevent them from being taken advantage of. Yet others felt that the feminization was the best course for them, but only if their husbands engaged in it voluntarily.

In the end, a resolution was passed which provided that while Mayor Gabby consulted *quietly* with outside experts, the manner in which any particular woman would handle the current crisis would be up to her. Commensurate with this, the women all agreed to accept the decisions of the others and not to interfere with other males by giving them orders or trying to change the way they behaved. In effect, the town agreed to let every woman chart her own course.

They further agreed to meet every three weeks to discuss their progress. They hoped that someone would stumble upon a solution they could all then share. In the meantime, they would watch for any new physical changes – the geneticist had warned those could be coming – and any psychological changes. At this point, however, it seemed that the virus had run its course.

—o—

Violet Miller sat on the couch in her living room. Her husband Henry was working in the kitchen. He was preparing a meal, per her instructions. When the meal was ready, they would sit at the table, with her at the head of it, and they would have a lovely conversation about the shows she picked for them to watch and the fashion magazines she made him read.

Although life had gone back to normal for almost all the attorneys at the firm, Henry's had not. Violet had been bothered deeply by Henry's sexist behavior, particularly his harassment of Sidney, and she wanted to teach him a lesson. To that end, she decided not to return him to dressing and acting like a man, even as every other attorney and most of the males in town had. Violet decided that it would be best if Henry continued acting as the underling of all the other women around him until he learned to abandon his sexist ways.

It would take a very long time.

—o—

Amber sat on the couch, wrapped in Jason's arms. Both wore matching white night gowns and high-heeled wedges. Jason no longer needed to wear women's clothes, so he didn't at home or at school, but he still did whenever he and Amber were alone; this remained their secret. Right now, they were at Amber's apartment.

"Hopefully, they'll find a cure," said Amber.

"I'm sure they will, now that someone's actually looking for one," said Jason. "I can't believe people didn't see through Morgan sooner."

"I know," said Amber.

They watched a few minutes of television.

"Things seem to be getting better at the school lately. Well, as good as can be expected," said Amber.

"Yeah, definitely. There are still some boys who are stuck dressed as girl or whatever, and there is definitely still a sense that the girls are completely in charge, but all in all, most people are happier."

"I'm glad you're back to normal. Though if I'm being honest, I miss you wearing girl's clothes," said Amber.

Jason looked down his body at his nightgown and his heels. "Uh, what am I wearing? This isn't exactly a football jersey!"

"I know, but I mean all the time. I liked seeing you in your cute little uniform," said Amber. She felt a rush deep within her pussy as she thought of it and how she *loved* the sound of his high heels as they walked home. That was always guaranteed to turn her on. She kissed Jason.

"I still have it... the uniform. I can wear it

any time you like."

"To the store?" asked Amber only half joking.

Jason blushed. "Well, almost any time."

"I can make you do it," said Amber with a sly smile.

Jason looked deeply into Amber's eyes and shook his head. "You could, but you wouldn't. And that's why I love you."

Amber flashed a fake frown. "Darn. You got me!" she said with a laugh.

"Of course, you could make me wear it when we're alone," said Jason.

"You just said I couldn't use the power on you!" protested Amber. "How do I make you wear it?"

Jason smiled. "You just need to ask."

"Really?"

"Yep."

Amber blushed. Then they kissed. In perhaps the greatest irony of all, Melanie and her insane plan had brought them both happiness.

—o—

Brenda Cole sat on her couch and watched her husband and her daughter dust the living room. She was punishing both. Greg was being punished for his sexist attitude. To that end,

Brenda decided to keep him feminized and sissified until he learned his lesson. She wanted to break his macho jerk attitude and make him back into the man he claimed he was before they married; and in truth, she didn't mind a little payback either, so she wanted to make this as humiliating as possible for him. Consequently, he was dressed as a French maid at the moment in ridiculously high heels.

He would be freed when he finally stopped being sexist. Unfortunately for him, he wasn't good at not being sexist.

Cindy was being punished for the things she did. Brenda had learned through a lengthy discussion with Jason and Amber all about how Cindy had treated Jason, and that she did it long before Melanie's insane plan became an excuse. Brenda saw this as no different than the way Greg had behaved. Consequently, since Cindy was a very girly-girl, Brenda now made her dress like a boy, cut her hair like a boy, and act like a boy. Although, saying that she was dressed "as a boy" wasn't entirely right. Brenda had rather dressed Cindy as a butler, only with short pants. She looked a little like an organ grinder's monkey and she looked ridiculous, but that was the point.

What's more, Brenda warned Cindy that if she ever gave anything that Greg or Jason interpreted as an order then she would be spanked harshly by Brenda and a week would be added to her sentence. Unfortunately for Cindy, Cindy wasn't good at refraining.

Greg and Cindy were going to do this for a very long time.

—o—

A few weeks had passed since Melanie vanished. Things had settled down around the town. Most of the men had returned to normal male attire and everyone was doing their best to cope with the changes. There were few reports of trouble. All told, the town was a good deal more calm and happier than it had been in weeks. It wasn't perfect, not by any means, but everyone was doing their best.

Today was the day of Sidney and Eric's wedding.

The wedding was booked at a small luxury hotel on the outskirts of town. The hotel sat on the side of a mountain, near a waterfall, and had an amazing view down into the valley and Satin Falls. The ceremony would take place on the veranda.

Sidney stood at the altar. She had always envisioned herself to be the blushing bride when she was finally married, but things would be a little different today. Indeed, she wasn't even wearing a dress. Instead, Sidney wore a black tuxedo and black open-toed slingbacks. Her nails were dark red and she had done her hair up with a sort of bun on the back of her head pierced by roses. The roses were meant to match the rose shape of Eric's dress.

Next to Sidney stood Mayor Gabby, who had volunteered to officiate the wedding. She wore white and silver decorative Mayoral robes. Holding the ring was Amber, who wore a pink Spring dress with matching pink sandals. Jason had painted her toenails for her. The ring itself was gorgeous, having a beautiful setting of three diamonds. Sidney would place this ring on Eric's finger. He would then place a similar ring on her finger.

In the audience were friends and family. For the most part, there was nothing unusual about them. There was one exception, however.

"I can't believe you're doing this to me!" growled Henry to his wife. Henry wore the body-hugging purple dress Sidney found for him when they went clothing shopping and garish yellow high-heeled sandals with a two-inch platform decorated with flowers. He looked like a fool, especially with his male haircut and limited makeup.

Violet patted Henry on the knee. "Oh Henry, just accept it."

"But I'm the only one in a dress!"

Violet looked around the room and smirked. "Not quite, dear. Close, but not quite."

"This is humiliating!"

"I'm sure it is, but if you weren't such a sexist and you weren't so nasty to Sidney, then none of this would be happening," said Violet.

"I knew she was behind this," growled Henry.

"No Henry, this was my decision. I wanted you dressed as a girl and I will keep you dressed as a girl even as every other man in town returns to being male until you learn not to be such a sexist pig," said Violet.

Just then, the music began. Everyone turned to face the back of the room. In walked Eric, led by Kayleigh, his little sister. Kayleigh wore the same dress and heels that Amber wore. As she walked, she spread rose pedals on the floor. Eric followed her in his white dress. It was an amazing dress. It was a mermaid dress with a fitted bodice and a flowing tail. The bosom was shaped like two roses placed side-by-side. Eric's hair was dyed light brunette and, like Sidney, he wore roses in it.

"Oh my God! She's made him wear a dress!" growled Henry.

Violet glared at her husband. "It was his own choice."

"Not my son it wasn't!"

"Yes, it was, Henry," said Violet. "And there's more bad news for you too. He's taking her name. He's going to become 'Eric Blake' and he's going to stay home and care for their family."

Henry looked like he would explode. Being the only man forced to wear a dress to this wedding, a wedding where his own son, the groom, had been turned into the bride and was giving up his manhood, was the most humiliating thing he could ever possibly imagine.

Meanwhile, Eric made his way to the altar. He felt his feet in their high heels balance delicately as he made his way down the aisle. He felt the tug of the dress on his legs and rear. He smelled the perfume that had been placed on him and the smell of the roses in his hair. His vision was slightly blurred through the veil he wore. He was hard as a rock. This was a fantasy come true and he would have whipped out his penis right then and there and jerked himself off to the biggest explosion ever if he had could have in that moment... but he didn't. He didn't want to ruin the most perfect day ever in his life. This was his dream come true. And when he reached the altar, and Sidney removed his veil and brushed his cheek with her fingers, he actually cried it was all so perfect.

—o—

A few hours later, Eric lay on the bed in the hotel room they rented. He wore white silky lingerie and a pair of satin mules. His pink toenails showed through the open fronts of the shoes; this excited him. His erection stood up tall and proud where Sidney had pulled it out from beneath his lingerie. Sidney wrapped her fingers around it and stroked it.

"So, *Mr. Blake*... how does it feel to be my wife?" asked Sidney.

"It feels good, Mrs. Blake."

"I thought old Henry was going to blow a gasket when you swore to honor and obey me." Sidney laughed. "Not to mention, when he saw you in your dress... not that he had room to speak."

"He did not look happy. But it sounds like mom has him well under control these days."

"So it seems," said Sidney. She kissed Eric and she sped up her stroking. "You looked amazing in your dress."

"Thank you, Miss. It was a dream come true."

"I'm glad. You know, this whole virus thing has actually worked out well for many people," said Sidney.

"How so?"

"Well, it gave you the freedom to come out of my closet and let your family know the real you. It's helped people like me overcome sexist jerks like Henry. Not to mention, it's made your mother happier."

"True."

"There are other people too," said Sidney. "A lot of the men learned to be more sensitive. A lot of the women learned to be better people."

"That's true to."

"Of course, it could have been worse too," said Sidney.

"How so?" asked Eric doubtfully. "I can't image it could have been worse for the men. They became completely helpless and within the power of every woman in town. That's intensely humiliating for most men."

"It's not humiliating for you."

Eric blushed. "Actually, it is," he said. "I just kind of like it when it's you I submit to."

Sidney chuckled and threw her arms around her husband. "Good, because that's the story for the rest of your life: *submissive to me.* You're going to be my little wife from now on, Mr. Blake, and there's nothing you can do about it!"

As Sidney said this, it sent a chill down Eric's spine. Could he really endure an entire life of submission? He hoped so because the idea excited him. It brought him peace too to let

Sidney control his life in every detail. It felt right.

"Still, it could have been worse," said Sidney, returning to the virus.

"How?" asked Eric again.

"The geneticist said that other changes were likely as well. We didn't generally spread that around though, because we didn't want people freaking out."

Eric furrowed his brow. "What kind of changes?"

"No one knew," said Sidney. "It could have been anything. But their best guess was that you boys might have slowly turned into women with tiny penises." Sidney returned her hand to her husband's penis and stroked faster than before. He began breathing harder. "Could you imagine growing breasts? Your penis shrinking? Losing your body hair? Losing your muscles? Maybe even growing smaller?"

Eric shuddered at these possibilities. "That would have been horrible!"

Sidney smirked. "I don't know. I wouldn't mind you being a little shorter and having boobs. Though your penis shrinking would have been a tragedy," she said with a wink as she kept stroking him.

Eric changed the topic. "Do you think they'll ever find a cure?" asked Eric.

Sidney shrugged her shoulders. "I suppose

so. But so far, they haven't."

Eric spread his legs slightly and arched his back. His balls pulled upward and felt like they were tightening. His erection throbbed within Sidney's warm, soft hand. He sucked in air and then held his breath. His penis shook and throbbed and then erupted. His hot, white juices shot out of him and covered Sidney's hand.

She smiled, and so did Eric.

"Happy?" asked Sidney.

"Yes, Miss," purred Eric.

Sidney wiped her hand and snuggled up next to her husband. She played with his nipple as she tucked his penis back beneath his lingerie. His nipples seemed larger than normal to her, perhaps a little inflated too. She didn't think anything of this, however. Instead, she put this off to his being super excited.

"Are you serious about the changes?" asked Eric.

"Yes, I am. That's what the geneticist told us."

Eric swallowed hard. "Well, I hope they find a cure.

Sidney smiled at her feminized husband. She felt so happy to have him this way. "I love you honey," said Sidney.

They kissed.

"Do you know what we should do?" asked

Sidney excitedly.

"What?" asked Eric.

"We should sit out on the balcony and watch the sun go down over the mountains!" said Sidney.

Eric agreed.

They rose and Sidney took Eric's hand. She led him out to the balcony. As they walked, Eric realized that Sidney seemed an inch or two taller than normal. He looked down at her feet but saw that her heels weren't unusually high. Nor were his lower than he normally wore.

"That's strange," he thought. "I must be imagining it."

Or was he?

Epilogue
—o—

Melanie Morgan ducked into the building and made her way up the back staircase to her room. There was definitely an arrest warrant issued for her. The behavior of that cop proved it. Melanie had been lucky to escape. She would need to be more careful in the future. Still, she laughed at her good luck.

"Somebody's looking out for me," she said with a chuckle.

Melanie walked over to the bed and ran her hand over her suitcase. The three vials of pure virus she had gotten from her biologist friend were inside this suitcase. He had given her the vials so she could have them analyzed by the CDC; he had no idea she never intended to pass them along. She chuckled about that too.

She unzipped the suitcase.

"All I have to do is drop a vial in the water supply and millions of men will fall victim to the virus," thought Melanie.

She giggled. Then she removed the leather pouch which held the vials. That was why Melanie and her new girlfriend Candi had come to the big city: to spread the virus. Though Candi knew nothing about it. Melanie thought it best not to tell Candi anything because she wasn't very bright and couldn't be trusted to keep a secret.

"She's a nice girl, but rock stupid. Candi is eye-candy only," thought Melanie condescendingly. "It's a good thing she's not smart enough to put anything together from what she's seen."

Melanie opened the leather pouch.

It was empty!

Actually, it wasn't entirely empty. There was a note. It read:

Dear Melanie,

The more you talked, the more interested I became in this crazy virus you kept dropping hints about. After a while, I decided that I wanted to own it. Sorry, lover. Maybe you shouldn't have underestimated me.

With love,
Candi

Melanie's jaw dropped. She couldn't believe what had happened. She was furious. She needed to find Candi and get those vials back! She grabbed her purse, which she had set down when she entered the room, and she raced to the front door. She threw open the door to her room. On the other side of the door stood two police detectives. They were here because of a tip they had received from someone named Candi.

The End.

Thanks for reading my book!
I hope you enjoyed it!

Please sign up for my newsletter!

Get news, updates on new books, captioned images, author interviews, and more.

You can also win free books.

All you need is an email address. Sign up here:

https://annmichellebooks.wixsite.com/website

You can see a sample newsletter here:

https://mailchi.mp/d81fa5f2218c/october-newsletter

Don't forget to check out my other books. The complete list is at my Amazon homepage:

https://www.amazon.com/Ann-Michelle/e/B007JLQ9RG/

—o—

Blackmailed Sissy Maid

Powerful men like Christopher Jordan need ways to unwind. For Christopher, who planned to run for governor in the next election, this meant having a safe, anonymous internet mistress. But this mistress wasn't as anonymous as he thought. Christopher would now learn a hard lesson as this mysterious mistress slowly placed him at the mercy of the women in his life.

August 2013 No. 1 Best Seller in Transgender Erotica at Amazon!

—o—

Caught By His Roommate

Mitch thought Katie was the perfect woman. She was beautiful. She was innocent. She was naive. And best of all, she dressed the way young women should dress in heels and dresses. So Mitch tricked Katie into becoming roommates so he could explore her closet. Unfortunately for Mitch, Katie would catch him red handed. That's when things got really strange for

Mitch. See, Katie wasn't as innocent and naive as he thought, and she had plans for her new sissy!

June 2017 and July 2017 No. 1 Best Seller in Transgender Erotica at Amazon!

—o—

Caught In Her Closet

Jimmy always enjoyed cross-dressing secretly when no one else was home. Then he gets caught by Christine and her friend. What will Christine do with her new stepsissy?

June 2017 and July 2017 No. 1 Best Seller in Transgender Erotica at Amazon!

—o—

A Collection of Short Stories, Volume One: Three Tales of Halloween Magic

They Messed With The Wrong Witch: Three rotten brothers learn a lesson they will never forget when they wrongly accuse a woman of being a witch.

The Magic Ring: A husband and wife argue over a magic ring only to discover that magic can be a dangerous and tricky thing. Soon they learn what happens when the shoe ends up on the other foot.

I Wasn't Myself: The tale of a man who finds himself in the body of his ex-wife. That's not the worst part though. The worst part is that his ex-wife is now in his!

—o—

A Collection of Short Stories, Volume Two: Tales of Feminization By Hypnosis

Save Us Sis!: Candice gets a plea from her brother to come save him and their father. Is this a joke? Or is something sinister going on at home?

Controlled By His Roommate: Dave is about to learn that his roommate Katie has more control over him than he thought!

The 'Disappearance' of Alpha Mu: A college committee investigates the 'disappearance' of Alpha Mu fraternity. Though, 'disappearance' might be the wrong word.

Hypnotized Husband: Diane is shocked when her husband starts dressing like a woman after he participates in a hypnosis stage show. But all may not be as it seems.

September 2018 No. 1 Best Seller in Transgender Erotica at Amazon!

—o—

Dress Coded

Written in the spirit of *Grounded in Heels*, this is the story of Charlie Mitchell. Charlie wants to wear shorts, but the dress code doesn't allow it. He tries it anyway, figuring that the worst the principal can do is send him home for the day. Boy, was he wrong! Before he knows it, Charlie finds himself stuck in skirts and dresses and worse. What will the other students think? Will this complicate his run for class president against his nemesis... Stephanie Mills?

May 2018 and June 2018 No. 1 Best Seller in Transgender Erotica at Amazon!

—o—

Emasculating My Husband

When I married Mike, I thought I had found my fairy-tale prince. He seemed to be strong and confident and the kind of man you wanted to lead the family you hoped to build. Sadly, I soon learned that he was none of those things. Still, I did my best to be the submissive little housewife I had been taught to be. Then one day, just as I could take no more, I came upon a hormone cream that would change everything. Before my plans were finished, Mike would be the submissive little housewife in the four-inch heels!

June 2015 and July 2015 No. 1 Best Seller in Transgender Erotica at Amazon!

—o—

Femford School for Girls (Part One)

Lewis Stevens thinks his fiancée is having an affair at the secretive girl's school where she works. He decides to sneak into the school to find out. Little does he realize that this girl's school has another purpose. Now he finds himself trapped and going through their program. Can his fiancée help him? Will she want to?

May 2017 and June 2017 No. 1 Best Seller in Transgender Erotica at Amazon!

—o—

The Femford School (Part Two)

Each day Lewis remains trapped at the Femford School, he finds himself feminized further. Bit by bit, his masculinity is being stripped away. What's more, Vera has set into motion a series of changes that will forever alter Lewis's mind and body to make him Maria's submissive pet. Only Maria can save him now, but why does she keep dragging her feet? Can Lewis resist long enough to convince her to save his manhood?

June 2017 No. 1 Best Seller in Transgender Erotica at Amazon!

—o—

Feminized and Cuckolded

Junior Executive Brent Jones watches as their new boss Rebecca seduces and marries his friend John. Before Brent's very eyes, she begins to feminize his friend. So why doesn't Brent do something to stop her? Well, it's complicated. See, he wants her for himself, and if John's a girl, that might make it easier. This can't end well.

April 2017 No. 1 Best Seller in Transgender Erotica at

Amazon!

—o—

Feminized By His Mother-in-Law: Part One: Not Man Enough

Christopher has a problem. He has a beautiful new wife who loves him, but his mother-in-law thinks he's not man enough for her. Even worse, she's set out to prove it. Can Christopher stop her from making him not a man at all?

February 2018 and March 2018 No. 1 Best Seller in Transgender Erotica at Amazon!

—o—

Feminized By His Mother-in-Law: Part Two: Not Woman Enough

Christopher's problem is getting worse. Not only is his mother-in-law still determined to prove that he's not man enough for his wife, but now his wife is starting to think she wants him feminized. Can 'Chrissy' escape his increasingly feminine fate?

March 2018 No. 1 Best Seller in Transgender Erotica at Amazon!

—o—

Feminized By Hypnosis

Jess and his stepmother never got along, at least until she brought him a new CD. Now they get along great, and Jess and his father are changing fast. Everyone seems to be noticing the changes too, except them. Can Jess's mother save Jess and his father from his evil stepmother? Or are they destined to become sissy maids... or worse?

September 2012 No. 1 Best Seller in Transgender Erotica at Amazon!

—o—

Feminized Cuckold

When powerbroker Paul Jackson loses his job, he finds himself at the mercy of his trophy wife. Little by little, she feminizes Paul as she turns him from domineering husband into submissive housewife. She even invites his former best friend to move into their home, and she cuckolds him. Will this be his new life or can he escape his fate?

September 2012 No. 1 Best Seller in Transgender Erotica at Amazon!

—o—

Feminized Fiancé

When Victoria Martin built 'The Martin Firm' into one of the most prestigious firms in the world, she expected that her daughter Sarah would one day follow in her high-heeled footsteps and take over the business. When she learns that Sarah is planning to marry a young man Victoria considers entirely unsuitable, however, Victoria sets out to make sure Sarah will never want to marry him... by turning him into a woman.

November 2013 No. 1 Best Seller in Transgender Erotica at Amazon!

—o—

Serving His Fiancée (Part Two of *Feminized Fiancé*)

Rick is now trapped in a rigged bet with the powerful Victoria Martin. Rick must win his fiancée back to regain his freedom or he'll be trapped as Victoria's sissy maid forever! Complicating Rick's plight, Victoria is forcing him to masquerade as his fiancée's personal maid 'Sissy', and he can't tell her who he really is. But does she already know?

January 2014 and February 2014 No. 1 Best Seller in Transgender Erotica at Amazon!

—o—

Feminizing Her Husband (The Complete Story – Parts 1 & 2)

Part One: How Megan Avoided Pregnancy: Megan and Mark can't agree. Mark wants a baby, but Megan does not. When Mark issues an ultimatum to his wife demanding a baby, she counters by demanding that he dress as a woman for nine months before she will agree to get pregnant. Naturally, she assumes her macho husband will never agree. Imagine her surprise when he does. What follows is a cat and mouse game as each tries to trick the other into giving up.

Part Two: How Megan Got Pregnant: Things are changing fast now as Mark begins to 'grow' into the role of 'Princess.' But Mark isn't the only one changing. Megan is about to undergo a major change as well. Will Mark get the baby he wants? Will Megan let him escape with his masculinity intact?

May 2016 and June 2016 No. 1 Best Seller in Transgender Erotica at Amazon!

—o—

Grounded in Heels

When Sam's stepmother discovers the perfect way to keep her stepson out of trouble, she unknowingly puts him at the mercy of his worst enemy... his vengeful stepsister Diane. Now Diane has plans to make sure he never escapes. Can Sam find a way to save himself or will his summer in heels become a lifetime sentence?

April 2013 and December 2015 No. 1 Best Seller in Transgender Erotica at Amazon!

—o—

Grounded In Heels (Part Two: Back To School)

With Sam's stepmother forcing Sam to return to school as 'Samantha' until she can find a way to undo the feminine changes Diane has done to his body, Sam must learn to deal with being a young woman surrounded by the people who knew him as Sam. Can he keep his secret? Even worse, Sam still finds himself under the absolutely power of his vengeful stepsister Diane, who has plans for the helpless feminized Sam and is determined to humiliate him and to make his time in heels permanent. But her plans might now work out so well this time.

December 2015 and January 2016 No. 1 Best Seller in Transgender Erotica at Amazon!

—o—

Her High-Heeled Solution

John's wife Suzie wrongly thinks she's caught her husband having an affair. With the help of a friend, she comes up with an ingenious way to guarantee that John will never have another affair: she locks him into a pair of high heels. This simple solution goes wrong, however, as husband and wife both try to outwit each other. Soon events are spinning out of control. What's more, standing in the middle of all of this is Crystal, Suzie's best friend, who is having a grand time manipulating them both to make sure John gets slowly feminized.

November 2015 and December 2015 No. 1 Best Seller in Transgender Erotica at Amazon!

—o—

The House On Femford Hill

Would you stay in a haunted house? What if the house was known for turning men into women? Professor Eric Meyer plans to stay. See, Professor

Meyer studies the strange, the supernatural, and the paranormal, and he can't wait to investigate the famed House on Femford Hill, which is rumored to turn those who stay overnight into women. Could this be true? Professor Meyer intends to find out.

October 2018 No. 1 Best Seller in Transgender Erotica at Amazon!

—o—

Humiliation At The Office

For too long, corporate hotshot Andrew Boden treated the women of the office like sex objects. Now his secretary is out to settle the score as she slowly feminizes him and traps him in an inescapable web of femininity and humiliation. Little by little, Andrew loses his power, his freedom, and his masculinity, and everyone at the office is noticing.

March 2012 No. 1 Best Seller in Transgender Erotica at Amazon!

—o—

The Making of Danielle (Parts One Through Five)

This is my take on a very classic idea that comes up often in our genre: the idea of the young man transformed by an evil "Aunt." Daniel is an unruly young man who fights constantly with his stepmother. To end the fighting once and for all, his stepmother sends Daniel to an Aunt he's never met who will teach him discipline. Imagine his surprise when he finds himself put into skirts and he is trained to become a girl.

November 2016, December 2016, January 2017, February 2017 No. 1 Best Sellers in Transgender Erotica at Amazon!

—o—

The Making of Danielle, The Illustrations

The Making of Danielle series is now illustrated! It took almost a year to complete that project, but it was well worth the wait. All told, there are thirty images total across all five books and they are amazing! Drawn by Andy from andysdames, the images tell the story perfectly! They are well worth adding to your collection.

June 2017 No. 1 Best Seller in Transgender Erotica at Amazon!

—o—

The Story of William, From The Making of Danielle

This is the story of William and how he was transformed into Wilma. These are the things Daniel never knew. *It is also the conclusion to Daniel's story.* How does Daniel's story end? In a word: a wedding. To whom is the question though!

June 2018 and July 2018 No. 1 Best Seller in Transgender Erotica at Amazon!

—o—

Miss-ing Billionaire

Reporter Martin Ward has uncovered an incredible story. The billionaire founder of Ing Co. is missing, and Martin's source tells him the billionaire's new wife is behind it. Unfortunately, the only way Martin can investigate this story is to disguise himself as a woman. Can he do it? Should he do it?

August 2016 Best Seller in Transgender Erotica at Amazon UK!

—o—

More Than He Bargained For

Jeff wanted to change his wife. He wanted her to be more adventurous in the bedroom, so he took a long shot on some hypnosis tapes. Only, she found out what he was doing. That's when she decided to teach him a lesson he would never forget by giving him exactly what he wants and so much more. His life at home and at the office will never be the same. (This includes the alternate cuckold ending as a bonus.)

March 2013 No. 1 Best Seller in Transgender Erotica at Amazon!

—o—

My Femdom Marriage (Part One)

This is the true story of how my wife took over our

marriage and made me her feminized slave.

March 2018 and April 2018 No. 1 Best Seller in Transgender Erotica at Amazon!

—o—

My Femdom Marriage (Part Two)

This is the rest of the true story of how my wife took over our marriage and feminized me.

May 2018 No. 1 Best Seller in Transgender Erotica at Amazon!

—o—

My Lactating Husband (Part One)

What would you do if you started growing breasts? That's the problem Andrew faces. His life was great. He had a loving wife and a good job. He was even up for a promotion. Then he took an experimental treatment meant to grow hair... but something else grew instead. As his chest slowly expands into a pair of classic breasts, he finds his wife taking over and himself demoted. What's more, his boss wants him to report to work as a secretary! Where will this end?

September 2018 and October 2018 No. 1 Best Seller in Transgender Erotica at Amazon!

—o—

My Lactating Husband (Part Two)

Things are really headed in the wrong direction now for Andrew. Not only can he no longer hide the "growths" on his chest, but now he needs to report to work as a secretary... dressed as a woman. Even worse, his new boss is not exactly the nicest woman. How bad can she be though? Andrew is about to find out. Hopefully, he can remember the things his wife taught him about being a woman.

October 2018 No. 1 Best Seller in Transgender Erotica at Amazon!

—o—

Satin Falls (Part One)

Satin Falls is the story of a small mountain town where the males slowly lose their ability to resist any command given by the females after an unknown virus infects the water supply.

July 2015 and August 2015 No. 1 Best Seller in Transgender Erotica at Amazon!

—o—

Satin Falls (Part Two)

With all the men of Satin Falls now infected by a virus that causes them to lose their ability to resist any command given by any woman, the women of Satin Falls take over. Following Dr. Melanie Morgan's plan, the women remove the men from positions of authority and then feminize them for their own good. Unfortunately, none of them yet suspects what Melanie is really up to.

August 2015 No. 1 Best Seller in Transgender Erotica at Amazon!

—o—

Short Story: The Magic Journal

After macho football player Brad ruins her date, Rachel gets even using a magic journal which lets her change his body as she wishes. Brad is about to learn a lesson in feminization he will never forget.

—o—

Summer in Skirts (Part One: Becoming Summer)

Paul is sent to spend the summer with a crazy old acquaintance of his parents. He's not too happy about it either. Making matters worse, he finds a pair of twins already living there, and they have designs on him. They seem to think he should be obeying them. Naturally, he has a different view on the matter. Before long, they teach him the meaning of petticoat punishment. Things go increasingly more wrong – or right – from there.

July 2018 and August 2018 No. 1 Best Seller in Transgender Erotica at Amazon!

—o—

Summer in Skirts (Part Two: Queen of the Fair)

Now that Paul is firmly stuck as 'Summer' for the rest of the summer, it's time he explored his new relationship with the wonderful Ellie. Unfortunately, the twins are about to take center stage in his life again, and Paul isn't going to escape them this time. Ellie has a plan, however, but Paul isn't going to like it.

August 2018 No. 1 Best Seller in Transgender Erotica at Amazon!

—o—

Two Weeks As His Wife's Feminized Submissive

Paul Wallace is a powerful man. But Paul has a secret. While Paul appears to be a man in charge, his wife Amanda really holds the power. What's more, for two weeks every year, Amanda turns Paul into Paula, her feminized, submissive plaything... and he loves it.

November 2016 No. 1 Best Seller in Transgender Erotica at Amazon!

—o—

Wager Into Womanhood (The Complete Story – Parts 1 & 2)

Max is an arrogant sexist with a submissive wife and an inability to turn down any bet. Will is a househusband with a dominant wife who just caught him having an affair. Both of their lives are going to change significantly when they get tricked into entering a bet to prove that they can live as women for a week... or longer.

September 2017 No. 1 Best Seller in Transgender Erotica at Amazon!

—o—

The Writer's Secret

Loren had no idea what he was getting into when his agent suggested he write transvestite fiction. Nor did he realize how eagerly his wife Stephanie would embrace the idea of feminizing her husband. How far would they go?

March 2012 and October 2015 No. 1 Best Seller in Transgender Erotica at Amazon!

—o—

The Writer's Secret (Part Two: Blackmailed Sissy)

As Loren continues to adjust to living as a woman, his life becomes complicated when a young relative of Stephanie's comes to stay with them. This seemingly sweet and naive young woman turns out to have an unexpected dark side, and a penchant for blackmail. At the same time, Stephanie faces a boss who demands that she sleep with him if she wants to keep her job. How will Loren and Stephanie get out of these messes?

September 2015 and October 2015 No. 1 Best Seller in Transgender Erotica at Amazon!

Ann Michelle

Printed in Dunstable, United Kingdom

63634261R00198